Rhubarb & Revenge

A Tech-Free B&B Mystery #1

Jamie McAllister

ISBN-13: 979-8-9991713-1-3

Cover design by: Mariah Sinclair
For permissions or inquiries, contact:
jamie@mcallistermysteries.com

For my husband, James McAllister, for making all the dreams come true.

Chapter 1

Standing in the cozy kitchen of the rural Michigan farmhouse I had inherited from my grandmother, morning sunlight streaming through the windows, I kneaded a soft, fragrant lump of bread dough. The rhythmic movement of my hands left my mind free to play host to a flood of memories.

Once again, I was eight years old, wearing one of Grams' aprons, flour speckling my cheeks like powdery white freckles. In my memory I heard Grams' soothing voice and my childish laughter echoing in the kitchen, and it brought a smile to my lips. "Roll the dough like this, Rachel," Grams had said, as she demonstrated the act of kneading. Her long fingers expertly worked the dough after decades of practice. "Baking is how you transform the ordinary into the extraordinary," she always said. This farmhouse, with its creaky wooden floorboards and bright red front door, was not just a house—it was a treasure chest overflowing with my cherished childhood memories.

This morning, however, my stomach was knotted with anticipation. I rolled the dough once more on the floured wooden board, placed it in a greased glass bowl, and covered it with a clean kitchen towel so it could rise. I stepped back and cast a critical eye over the countertops and cabinets. "I need to make sure I get every speck of flour off the counter," I murmured to myself. I mentally added the task to the never-ending list of chores I needed to complete in time for the farmhouse's grand opening as the all-new Yesteryear Bed and Breakfast.

A mixture of excitement and anxiety swirled in my stomach. I had spent years managing chaotic kitchen restaurants. I recalled the hectic opening night of Origins, the restaurant I had owned in Chicago. Surrounded by the heady aroma of my signature dishes, I had paced the kitchen, dealing with one crisis after another. First, half of my staff had called in sick with a nasty strain of flu that had been making the rounds that year. Then, the restaurant's air-conditioning had gone out. Finally, just to make for an even more memorable first night, Mother Nature had sent a deluge of rain over the sweltering city.

I had jumped into kitchen duties: prepping plates, cleaning spills, even washing dishes and taking out the garbage at the end of the night. One of the waiters had a cousin who worked at a business that sold commercial fans. He called his cousin, who was able to drop off several fans to keep the restaurant cool. We weren't able to offer outdoor seating because of the pouring rain, but the patrons didn't seem to mind sitting inside. Despite so many things going wrong, the first night had been a huge success.

"You survived that, you can handle this," I reassured myself out loud.

But that was different, argued a little voice in my head. In addition to being my new business venture, this was also my new home. Fear bloomed in my chest, casting a dark cloud of doubt over the new direction I had chosen for my life. I wasn't in Chicago anymore. I was in Hillsville, Michigan, a small town in the middle of nowhere. And I wasn't running a restaurant this time, either.

Six months ago, Grams passed away. I had been consumed with grief over her death. She had been one of the most important people in my life, if not the most important. I had spent every summer of my childhood with Grams at the farmhouse, where she had taught me how to cook and bake. We spent countless hours together in the garden, pulling weeds and harvesting fruits and vegetables. We took long walks together through the woods that stretched for several acres behind the farmhouse. Those had been the happiest moments of my life. Grams' cooking lessons had fueled my desire to become a chef and to open my own restaurant, where I could make meals for other people to savor and enjoy.

After Grams' death I learned I had inherited the farmhouse and the forty-five acres of land—much of it forest—that came with it. The attorney handling Grams' estate, who knew I lived in Chicago, had automatically assumed I would sell the house and the land. At first, I had agreed with the attorney, although reluctantly. How could I ever keep up the farmhouse and the land if I were hundreds of miles away running a busy restaurant? I told the attorney I would sleep on it and get back with him in the morning. He had smiled, confident he knew what my decision would be.

Rather than getting a hotel room in a nearby town, I had opted to stay at Grams' farmhouse while in town for her funeral. I thought it would be overwhelming to stay in Grams' house, to be surrounded by everything that reminded me of her. But the exact opposite had happened. The moment I entered the red front door, I felt like I had come home. The kitchen was filled with warmth and sunshine, as well as the wonderful memories of our time together. Stepping into the kitchen was like stepping into one of Grams' special hugs.

The welcoming feeling was everywhere I went in the farmhouse. When I stepped into the living room, my gaze lingered on the family photographs hanging on the walls. There was a photo of Grams and Gramps on their wedding day, joy radiating from their youthful faces as they started out their new life together. Photos of them through the years showed a progression of gray hairs and thickening middles. The last photo of them was taken on their thirtieth wedding anniversary, just a few months before Gramps had died in a car accident.

Numerous photos of my mother, an only child, were included in the collection. A photo of Mom when she was about ten years old, perched atop a horse on the farm, bareback and barefoot. Another of her with Gramps after an afternoon spent fishing in the pond. Mom held a string of bluegill proudly in front of her while Gramps held up one lone fish, a mock frown on his face and his arm around Mom's shoulders. Mom had always been a daddy's girl. Another photo of Mom in a black gown and mortarboard, graduating, with honors, from college.

One entire wall of the living room was covered with photos of me, from the photo taken on the day I was born, with my funny expression and wrinkly pink skin, to the day I opened my restaurant. In between were school pictures of me ranging from a cute, innocent seven-year-old with barrettes in my hair to an awkward adolescent with permed hair and braces. As the only grandchild, I had always had all of Grams' love and attention.

I examined the last photo, the one of the grand opening of Origins. The photo had been taken by a professional photographer and I had it framed so I could send it to Grams. I stood at the front door of the restaurant, in the center of a group made up of my staff, friends, and, right next to me, my fiancé, Finn Peale. I had a huge grin on my face. Finn's arm was wrapped around my shoulders.

He too wore a smile, maybe even bigger than mine. I remembered the joy and happiness of that moment, as well as all the years of hard work that had led up to it. That photo had been taken only three years ago, but it felt like an entire lifetime had passed since that day.

My gaze lingered on Finn's face in the photo. I had postponed our wedding after learning I was the new owner of the farm. In fact, the B&B's grand opening, just a few days away, fell on the date we had planned for our nuptials. I felt a stab of guilt. Finn and I had not officially ended our relationship, but with me in Hillsville and he in Chicago, I had no idea where we stood with each other. I tore my gaze away from Finn's beaming face. I didn't have the time or the mental space to deal with my relationship status right now.

A photo of Grams and I standing in the garden caught my eye. I reached out a finger to touch the glass. Both of us were barefoot. Grams grasped several freshly picked carrots in one hand. I clutched a pail overflowing with raspberries. A halo of sunlight enveloped us in the photo. Looking at the photo, I could recall the warmth of the sun shining on my shoulders and the soft earth squishing between my toes.

"I'm not going to let you down," I whispered to the photo. Oh, how I longed for Grams to say something to me, but she remained static in the photo, smiling silently out at me.

In that instant I had made the decision to sell Origins and move to the farm. Although I had loved my life in Chicago, the farmhouse felt like home. I could not give up the memories and the happiness that surrounded me when I was within the farmhouse's four walls, standing in the garden, or walking in the woods. The attorney handling Grams' estate had been incredulous when I had called him the next morning to tell him my decision.

"Do you have any idea what you're getting yourself into?" he had asked. "The farmhouse needs a new roof. The septic system is ancient and will have to be replaced. The interior of the house is worn and dated. All of that work will cost tens of thousands of dollars."

"I don't care," I had replied. "Grams' house is worth more to me than any amount of money. I will do whatever it takes to keep her house. I will never sell it to strangers."

The attorney had huffed and puffed and tried to convince me to sell at least two more times. I finally put my foot down. "I'm not selling and that's that," I said. "Let me know what papers I need to sign and I will come into your office to sign them. Thank you." I had hung up the phone, a surge of adrenaline coursing through my veins. I had just made a huge commitment, and I had never felt so sure of myself before in my entire life.

After Grams' funeral I returned to Chicago to put my condo on the market and start looking for a buyer for Origins. I packed up what I thought I would need at the farmhouse and sold or donated the rest. I was amazed and a little bit saddened to find that my life in Chicago could be packed into several boxes and placed in a small U-Haul trailer.

One day shortly after I moved, I had been talking on the phone with Hillary, a friend of mine in Chicago, about my plans to transform the farmhouse into a bed and breakfast. I had been talking to her on the old yellow rotary phone hanging from the wall in the farmhouse's kitchen. I told Hillary that I was talking to her on an old rotary phone and she had squealed with delight.

"That's a riot," she had said. "I feel like I'm tethered to my cell phone." Her voice had taken on a wistful tone. "I wish I could experience life without my phone." She let out a giggle. "But someone would have to take my phone away from me because I don't have the willpower to part with it on my own."

Hillary's words struck a chord somewhere deep inside me. What if I could offer a place where my future guests could take a break from their cell phones and experience all the peace and relaxation I had always enjoyed at the farm? Grams had never had a computer or the internet at the house. In fact, she had never even owned a television set. At that moment I knew I had something special to offer the guests of my future B&B. I would turn Grams' one- hundred-and-fifty-year-old farmhouse into a bed and breakfast, but with a twist: no cell phones or modern gadgets allowed.

I used the money from the sale of the condo and the restaurant to make all the repairs the attorney had warned me about, and then some. I sank every last penny I owned into refurbishing and repairing the farmhouse to make it into a bed and breakfast.

Everything had happened so quickly. In just six months I had gone from the owner of a popular Chicago restaurant to the owner of a B&B. And now that the grand opening was just a week away, a parade of doubtful thoughts marched through my mind. What if my guests didn't like being without their cell phones? What if they hated staying at the B&B without any modern gadgets and were bored? What if they demanded their money back? Worst of all, what if I couldn't make any money from the venture and had to sell the farmhouse?

Fear gripped my gut. If this venture flopped, I wouldn't be able to keep the farmhouse. I wasn't worried about what I would do. I knew I could always get another restaurant job. I thought about the years of work and the grueling hours that had gone into starting my own restaurant. I didn't look forward to doing that again, but I could if I had to. However, if I lost the farmhouse I would lose the connection to Grams. I would no longer be surrounded by all of those happy childhood memories. I could not let that happen. I felt panic taking hold and took a deep breath to calm myself. The fears and doubts could show up, but that didn't mean I had to roll out the red carpet and encourage them to hang around.

"I can do this," I declared to the empty kitchen. "I will make this B&B feel as warm and inviting as Grams did. People won't even notice they don't have their cell phones. They will be too busy enjoying everything the farm has to offer." I conjured up an image of my first guests arriving. I envisioned greeting them at the door, the aroma of fresh-baked bread mingling with the bright scent of freshly mown grass.

As the image in my mind grew clearer, my jumpy nerves began to transform into a bubbling excitement. This farmhouse, my sanctuary, was ready to welcome others into its embrace. I knew in my heart I would pour every ounce of love and energy into making their stay meaningful. I would create an unforgettable experience for my guests, just like Grams had for me.

****

While I waited for the bread to rise, I scrubbed the kitchen counters. Once that task was done, I changed into my work clothes, a pair of torn jeans and a paint-splattered T-shirt. Weeding the flowerbed in front of the farmhouse was next on my list of tasks to finish before the grand opening. I pulled on a pair of gardening gloves and grabbed a pail I had stashed on the large front porch.

Today promised to be warm for early May. Already I could feel beads of sweat gathering on my forehead. I set the pail down next to the rectangular flowerbed in the front yard and pulled out the kneeling pad sticking up out of the pail. I shaded my eyes with one gloved hand and gazed around the farm.

The white farmhouse with the large front porch gleamed in the spring sunshine. Morning glory vines grew over the white lattice under the porch, their pink and blue blooms opening in the warmth of the sun. Behind the house was Grams' large garden where a number of vegetables were planted. I planned to use a great deal of the harvest from the garden in the meals I would prepare for guests. My mouth watered as I thought about the crispy, salty pickles I would make from the cucumbers growing in the rich soil. Thick, juicy raspberries would taste heavenly baked in a pie or just by themselves as a snack. From the front yard I could see the large leaves of the rhubarb plants waving in the gentle breeze. I had never cared for rhubarb as a child, but eventually my tastes had changed and now I loved the tangy crimson stalks either in a dessert or a savory dish. The options were endless.

The big red wooden barn stood to the left of the farmhouse. The barn had been repainted and looked better than ever. While I had tried to keep the farm and the farmhouse true to the way it had looked when Grams was alive, I had added a painted quilt square to the big red barn. I had chosen the Star of Hope quilt block in white and lavender. The soothing color tone contrasted nicely with the gleaming red barn. A local craftsman built the large wooden quilt blocks, and his wife painted them. I had visited a craft fair in downtown Hillsville and had fallen in love with the beautiful barn quilt. I also admired the name of the quilt block. I was filled with hope for this new chapter of my life, and I wanted a daily reminder of that hope. And, while I wanted to preserve the farm's history, I also wanted to incorporate some personal touches of my own. The Star of Hope barn quilt had been the perfect choice.

As I knelt in the flowerbed pulling weeds and tossing them into the pail, a beat-up tan Chevy pulled slowly onto the dirt road in front of the farmhouse. The car stopped at the mailbox and the woman inside waved. I lifted a gloved hand and waved back. Crumbs of dirt drifted off the glove and landed on my shirt. Brushing off my T-shirt, I stood up and walked to the mailbox.

11

The rural mail carrier, Holly Granger, sat in the front seat surrounded by plastic bins heaped with envelopes and flyers. Packages were piled high in the backseat. Holly was petite. Just a few inches shorter and she might not have been able to see over the steering wheel. She wore her thick dark hair pulled back in a ponytail. I tugged self-consciously at my plain brown hair tied in a messy bun at the back of my head. Holly's fair skin and vibrant green eyes provided a lovely contrast to her dark hair. She wore cutoff denim shorts and a T-shirt bearing the local high school's mascot, the Hillsville Hog Caller. On the front of the T-shirt was a portly man dressed in a plaid shirt and bib overalls. He had his hands cupped around his mouth. In a bubble next to his mouth was the word "Sooooo-eeeey!" Charging toward him was a huge pink pig with black spots. The mascot's name was in honor of one of the area's biggest agricultural businesses—swine farms.

I approached the rusty, dusty old car as Holly shuffled through a bin filled with envelopes perched on her lap. Holly had been delivering mail to Grams for about ten years. Grams talked of her often during our weekly calls. Grams had always looked forward to her daily chats with Holly and waited eagerly for her mail delivery. Sundays were tough for Grams because those were the days she didn't get to see her special friend, but as she told me, "Sundays are the day I get to talk to my only granddaughter, so that is special all by itself."

"Good morning," I said. Holly smiled and handed me a thick stack of mail. Lots of bills, no doubt. I shoved the stack under my left arm and stuck my right hand through the passenger's side window. "We haven't officially met yet," I said. "I'm Rachel Kent, Winona Walters' granddaughter."

Holly shook my hand, her grip tight. I unclasped my hand, but she held on a few seconds longer. "I'm Holly Granger," she said. "You're the new owner of the farm, right?"

I nodded. "Yes, I am." I gestured at the sign at the foot of the driveway. The words *Yesteryear B&B* were painted on it in a swirly black cursive font on a white background. Above the name was a cell phone in a circle with a thick black slash through it. Underneath the cell phone were the words "A tech-free B&B." The sign was brand-spanking new, installed just two days ago in anticipation of my very first guests arriving this Friday.

Holly gazed at the sign. "I saw the sign when they were putting it up," she said. She peered closer at the sign. "I'm not wearing my glasses. What's that say at the bottom?" She leaned forward and squinted. "'A tech-free B&B?' What does that mean?"

"There are no cell phones or other similar gadgets allowed at the B&B," I explained. Holly's left hand reached out to cup her cell phone, positioned on a holder attached to the center console. She clutched the phone tightly, as if she were afraid I might dive headfirst into the car and snatch it from her. "The B&B is for people who want to take a break from their devices for a little bit," I explained. "I lock up their phones so they can resist the temptation and enjoy life without being tied to their devices."

Holly slowly let go of her cell phone. "That sounds . . . interesting," she said.

"It's not for everyone," I said. "It's also not forever. People will get their phones back when they leave."

"I guess I can understand that," Holly said. She looked down at her phone. "I couldn't imagine being without my phone, though. I have to stay connected to my kids. I have two, a boy and a girl." She pulled the phone from its holder, swiped through a few screens, and showed me a photo of a little boy with dark brown hair wearing jeans and a striped T-shirt. He stood next to a little girl. She looked like a tiny version of her mother with her emerald-green eyes and thick black hair hanging loose around her face.

"They're cute," I said.

"Yeah, they're the best," Holly replied, tucking her phone back into the holder in the console. "I don't know what I would do without them."

Holly turned her head to gaze to me so abruptly that I almost dropped the mail still clutched under my arm. "You were a restaurant owner in Chicago, right?" Her green eyes were alight with excitement and interest, as if she wanted to take in every detail about me all at once. I was flattered and a little shocked. After years of living in a large city where most people barely took time to get to know their next-door neighbors, let alone strangers, someone taking such a keen interest in my life threw me off guard.

"That's right," I said. I pulled the stack of mail out from under my arm and used it to gesture at the farmhouse and the land surrounding it. "I loved my restaurant, but every day I spend here I feel more and more like I am truly home."

Holly gazed at the farmhouse and tears welled up in her eyes. "I miss Winnie so much," she whispered. She wiped at her eyes with the back of her hand. "She was so sweet to me. My mother's parents died before I was born and my father's parents died when I was just a baby, so I never really had grandparents. Winnie was like a grandmother to me. In fact, she even let me call her Grandma Winnie."

That sounded like something Grams would do. She had never mentioned that to me, but that was OK. Grams was entitled to a few secrets. "I'm so happy you could share that kind of bond with Grams," I said.

Holly nodded enthusiastically, her thick black ponytail bobbing. "One day she even referred to me as her 'adopted granddaughter.' It felt really good."

Tears sprang up in my own eyes and I felt a rush of grief hit my chest like a wrecking ball. Holly seemed overjoyed that Grams had used the term granddaughter for her. It was yet another reminder of Grams' kindness and compassion for others. She had always seemed to sense what others were feeling and instinctively knew what to say to make them feel good. I admired that trait and wished I had inherited a lot more of it.

Holly took note of my tears and let out a gasp. "I'm so sorry," she said. "You lost your grandmother just a few months ago and here I am going on about her and reminding you of your loss all over again." She settled the plastic bin filled with mail on the seat next to her.

Holly's expression turned serious and her green gaze bore deep into my brown gaze. "I can tell you belong here," she said. She shifted the car into drive and lifted her foot off the brake. "Welcome home, Rachel," she said before once again driving slowly down the gravel road. Clouds of dust lifted in her wake.

I raised a hand and waved at Holly's departing vehicle. Living in a small town was going to take some getting used to. I wasn't accustomed to people being so open and chatty with strangers. It felt good, though, to have a personal connection with the people around me.

I finished weeding the front flowerbed, then stood back to admire the bright, fragrant blooms. I pulled off the gardening gloves, tossed them in the pail along with the kneeler, then stashed the pail back on the porch. I had time to change my clothes, take a quick shower, and put the bread in the oven before the two interviews scheduled for the afternoon.

****

I sat down at the kitchen table and pulled the applications from a file folder. I had been searching for a part-time assistant for the B&B, but after talking with a handful of candidates, I had not been able to find anyone suitable to fill the position. If I was going to work with someone in not only my business but my home, I wanted to find someone I truly enjoyed and wanted to spend my time with. Some might say I was being picky, but I needed someone I not only trusted, but liked. That was turning out to be a very tall order indeed.

I wouldn't admit it out loud, but I was getting anxious. The grand opening was just a week away. I needed to find someone to help me with all the chores around the B&B, as well as help take care of the guests. I could do it all on my own if I had to, but I didn't want to be swamped with all of the duties. The grand opening would go a lot smoother and be more enjoyable for me if I had another set of hands to help me out.

The first interview was set for two o'clock and was with a woman named Veronica Larson. I glanced at the clock. I had about fifteen minutes before she was supposed to arrive. Just the right amount of time to familiarize myself with her work history and jot down a few questions.

Veronica was a Hillsville native. She had worked at several hotels in nearby towns, which was a definite plus. She had also been a waitress when she was younger, another point in her favor. Experience in the hospitality and food industries were an ideal combination for my future assistant. I made a few notes on Veronica's application and wrote a couple questions I wanted to remember to ask her. Glancing back up at the clock, I was surprised to see it was already a quarter after two. I frowned. No matter how great someone's work experience was, if she didn't show up on time it was definitely a strike against her.

I waited another fifteen minutes, then stood up and grabbed the phone. I dialed the number on Veronica's application. While the phone rang, I toyed with the curly yellow phone cord. After six rings a generic voicemail kicked in, telling me the voice mailbox was full. I sighed and replaced the receiver.

I hoped Veronica's absence wasn't a sign of things to come. I took my seat at the table again and pulled out the application for the next candidate, Bree Foster. Her interview was scheduled for three o'clock, about thirty minutes away. I scanned through her application. She was much younger than Veronica and had only one past job listed, a position at a local factory called Skyler Industries. Bree had graduated from Hillsville High School a few years before. Although she had not listed any jobs in the hospitality or food industries, I still chose to interview her because I had received so few responses to my job ad. My hopes drooped as I looked at the empty folder next to me. If Bree ghosted me, too, it looked like I would be handling the grand opening of the B&B all by myself.

A knock at the front door startled me out of my pity party. My gaze shot up to the wall clock. Hallelujah! Bree was not only on time, she was a few minutes early. I pushed away from the table and pulled open the front door. A young woman stood on the porch. She was a few inches taller than me and a good ten pounds heavier, but it looked like solid muscle. She had dishwater blonde hair pulled into two French braids on either side of her head and wide hazel eyes. She wore a pair of black dress pants and a simple pink blouse. A small silver nose ring flashed from her left nostril. She smiled when she saw me.

"Hi, I'm Bree Foster," she said. She stuck out her hand and I shook it.

"I'm Rachel Kent," I said, standing back and waving Bree into the farmhouse. "Please have a seat at the kitchen table. I'm so glad you're here."

Bree pulled her cell phone from her back pocket and took a seat in the chair across from mine. She held her phone in her lap and fiddled with it nervously. Uh-oh. I had a feeling Bree wasn't going to be happy when I explained the B&B's tech-free policy. I expected everyone to stick to the policy, including myself and any future employees. It wouldn't look good for my guests to have to go without their phones while myself or my employee could pull out our phones any time we needed a fix. I decided to address that issue only if I needed to. Based on Bree's job history, perhaps she wouldn't want to work at the B&B once I explained the tasks she would be doing.

I launched into a description of all the tasks I would need help with at the B&B: making beds, washing linens and towels, preparing food, washing dishes, cleaning, picking fruits and vegetables in the garden, and, of course, tending to any and all of my guests' needs. "Do you have any experience with those things?" I asked.

Bree nodded. "I do all of the laundry and cooking at home," she said. "I also wash all the dishes and clean the house." She paused and thought. "We don't have a garden, but I don't mind getting dirty. If you told me what you needed done, I'm sure I could do it."

"I would need your help with preparing breakfast and dinner every day," I said. "As well as putting together sack lunches for the guests." Even though I was operating a bed and *breakfast*, the farmhouse was too far out in the country for guests to easily travel to a restaurant for lunch and dinner. I would offer two home-cooked meals every day, as well as prepacked lunches so guests could help themselves.

"I can do that," Bree said.

"What about hospitality?" I asked. "Do you have any experience with customer service?"

"I love taking care of people," Bree said. "My mama lost both her legs and I have to take care of her. My father passed away from cancer a few years back, and I helped tend to him up until the end." She smiled shyly. "My dream is to someday go to nursing school."

I felt a twinge of sadness for the young woman sitting across from me. She was so young and already feeling the weight of such tremendous responsibility. However, I also admired Bree's dedication to her family. "Will working at the B&B interfere with you taking care of your mother?" I asked. The job was only part time, about twenty hours a week, because that was all I could afford at the moment. But I didn't want Bree to take the job if she thought it would conflict with caring for her mother.

Bree shook her head. "No. Mama and I have worked it out with a neighbor down the road. She can be with Mama during the time I will be at work."

I looked again at Bree's application and noted the dates she had been employed at Skyler Industries. "It says here you only worked at the factory for about four months," I said, lifting my head to look at Bree. "What made you leave after so short a time?"

Bree dropped her head and stared at the tabletop, squirming in her chair. "Working at a factory just wasn't a good fit for me," she mumbled.

I found Bree's sudden attitude shift a little odd. Just seconds before she had been upbeat and talkative, but now she wouldn't even look me in the eye. I decided that Bree was right. Since she was such a caring person, a factory job wouldn't fit her personality.

I really liked the young woman sitting across the table from me. She seemed sweet and sincere, two qualities I admired. Her desire to care for others seemed genuine and would be invaluable when it came to helping out around the B&B. I watched as Bree fiddled with her phone in her lap. She wasn't looking at it, which made me think she wasn't even aware of what she was doing. Would telling her about the tech-free policy scare her off?

"There is one more thing you have to know about this job," I said. Bree looked at me, waiting for me to continue. "You aren't allowed to have your cell phone during work hours."

Bree frowned and looked down at her phone, then back up at me. "Why?"

A simple question. Bree probably thought I was a nut for even mentioning it. "Well, my new B&B is different from any other," I said. "No cell phones or other similar gadgets are allowed. People will pay to stay here so they can get away from the demands and distractions their phones create for them. I don't use my cell phone, and my employee wouldn't be able to, either." Bree hesitated and I rushed to offer a consolation. "It's only during business hours while you are here at the B&B," I said. "You can do whatever you want on your own time, of course."

Had my little speech made Bree change her mind about taking the job? She gazed around the kitchen, taking in the sunlight spilling through the window and onto the braided rag rug by the sink. The smell of baking bread hung in the air and in the silence the birds chirped loudly in the trees out front. The wall clock ticked as I waited for Bree's answer.

Bree finally nodded. "I can live without my phone a few hours a day," she said. "It might even be fun."

"Excellent," I said, feeling a burst of relief. "I think we will work very well together. Can you start bright and early tomorrow morning? The grand opening is only one week away."

Bree's eyes lit up and she jumped out of her seat. "Oh, yes!" she said. She hugged me impulsively and I laughed, hugging her back. I couldn't help but catch a little of Bree's youthful enthusiasm.

I shook Bree's hand. "Welcome aboard," I said. "Can you be here at six o'clock tomorrow morning?"

"Absolutely." Bree hugged me again. "Mama is going to be so excited when I tell her I got the job!"

I felt like a huge weight had been lifted from my shoulders. It felt incredible to finally find the perfect fit for the assistant role. Now I had one more task I could check off my to-do list. Not only that, I was genuinely looking forward to working with Bree. She seemed like a caring, responsible young woman. I had a good gut feeling about Bree.

After escorting Bree to the front door, I did a little happy dance in the middle of the kitchen. Things were definitely looking up. I had no doubt that everything would go smoothly and the grand opening of the Yesteryear B&B would go off without a hitch.

Chapter 2

The morning of the grand opening arrived. I peeked through the lace curtains in my small first-floor bedroom. Sunshine poured down from a clear blue sky. I took the amazing weather as a good omen and quickly dressed in a pair of jeans and a white tank top embroidered with flowers along the neckline. Bree arrived and we set to work taking care of a few last-minute tasks around the farmhouse. The very first guests were expected to arrive in the early afternoon.

Around one o'clock I heard a car pull into the driveway, tires crunching over the gravel. I glanced out the kitchen window and saw my dad, Al Kent, and his new wife, Kelsey, sitting in a rental car. Before they could even step out of the car, I rushed out the front door of the farmhouse. I hugged Dad when he emerged from the driver's seat.

"Whoa, Rache," he said, hugging me back. "It was a long drive from the airport. Let an old man work the kinks out of his back first." He made an exaggerated grimace and gripped his lower back with both hands. Dad didn't look like an old man. He still had thick brown hair with a touch of gray at the temples. Fine lines crinkled around his eyes when he smiled. He was dressed in a green polo shirt and khakis.

I laughed and hurried over to the passenger side to embrace Kelsey. "Welcome to the Yesteryear B&B!" I exclaimed. "How was the cruise? How did the wedding go?"

Two weeks ago, Dad and Kelsey had gotten married on a cruise to the Bahamas. She had been Dad's dental hygienist and I guess he liked the way she cleaned his teeth because he proposed after only three dates. Within a few months, the two were saying "I do" on a cruise ship. I wasn't able to join them for their wedding because of all the preparations for the B&B, so I was thrilled to have them staying with me for the final leg of their honeymoon before returning to their home in Seattle. Having Dad living on the other side of the country was tough. I often wished he were closer so we could see each other more often.

"The cruise was incredible," Kelsey said, smiling at me. "And the wedding ceremony was perfect." She gazed over at Dad, who was busy unloading suitcases from the trunk of the rental car. "Well, almost perfect. Your father said 'With this wing, I thee wed' instead of 'With this ring' during the ceremony."

"Really, Dad?" I asked, laughing.

Dad pulled the last bag from the back of the car and slammed the trunk lid closed. "I was so excited to be marrying such a gorgeous woman that I couldn't even speak properly," Dad said, gazing fondly at Kelsey.

Kelsey giggled and hoisted her overnight bag over her shoulder. "Good answer," she said.

Kelsey had shoulder-length brown hair and wide green eyes. She was thirty-five, only four years older than me. Honestly, the age difference didn't bother me. After my parents divorced, my father had gotten married three more times. I really liked Kelsey and hoped the fifth time was a charm and that this was the marriage that would endure for Dad.

I helped Dad and Kelsey carry their luggage into the farmhouse. We stopped in the mudroom, where I had set up a small check-in area, complete with a counter and a guest book. Dad signed his and Kelsey's names.

Bree popped her head into the mudroom and I introduced her to Dad and Kelsey. "It's a pleasure to meet you," Bree said. The phone rang. "I'll get it," Bree said, hustling back into the kitchen.

"You did a great job fixing this place up," Dad said, peering into the kitchen where Bree was taking down a message on the notepad hanging on the wall next to the yellow rotary phone. "It looks newer, but somehow it still looks exactly the same as when your grandmother lived here."

"Thanks," I said. "I had to get everything up to code, especially the kitchen, but I also wanted to preserve the house just like Grams had it."

"Well, you did a phenomenal job," Dad said. I handed him the keys for his room and the front door of the farmhouse and he slipped them into his pocket. "Aren't we supposed to surrender our phones?" he asked jokingly. "Or are you going to take them by force?"

I laughed. "No force." I had explained the tech-free concept to Dad when he asked to make a reservation, and he and Kelsey had both agreed they were open to the idea of unplugging from their devices during their stay. Of course, that had been a few months ago, when they had been caught up in all the excitement of planning a wedding. Would the idea of living without a cell phone for an entire week still seem as appealing to them?

Dad pulled his cell phone from his back pocket and Kelsey lifted hers from her purse. Dad heaved an exaggerated sigh as he placed the phone on the check-in counter. "So long, old friend," he said, gazing solemnly at the device. "I will see you again soon."

Kelsey punched Dad lightly on the shoulder. "Stop being so melodramatic," she said. "You can live without your cell phone for a few days. It won't kill you." Kelsey placed her phone next to Dad's.

"Maybe, maybe not," Dad said.

I wrapped Dad's and Kelsey's cell phones in soft cloths and placed them together in a small box. I pulled a marker from the canister on the check-in counter and labeled the box with the name *Kent*. I dialed the combination, pulled open the door, and placed the box in the safe.

Turning back to Dad and Kelsey, I said, "I have you two in the Sweet Cherry room." All three of us grabbed suitcases and bags and I led the way up the stairs.

"Watch your step," I cautioned. "These stairs are a little steep." I recalled playing with a Slinky one summer and taking a tumble down the stairs, passing the curly metal toy as I fell. I didn't want anyone else to repeat that experience.

When we reached the upstairs landing, I took a right and walked to the end of the hallway. I set the suitcases I had been carrying on the floor and pushed open the door to the Sweet Cherry room. "I hope you like it," I said, stepping aside so Dad and Kelsey could enter.

The walls of the room had been painted a bright cherry-red, with a matching accent rug spread over the polished hardwood

22

floors. One of Grams' handmade quilts, worked in shades of red and cream, was spread over the bed. Framed vintage prints of cherries hung on the walls. The large window in the room offered a lovely view of the big red barn rising into the clear blue sky.

While Kelsey admired the stitching in Grams' quilt, Dad took me aside. "Has your mother visited the farm yet?" he asked in a whisper.

I shook my head. "No. I invited her, but she would never let me pin her down for an exact day when she could come for a visit."

Even though they are divorced, my parents get along well. They don't see each other often, and when they do they tend to treat each other like business associates. They are polite and cordial, but rarely discuss anything personal.

Grams' farm was a painful subject to discuss with Mom. She was not happy when she found out about my plans to move into the farmhouse. She had told me to sell the farmhouse and the land the instant she found out Grams had left them to me in her will. Even though I knew Mom and Grams had had a strained relationship and that Mom wasn't particularly fond of her rural upbringing, I was taken aback by how quickly she wanted to dispose of the farm, a place she knew I loved. When I was growing up, I had often asked Mom why she didn't want to stay at the farm, too. She had come up with excuse after excuse, and finally I had just stopped asking.

"This room is absolutely perfect," Kelsey said, stepping into the small bathroom and putting her toiletries case on the sink.

"Glad you like it," I said.

Dad gazed out the window, surveying the lush green grass and the acres of woods behind the farmhouse. "Hey, Kels," he said, turning away from the window. "Want to take a walk? It's a beautiful day for a stroll."

Kelsey nodded. "Just let me change my clothes and put on different shoes." She walked over to the bed and unzipped one of the suitcases.

"Looks like my cue to get back to work," I said, backing out of the room. "Have fun on your walk."

Kelsey smiled and Dad waved as I closed the door. It was time to head back downstairs to wait for my next guests to arrive.

****

Half an hour later another car pulled into the driveway. A woman stepped out of the passenger side. She looked to be in her mid-forties and was dressed for summer in white capris with a silky pink sleeveless blouse showing off sculpted shoulders and biceps. On her feet she wore strappy white sandals. Her toes were painted the same shade of pink as her blouse. She carried herself casually, but she looked like a woman who knew exactly what she wanted and exactly how to get it.

A man emerged from behind the wheel. He wore wrinkled khaki cargo pants, along with an even more wrinkled gray T-shirt. The majority of the front of the T-shirt was taken up by the image of a large-breasted, raven-haired woman wearing the tiniest bikini I had ever seen. She clutched a frothy mug of beer in one hand, the other hand propped up on her curvy hip. I caught a glimpse of the name of a brewery and the words *Denver, Colorado*, emblazoned on the back of the shirt as the man walked toward the trunk of the car. Salt-and-pepper stubble sprouted on the man's cheeks, on his chin, and around his mouth. His brown hair looked as if he had used a leaf blower on it instead of a comb. The wild strands stuck up in every direction on his head.

I watched the man pull several suitcases, an overnight bag, and a cosmetics case out of the trunk. All of the luggage matched and was a shade of creamy pink. I gasped when I saw the designer logo on the bags. What was a woman with a set of six-figure luggage doing at my B&B? Nervousness bubbled up in my stomach. Would this high-end couple enjoy staying at a rustic B&B with no cell phones, no computers, and no TV?

The man opened the back door of the car and pulled out a dingy, olive drab duffel bag. He slung the strap of the duffel bag around his neck, draped the pink overnight bag over his shoulder, stuck a suitcase under each arm, and grabbed two more suitcases, one in each hand. The woman pulled a designer handbag from the car and placed it over her shoulder. She walked up the B&B's front steps, the man following in her wake like an overloaded barge.

I rushed to open the front door. "You must be Kathryn and Simon Dillon," I said, standing back so Kathryn could enter the farmhouse. "I'm Rachel Kent. Welcome to the Yesteryear B&B. I'm so glad you're here."

Kathryn's gaze swept around the mudroom and the kitchen. Her immaculately plucked eyebrows raised as she took in the old-fashioned hardwood floors and the sturdy kitchen table. She turned to look at me and I held my breath. Would my very first real guests not like what they saw? Would they turn around and drive to the nearest large town where they could find a nice hotel with a swimming pool, room service, and all the amenities they could ever want? Worst of all, would they demand a full refund?

The woman's lips lifted at the corners in what I took to be a smile. "Thank you," she said. "This place is so . . . quaint."

I took *quaint* to be a compliment. I held the door open for Simon, who was bent double under the weight of Kathryn's luggage. He stepped into the house with a gasp and dropped the luggage to the floor. Kathryn winced but didn't speak. I rushed to fill the awkward silence.

"If you could just step over here, I will get you checked in," I said. My hands shook as I lifted the guest book from the top of the counter. I made a checkmark next to the Dillons' entry and noted the time they had arrived. I turned the book around so they could each sign their names.

"Now if you will each give me your cell phone, I will lock them away in the safe."

"What is she talking about?" Simon, still panting slightly, sagged against the doorframe between the mudroom and the kitchen. He pulled his phone from his pocket and clutched it to his chest as if it were a newborn infant I had threatened to snatch from his hands. Kathryn laid a hand gently on his shoulder. "Remember, *dear*, I asked you to do this for me. For our *anniversary*."

When Simon balked at surrendering his phone, my heart went crashing all the way down to my toes like a runaway elevator. I held my breath as I waited to see how Simon would respond.

"You didn't tell me I would have to give up my phone," Simon said, a petulant tone seeping into his voice. "This isn't what I signed up for. I thought I'd just have to go without TV for a few days."

I will give Kathryn credit — she kept her cool. She smiled sweetly and tucked a strand of her sleek, shoulder-length blonde hair behind one ear.

"This was part of our agreement," Kathryn said. The manicured hand on her husband's shoulder tightened and he winced slightly. "Remember?"

Simon scowled but then his expression cleared. "Right. You get what you want, and then later I get what I want."

I wasn't sure how to take that last comment so chose to pretend I hadn't heard, even though I was standing directly in front of the couple. I didn't need any intimate bedroom images lingering in my mind.

Simon held out his phone for me to take. I wrapped my hand around the device, but his grip was firm. "You won't even notice it's gone," I said, tugging the phone a little harder. Simon didn't look like he believed me, but he did let go of the phone.

Kathryn had already placed her phone on the counter. I wrapped each phone in a cloth and nestled them both in a shoebox. I settled the lid on the box and grabbed a black marker from a nearby glass jar filled with a variety of pens, pencils, and markers. I wrote the name "Dillon" on the front of the box and put the box in the safe behind the check-in counter and under a window facing the side yard. I shut the door and spun the dial on the safe.

"Are we the first guests to arrive?" Kathryn asked.

I shook my head. "No. My father and his new wife, Kelsey, arrived just a bit ago and are out for a walk. I am expecting a full house for the grand opening. The other guests should be here shortly."

"We look forward to meeting everyone," Kathryn said. She picked up her overnight bag. "Which room will we be staying in?"

I lifted a key from the pegboard next to me, which contained all the room keys as well as the keys to the outbuildings, all neatly organized and labeled. "Would you like one set of keys or two?" I asked.

"One should be fine," Kathryn replied. "We plan on sticking close to each other during our stay." She smiled at Simon. The corners of his mouth flicked up briefly in return. Poor guy. He was probably still mourning the loss of his phone.

I handed Kathryn the keys. She clutched them in her hand and laughed. "It's been a long time since I have stayed anywhere that used actual keys."

I laughed, too. "The key with the green tab is for your room. The key with the white tab opens the front door, which I lock every night at ten o'clock. You are free to stay out as long as you like, but keep in mind the front door will be locked promptly at ten."

Kathryn nodded. Simon slung the duffel bag over one shoulder then, with a grunt, once again hefted all of Kathryn's designer luggage. Kathryn readjusted the strap of her designer purse on her shoulder.

"Would you like me to carry one of those?" I asked. Simon shook his head. "Then allow me to show you to your room."

I took several steps away from the front entry, Kathryn next to me. I looked back to make sure Simon truly could handle all the luggage, and saw him staring at the safe, a pained look in his eyes.

"I assure you that your cell phone is one hundred percent secure," I said, smiling. I figured Simon wouldn't be the first anxious guest who needed to be consoled after parting with his phone. "I am the only one with the combination."

Simon still didn't look happy, but he hefted the luggage and followed Kathryn and I. I led the couple through the farmhouse's kitchen to the wooden staircase leading to the second story. The stairs were painted a crisp white and a starched white lace curtain covered the window at the bottom of the stairs.

"You will be staying in the Green Apple Room," I said when we reached the top of the stairs. I crossed the hallway and pushed open the door to their room. The couple trailed in behind me. The room had been painted bright green, as crisp as a tart green apple. A queen bed took up most of the room. A white chenille spread covered the bed. A small wooden nightstand stood on either side of the bed and a small wooden wardrobe had been placed in the corner. "The bathroom is here," I said, gesturing at the door leading to the small bathroom.

Simon dropped the luggage on the floor with a thump. Kathryn scooted quickly over to his side to retrieve the makeup case. She stepped into the bathroom and placed the case on the sink. Simon, finally free of the heavy luggage, collapsed on the bed.

Kathryn poked her head out of the bathroom. "Don't lay on the bed!" she snapped.

I had been just about to invite the two downstairs for iced tea when Simon rolled off the bed and onto the floor after Kathryn's sharp rebuke.

I glanced up at Kathryn standing in the bathroom doorway. Her cheeks were tinged hot pink and her nostrils flared. She looked like a completely different person. Shaken by Kathryn's abrupt mood swing, I hurried around the other side of the bed to check on Simon. He had landed in a heap on the floor and was quickly scrambling to his feet. He waved away my hand when I offered to help him stand up.

Kathryn swiftly regained her composure and the flush faded from her cheeks. "Shoes on the bed is one of my biggest pet peeves," she said. She smiled, but the warmth didn't reach her green eyes.

Oooookaay. "Totally understandable," I said. "No worries." Simon slouched against the wall. "Is there anything I can do for you?" I asked. "Anything I can get for you or questions I can answer?"

Kathryn gazed around the room. Her upper lip curled slightly as she took in Grams' white chenille spread on the bed. "We will be fine," she said, her composure firmly back in place and her flare-up from moments ago forgotten.

I smiled, waved, and backed out of the room. As I pushed the door closed, I heard Kathryn's harsh whisper, but wasn't able to make out the words. With the door shut, I couldn't hear Simon's reply at all.

Kathryn must really have a hang-up about shoes on the bed, I thought, stepping down the stairs to resume my post at the front door so I could greet the next guests.

****

Before the next guests arrived, I made a quick trip upstairs to place a stack of freshly laundered and folded towels in the linen closet. Just as my foot touched the upstairs landing, Simon and Kathryn emerged from their room. Simon had changed his shirt and combed his hair, but he was still wearing the wrinkled khaki shorts. Kathryn seemed to be in better spirits than the last time I had seen her, when she was chastising Simon for lying on the bed with his shoes on. "We're going to take a walk around the grounds," Kathryn said. "Is that alright?"

"Absolutely," I replied. "After dinner you can join the guided tour I will be giving for all the guests." Kathryn nodded and headed down the stairs, Simon right behind her.

"If you want to stop in at the big red barn, there is a herd of barn cats in there that is super friendly," I called down the stairs after them.

Simon stopped mid-step and almost lost his footing on the stairs. "I hate cats!" he said. "There aren't any cats in the house, are there?" he asked, whipping his head up to look at the ceiling as if he expected a cat to parachute down on him at any moment. "I'm severely allergic to cat dander and I won't get within spitting distance of any cat."

I rushed to reassure him before he ran screaming out of the B&B. "All of the cats are in the barn," I said. "As long as you stay out of the barn, you will be safe."

"I'm going to keep an eye out for any cats that might stray from the barn," he said. I agreed that was a good idea. Kathryn glided down the stairs, Simon trailing in her wake, stepping carefully and looking all around him for any ninja cats that might try to sneak up on him.

I placed the towels in the linen closet and hustled downstairs just in time to greet the next guests to arrive. Aries and Leo Sanchez were a brother-sister pair from California. When they had called to make their reservations, they had squealed with delight about surrendering their phones for seven whole days. I wasn't so sure they would be that enthusiastic when the time actually came for them to give up their devices, but I was wrong.

"Ohmigod, I can't believe we're doing this!" Aries squealed. Her curly dark hair bobbed around her shoulders as she bounced up and down. She whipped her cell phone out of a hemp bag she wore across her chest and thrust the device across the counter toward me.

Leo followed suit, pulling his phone from his hip pocket and placing it next to his sister's. "Bye-bye," he said, waving at the phone and laughing. "See you in seven days."

The siblings looked to be in their early 20s. They both shared the same large brown eyes, curly black hair, and smooth brown skin. Aries wore her hair loose, but Leo's locks were tied up on top of his head in a man bun.

"We're fraternal twins," Aries said, noticing I was studying them. "People always say we look a lot alike."

"You do," I said, handing Aries a pen so she could sign the guest book. She signed for both herself and her brother.

"I'm older," Aries said proudly. She smiled fondly at her brother. "Leo was born three minutes after me."

Leo nodded. "We're here because we want to do a tech detox," he said. "Someday Aries and I want to live off the grid on a —"

"Farm!" Aries exclaimed, interrupting her brother midsentence. She closed her eyes and hugged herself. "I can see it now! We're going to find a remote location where we can live without all of the distractions of modern life. We can grow our own food, raise animals, make our own clothes." She opened her eyes and looked at me. "Live as one with the earth, you know?"

I nodded. The twins certainly seemed passionate about their future plans, but I wondered if they truly understood how much work and sacrifice a lifestyle like that would require. "What do your parents think about your plans?" I asked, trying to be diplomatic.

Aries and Leo rolled their eyes at the same time. "Our parents own a large security business in Los Angeles," Aries said, as if the very thought nauseated her. "They think we're crazy. They can't understand why we don't want to stay in California and work with them in the family business. We—" she pointed at first herself, then her brother, "can't *wait* to start a new life living off the grid."

"Well, you certainly sound like you know what you want," I said. Aries smiled smugly. "I hope you love it here at the Yesteryear B&B."

"Oh, we will," Aries assured me.

I pulled two sets of keys off the pegboard on the wall and handed one to each sibling. "Do you need any help with your luggage?" I asked.

Aries shook her head. "We travel light," she said, thumping the one suitcase she held in her hand. Leo lifted his suitcase to show it to me. "Great," I said. "Follow me and I will show you to your room."

I led Aries and Leo through the kitchen. Aries squealed when she saw Grams' braided rag rugs on the floor. "Beautiful *and* sustainable," she proclaimed.

We went up the stairs and took a left at the landing. I pushed open the door to the twins' room. "You two will be staying in the Strawberries and Cream room," I said, stepping aside so the twins could walk into the room.

Aries placed her suitcase on the floor next to one of the twin beds. Leo set his suitcase at the foot of the second bed. "It's perfect," Aries said. She ran her fingers over the curves of the chipped white metal headboard, then sat on the pink chenille bedspread. "It's so quaint and rustic," she said. She gazed up at Leo. "What do you think, bro-bro?"

Leo admired a small mosaic of a strawberry made out of smooth pieces of colored glass that hung on the wall. He grinned. "I love it. No computer, no TV, not even a radio." He sat on his bed and let out a sigh. "No distractions from the modern world."

"Do you need anything right now?" I asked. Leo and Aries shook their heads. "I'm going to be leading a tour of the farm after dinner," I continued. "You are more than welcome to join us if you'd like."

The twins' eyes lit up. "We can't wait!" they shouted in unison.

I closed the door behind me and ran lightly down the stairs. It felt great to have two such enthusiastic guests staying at the B&B. I had liked the twins immediately and was pleased they were taking the tech-free experience to heart. Maybe their enthusiasm would infect the other guests, like Simon, who might not be so giddy about giving up their phones.

****

The phone rang and Bree called out, "Rachel, it's for you."

"Thanks! I'll answer it in the mudroom." I didn't want to disturb Bree, who was hard at work chopping vegetables in the kitchen. I lifted the handset off the base on the check-in counter. While I had retained the wall-mounted rotary telephone, complete with curly yellow cord, hanging in the kitchen, Grams had also chosen to purchase a cordless phone to take with her when she worked in the garden.

"Thank you for calling the Yesteryear B&B," I said. "How can I help you?"

"Rachel? Is that you?"

"Finn? How are you?"

Finnegan Peale, known to his friends and financial clients as Finn, had been my fiancé back in Chicago. A rush of heat filled my chest, the result of several emotions all flaring to life at once. I still felt massive amounts of guilt for calling off our engagement. Even though I knew it had been the right thing to do, that didn't make it any easier. We had been in the middle of planning a wedding when I had left town to attend Grams' funeral. Finn hadn't been able to get away from work to come with me, and I had promised to return after the funeral. When I made that promise I had no idea Grams had bequeathed the farm to me.

"I miss you," Finn said, his tone soft and tender. "I need you here, Rachel. When are you coming home?"

At the mention of the word *home*, a new rush of emotions joined the current batch vying for attention. Just six months ago I would have said that Chicago was my home. Everything I loved was there: my condo, my thriving restaurant, my friends, Finn. But now, anytime I heard the word *home*, images of the farm filled my mind: the farmhouse at night, an ocean of stars twinkling high above. The creaking sound the door of the big red barn made as it swung open. The smell of damp earth and the birds chirping as I worked in the garden early in the morning. I had tried to explain to Finn just how much Grams' farm meant to me, but apparently he still didn't understand.

I glanced at the clock. There was still one more guest who hadn't arrived, and I didn't want to be stuck on the phone arguing with Finn when he showed up.

"Now isn't really a good time for me, Finn. Can I call you later?" My guilt swelled again. Finn had been the man I was going to spend the rest of my life with. Even though I had called off the engagement, we hadn't officially broken up. But with getting the B&B up and running and now welcoming guests, it seemed like there was never enough time for long talks with Finn about our future together. I felt terrible for not having time to be there for him when he needed me.

"Fine." I winced at Finn's clipped tone. He was obviously hurting, which made me feel even more guilty.

"I will call you tonight. I promise."

Finn let out a deep sigh. "OK, Rachel. I love you."

Tears pricked at my eyelids. "Love you, too."

Before I could say good-bye, Finn hung up.

I clicked the off button and slowly placed the handset on the counter. Even though my emotions were swishing around inside of my chest like an overloaded washing machine, I had a job to do. I would make it up to Finn later. For sure.

****

The last guest arrived about forty-five minutes later. I had almost written him off as a no-show when he knocked at the door.

"Come in," I called.

A middle-aged man pushed open the front door and stepped inside. He wore a red kerchief knotted around his neck, an expensive-looking pair of binoculars slung over one shoulder. On his head was a ball cap with the words "Bird Nerd" stitched in green next to a patch in the shape of an owl.

"Is this the Yesteryear B&B?"

"It is." I stepped into the mudroom. "Welcome."

"I'm Ned Blankenberger," the man said. His hand reached up to adjust his hat, and his fingers traced the outline of the owl patch.

"Nice to meet you. Did you have any troubles finding the B&B?"

Ned shook his head. "No. What time is it? Am I late?"

I smiled reassuringly. "No need to worry about the clock here, Mr. Blankenberger."

"You can call me Ned."

"Alright, Ned." I pulled my guest book from its spot on the shelf so I could check in the new guest.

Ned signed his name with a flourish. When I asked for his cell phone, he patted the many pockets in his shorts. When he didn't find his phone in one of the pockets, he frowned and dug into a small bag attached to the straps of his backpack with Velcro. He pulled a battered flip phone from the pouch and handed it to me.

I accepted the phone and stared at the deep scratches marring the silver phone's surface. The small rectangular display window on the front of the phone was cracked. Amazed, I tugged at the antenna on the right side of the phone and gently pulled it up. I felt like an archaeologist unearthing a relic from the ancient past.

"This is your cell phone?" I asked, trying to keep my voice neutral so as not to offend a paying guest. "Don't you have something a bit . . . uh . . . more recent?"

Ned shook his head. "Nope. That's my phone. Never did see the point with all that social media stuff. Tweeting is for the birds." He laughed loudly and slapped his knee. "I hardly ever use my phone. Usually too busy out in the woods taking photographs of birds or sketching birds." He thumped a fist against his chest and declared proudly, "I sell my photos and sketches to all the best birding magazines in the world."

I had to ask the next question, even though it was really none of my business. "If you aren't interested in taking a break from your phone, then why are you staying here?"

Ned lifted his Bird Nerd hat and readjusted it on his head. "I have been assigned to draw a series of sketches for an ornithology textbook and this is a great place to see both barred owls and the Eastern screech owl in their natural habitat," he explained. "Plus, I hate hotels. Too many people. Not enough nature." He gestured toward the front door, presumably toward the acres of woods stretching away behind the farmhouse. "Lots of trees means lots of birds."

I couldn't argue with that logic. I smiled and carefully wrapped the old cell phone in cloth before tucking it into its own box. I wrote the name *Blankenberger* on the front of the box with a black marker and placed it in the safe, directly on top of the box holding Kathryn's and Simon's much newer phones. I felt like I was placing a dried-out mummy in the safe.

I closed the safe and made sure it was locked, then reached for a set of keys on the board. "Here are your room keys," I said, handing the set to Ned. He took the keys and placed them in one of his many pockets. "The key with the red tab is for your room. The key with the white tab is for the front door, which I lock every night at ten o'clock. Since it sounds like you will be out late watching for owls, remember to keep that key with you so you can get back in."

Ned nodded. "No problem." He held a large bag in each hand. A bulging, olive-green backpack sprouted from his back like a giant fungus. He carefully lowered the bags to the floor and gently eased the pack off his back. He lifted the Bird Nerd hat off his head and scratched his balding scalp. A long brown braid hung halfway down his back. "I tend to get distracted," he said, leaning against the doorjamb between the mudroom and the kitchen.

"It happens to the best of us," I said. I finished with the guest book and returned it to the shelf. "Let me show you to your room. Would you like some help with your bags?"

Ned didn't answer. He had stopped leaning against the door frame and now his posture was ramrod straight. He stared at something behind me and I turned, terrified I would see some horrible creature ready to pounce.

The only thing behind me was the window facing the side yard, where I had installed a hummingbird feeder. Several of the colorful birds buzzed around the feeder, darting in and out to take sips of the bright red sugar water.

"Beautiful," Ned breathed. He was transfixed by the birds, smiling with joy each time one stuck its long slender beak into one of the small plastic flowers ringing the bottom of the feeder.

"Um, Ned?" I was afraid to break his trancelike state.

Ned shook his head and stared at me. For a split second I thought he didn't even remember me, but then he smiled and grabbed his binoculars. "Like I said, sometimes I get distracted. I have loved watching birds for as long as I can remember. My mother said I would sit in the garden when I was little and watch the sparrows in the birdbath for hours. She had to drag me inside and force me to wash my hands and eat dinner." He chuckled.

I smiled. Ned Blankenberger was definitely an odd bird, pun intended, but he seemed nice enough. "Would you like some help carrying your luggage to your room?"

Ned shot one last glance at the hummingbirds. I got the feeling he would much rather be out there flying around and drinking nectar than inside dealing with humans. "No, but thank you. I have a lot of practice lugging around all my gear."

I stepped in front of Ned so I could lead him up the stairs. We reached the second story and turned right. I had placed Ned in the Blueberry Room, which happened to overlook the side yard where the hummingbirds were still enjoying their mid-afternoon meal. The room had been painted a deep, rich blue. A white crocheted coverlet covered the twin bed in its white metal frame. One of Grams' old wooden cabinets sat in a corner with a ceramic basin on top, a matching pitcher nestled inside it. Both the basin and the pitcher were white with pink flowers painted on them. I loved the old-fashioned touch the décor gave to the room. One of Grams' braided rag rugs was on the floor next to the bed. I started to show Ned the small washroom, but he moved quickly to the window and pressed his face to the glass.

"This room is perfect!" Ned exclaimed. He watched the hummingbirds down below for a minute. I didn't want to interrupt, and I was about to step out of the room when his head jerked suddenly upward. Before I could ask if he was alright, Ned let out a whoop. He turned and fumbled with the zipper on his backpack.

"Oh, I have to sketch this image before I lose it forever." He pulled a small sketchbook from his backpack. His pencil zipped over the paper, roughing in the outline of a hummingbird in flight. I backed out of the room and stepped quietly down the stairs.

Chapter 3

After dinner I opened the farmhouse's red front door, letting in a refreshing breeze through the screen door. I exhaled slowly, glancing around the kitchen. My head was spinning with half-finished tasks and the lingering frustration from my conversation with Finn earlier in the day. I heard a soft knock and was shocked when I saw who was standing on the other side of the screen door.

"Mom!" I dried my hands on a dishtowel as I rushed to the front door. My mother stood timidly on the porch. I gasped when I opened the screen door and she stepped into the farmhouse. Mom is normally a textbook example of a Type A personality. She is always on time and never has a hair out of place. Today her appearance shocked me. A streak of mascara cut across her left cheek like a thick black scar and her red-rimmed eyes were bloodshot. Her light brown hair, cut in a chin-length pageboy, was sticking straight up a la Bart Simpson. The sleeves of her purple blouse were smeared with makeup, as if she had used them to scrub her face. Her charcoal-colored slacks were rumpled and her ankle boots were covered in dirt.

"Hello, Rachel," Mom said. She straightened her spine and lifted her chin, as if daring me to mention her rough appearance. I felt my heartrate slow a bit. Mom looked like she had been dragged behind a truck, but she still acted and sounded like her usual self.

"It's good to see you, Mom," I said. I gave her a hug. She hugged me back and I stifled a gasp of surprise. Usually my mother's hugs are brief and loose, but compared to her usual embrace this felt like a vise grip. After almost a full minute I finally pulled away.

"So . . . what's up?" I wanted to ask *Why are you here?* but I didn't want to be rude.

Mom cleared her throat and tucked her blouse into her slacks. Almost before my eyes she was slowly morphing back into the put-together woman I recognized as my mother. "I was in the neighborhood and thought I would stop by," she said.

I used up every last ounce of my restraint when I managed to keep a straight face. Mom scheduled her life down to when she would use the bathroom, so I didn't believe for a minute that she had decided to just "stop by." She also lived in Grand Rapids, a good three hours from the tiny town of Hillsville. She didn't drive all this way for a casual visit.

I decided there was no sense in voicing my doubts. "It's great to see you," I said. "Come on in."

Mom stepped into the kitchen and visibly flinched. While Mom had never come right out and said it, I knew she didn't enjoy visiting the farm where she had grown up. She had never told me why, but I guessed it had something to do with her desire to always appear worldly and sophisticated. Things I saw as "quaint" Mom interpreted as "hillbilly." Mom had been adamant that I sell the farmhouse and the land, and my decision to move to Hillsville and turn the farm into a B&B had caused a great deal of tension between the two of us. I batted those thoughts aside for the moment.

"So, Mom, what brings you to this neck of the woods?" I asked. I resumed my spot at the sink, finishing up the dinner dishes. Bree was upstairs, delivering more towels to Kathryn and Simon's room.

Mom pursed her lips so hard I thought she would swallow them. She took a seat at the kitchen table and fiddled with the salt shaker. "I had some business to attend to," she said, looking at the table and avoiding my eyes. "I thought I would stop by to see you. Is that OK?"

I winced at Mom's accusing tone. "Of course it's OK," I said. "It's always great to see you. Will you be joining us for dinner?"

Mom still wouldn't meet my eyes. She stopped toying with the salt shaker and grabbed the pepper shaker. "Actually, Rachel, I was hoping I could spend a few days here."

Surely this was some sort of joke. I glanced around the kitchen, looking for a hidden camera. Was some annoying D-list actor going to burst out from behind a door and shout "Gotcha!"? Or maybe Mom's body had been taken over by aliens. That would certainly explain her disheveled appearance.

My silence was not sitting well with Mom. "If you don't want me to stay here, I can get a hotel room somewhere else." She stopped fiddling with the salt and pepper shakers and now had her palms pressed firmly against the tabletop. She held herself erect, but I could see tears pooling in her eyes.

"Of course I want you here," I said. Then I remembered all of my guest rooms were occupied. I couldn't turn away my own mother, though. I mentally scrambled for a solution, then came up with the only answer. "All of my guest rooms are full, so how about you bunk with me?"

Mom raised an eyebrow. "In the same bed?"

"No, of course not," I said. My back muscles spasmed at the thought of sleeping on the hard wooden floor, then my mind flashed to an image of an old cot I had found jammed into the back of a closet. "You can sleep on the folding bed."

Mom raised one eyebrow. I tried to remain strong, but couldn't. I had too many other things going on with the grand opening that it wasn't worth a fight. "I can sleep on the folding bed," I amended.

Mom smiled. "Thank you, Rachel," she said.

Mom went out to her car to grab her overnight bag. I pulled the folding bed from the closet and unfolded it next to my bed. During the renovations to turn the old farmhouse into a B&B, I had turned the old sitting room into a bedroom for myself. The bedroom was small, but I figured I wouldn't be spending much time there, so it wouldn't matter. Sharing the tiny space with Mom was going to be a tight squeeze, but I figured I could deal with it for a few nights.

Mom came into the room and placed her overnight bag on the floor next to the bed. I tucked a fitted sheet over the cot, along with the top sheet and a blanket. I pulled a pillow from my bed and dropped it on the cot.

"I am going to be leading a tour of the farm in a few minutes," I said. "Would you like to join us?"

Mom looked doubtful, but then nodded. "Just let me freshen up a little bit first," she said.

I left Mom in the bedroom and, along with Bree, gathered the guests in the front yard. A few minutes later Mom, dressed in jeans and a fresh blouse, joined the group. I made introductions all around. Dad looked surprised to see Mom, but he quickly turned his quizzical expression into a smile. Mom greeted Dad and Kelsey without a trace of discomfort, which I appreciated.

The first stop on the tour of the farm was the red wooden barn. When Simon saw me pulling open the large barn door, he planted his feet firmly in the gravel of the driveway and crossed his arms over his chest. "I'm not going in there," he said. "That's where all those evil cats live."

I bristled at Simon calling my sweet barn cats evil, but I didn't let it show. "No problem," I said lightly. "You can hang out for a few minutes and we will be back shortly."

Simon remained outside while the rest of the group trooped into the big red barn. I pointed out the stalls that had, once upon a time, housed horses and a milk cow. I let the guests climb the ladder into the now-empty hayloft. Several pairs of feet stirring up the dirt floor of the barn made me sneeze. Simon had been wise to stay outside. All of the dust and straw, not to mention cat dander, floating in the air would have wreaked havoc on his allergies.

"And this is where the barn cats live," I said, stepping into a section of the barn filled with bales of straw, several bowls of cat food, as well as several more bowls filled with water. As I spoke, a stampede of cats cascaded into the room. Black cats, orange cats, big cats, and little cats swirled around everyone's ankles. Kathryn didn't look interested in the furry felines, but everyone else knelt down or sat on straw bales to pet the cats.

In the midst of the kitty love fest, Mom let out a shriek. Startled, I turned to see if she was alright. Mom stood facing the barn wall where I had displayed several items I had found when cleaning out the barn. Hanging on the barn wall next to where the cats congregated were two wooden wagon wheels, several vintage license plates, and a pair of antique gardening shears.

Mom reached up and lifted the gardening shears from the bent nail on the wall. She hefted the shears in her hand and smiled. It was the first time I had seen her smile since she had arrived at the farm. "These gardening shears belonged to my Grandma Sophie," she said. "She used them to trim the rosebushes that grew in front of the house." Mom paused, looking sad. "The rosebushes aren't there anymore, but Grandma Sophie used to love them. She always asked me to help her tend the roses." As everyone watched, wide-eyed, Mom whipped out her phone and took a selfie of herself holding the shears.

I closed my eyes and groaned silently when I realized I forgot to put Mom's phone in the safe. I had been thrown off by Mom's unexpected arrival and I had forgotten all about putting her cell phone in the safe. Mom was grinning and taking shots of the shears. "I always loved trimming the rosebushes with Nana Sophie," Mom said. I never knew Mom had been so close to her grandmother, my great-grandmother. While I was happy the shears brought back so many wonderful memories for Mom, I couldn't have her using her cell phone in front of the other guests, who had all agreed to go tech-free.

"I can't wait to post these photos on Facebook," Mom said. The guests left the barn, and Simon rejoined the group. Bree led everyone over to explore the garden. Dad stopped and glanced longingly back over his shoulder at Mom's phone in her hand. Kelsey took Dad's arm and steered him toward the garden.

Mom reverently replaced the antique gardening shears on the nail protruding from the barn wall. I watched her, wondering how I would approach Mom about her phone. Mom had been acting so strangely since she had arrived. How would she react to my taking away her phone as if she were a misbehaving teenager?

Mom continued to flick through the selfies on her phone, smiling. "I can't believe how many memories those old shears bring back," she said. "Such happy times, before everything got so complicated."

"Um, Mom?"

"Yes, Rachel?" Mom lifted her gaze from the phone. Her eyes were hazy with memory and for a split second I wasn't even sure she recognized me. She was so caught up with being a preteen tending roses with her grandmother that she forgot she was now a middle-aged woman with a grown daughter of her own.

"This isn't just an ordinary B&B," I said, deciding the indirect approach would work best. Or maybe I was just being a wimp. "It's a tech-free B&B."

Mom stared at me and nodded, looking like she couldn't wait for me to stop talking so she could upload her photos on Facebook.

"Everyone has to give up their phones when they stay here," I blurted out. Mom looked confused. "*Everyone*," I emphasized, gesturing at her phone.

Mom looked down at her phone, then back up at me. "You can't be serious, Rachel," she said. Oh, great. *Now* she decided to sound like her usual headstrong self. "I'm a grown woman. You can't take my phone away from me like I'm a child."

A growing sense of helplessness swept over me, but I shook it off. "We are all adults here," I said, pointing at the group of guests now admiring the thriving rhubarb plants in the garden. We were having a bumper crop this year and Bree was showing everyone how to harvest the long, dark-pink stalks. I had asked her to pick the rhubarb, and I silently congratulated her on figuring out a way to get the guests to help her do it. "I realize you aren't a paying guest, but I can't let you use your phone while all the others have to go without. I'm sorry."

Mom looked angry, then terror stricken. "How will people get ahold of me?" she asked.

I pointed toward the house. "You can give them the phone number for the B&B and they can talk to you on the landline."

Mom lowered the hand holding her phone to her side. She gazed out at the excited guests snapping rhubarb stalks in the garden and sighed. "It's your home now, so I have to follow your rules." She didn't sound happy about it, but at least she didn't seem angry. She cast one last glance at her phone, then handed it to me.

"Thanks, Mom. I will put it in the safe with everyone else's phones."

I took Mom's phone and hurried into the house to place it in the safe. Once that was done, I rejoined the group tour. The guests were admiring the large pond on the property. "The pond is perfect for taking a dip, doing some fishing, or paddling around in a canoe," I said, slightly out of breath after having jogged from the house. I pointed to the flipped-over canoes nearby.

Aries and Leo took off their shoes and waded into the pond. Dad and Kelsey checked out the canoes, while Kathryn and Simon stood off to the side, watching everyone. Mom stood next to me, a frown creasing her face. I wasn't sure if she was still mad that I had taken her phone.

Aries and Leo splashed out of the pond, holding their shoes and socks in one hand. I led the group over to the tree line. "You are welcome to talk a walk in the woods," I said. "We share a property line with a nearby campground, so when you see the signs saying *No Trespassing*, please turn back."

Everyone but Ned nodded. He was busy scanning the trees. "A pristine owl habitat," he proclaimed with a smile. "I can't wait to get out there tonight."

The group headed back to the farmhouse. Aries gazed dreamily at the house, then her eyes rested on a set of white double doors at the base of the house nearest the driveway. "Is that a root cellar?" she asked. She raced over to the doors.

Just as she was about to yank on the handle, I let out a scream. "Don't go in there!"

Aries froze with her fingers grazing the door handle. "Why not?" she asked.

Numb with terror, I couldn't open my mouth to respond. The summer I was ten years old I played with a neighbor girl named Amy Custer. Amy had stringy, greasy blonde hair, a piggy nose, and puffy cheeks. She wore grubby clothes and often smelled like pee. I played with her even though I didn't like her all that much because there weren't a lot of other kids nearby, so it's not like I could be choosy. Amy had ripped the heads off two of my Barbie dolls and had spilled grape soda all over the Monopoly board. She had also broken several of Grams' knickknacks. Grams had banished her from the house, so the two of us played outside.

One day we decided to play hide-and-go-seek, one of my favorite games. Amy always guessed my hiding spots, though, and I was mad about it. Amy was being a sore winner, too, taunting me. I decided I would find a really great spot to hide, so I went to the root cellar. Grams had told me not to go in there, but with my seemingly infallible ten-year-old wisdom, I didn't think it was a big deal. I pulled open one of the peeling white doors and closed it quietly behind me. The cellar was flooded with darkness and I was instantly terrified of whatever creepy-crawlies might be lying in wait for me. I pushed the door open, spotted a brick nearby, balanced on a small pile of large rocks, and used that to prop the door open so I could have a little bit of sunlight and some air while

I hid. The steps were old and rickety. The cellar was seldom used, but at one time it had been where the family stored their canned preserves and root vegetables. The walls were dirt, as was the floor. The whole place smelled of sour earth.

Amy Custer was a cheater, though, and she was watching me. (That was how she always managed to figure out my hiding places – she peeked. It took me a long time to finally figure out the kid was a dirty rotten cheater.) I heard a scuffling noise around the cellar door and was angry that Amy had once again found my hiding spot. I kept quiet, though, hoping Amy was just passing by and I could still win the game of hide-and-go-seek. I *really* wanted to win.

Suddenly the small bit of light vanished. Amy had closed the cellar door! I rushed up the rotting wooden stairs but my foot went through one of the treads, a long rusty nail gouging my right calf. I grabbed for the railing with both hands and felt several slivers embed themselves in my palms and fingers. I cried out to Amy and wrenched my foot out of the broken tread. With blood trickling down my leg and into my sock, I lurched up the steps. I could hear loud thuds. Was Amy pounding on the cellar door? I finally reached the top of the stairs and pushed against the door. I couldn't wait to see sunlight and feel fresh air on my face. But the door wouldn't budge. I heard Amy let out a big grunt and then the loudest thud yet against the door. I kept pushing against the door and yelling, but I couldn't hear anything. No response from Amy.

Then I felt a spider drop onto my neck and down my shirt. I screamed then, deep, primal screams of terror. I flailed my arms at the spider but couldn't get the feel of it off my skin. I felt something else drop down from the wall into the back of my Scooby-Doo T-shirt. Something with millions of little legs and I could feel every one of them wriggling against my bare flesh. I ripped at my shirt to dislodge the creature and toppled backward down the stairs. I landed in a heap on the dirt floor, screaming and sobbing.

I don't know how long I was trapped down there in the cellar. My bloody leg throbbed, my head ached, and the splinters lodged in my palms and fingers burned. I screamed until I was hoarse. Finally I heard voices, someone calling my name. Grams! I stood up and yelled, "I'm down here! Save me!" Grams wasn't strong enough to remove all of the large rocks by herself, so she called down to me that she was going to go get help. It felt like an eternity before Grams returned with a neighbor man to help remove the rocks.

Grams talked to me the entire time the two worked to free me. Grams's soothing voice calmed my terror, but I still couldn't wait to get out of that cellar. When the door finally opened I hobbled up the stairs with my injured leg, avoiding the broken tread. Grams wrapped me in her arms and I sobbed into her shoulder. I told Grams what happened, that Amy and I had been playing hide-and-go-seek and Amy had trapped me in the cellar. Grams usually didn't so much as frown, but in that moment she looked enraged. She didn't say anything to me about Amy. She hugged me tight, told me she loved me, and then took me to the hospital, where I had to get a tetanus shot and X-rays. I got seven stitches in my right calf where the nail ripped my skin. I also had a slight concussion from falling down the stairs, as well as a sprained wrist.

Since that moment I have been deathly terrified of the cellar. After the incident Grams put a padlock on the cellar door and didn't tell me where she hid the key. That was many years ago, though, and the padlock was long since gone. The cellar was empty and hadn't been used in years. I am an adult now and I know the cellar can't hurt me, but I still shudder to think what horrible creatures might be living down there these days, the descendants of the insects that terrorized me when I was a child.

All of the memories from being trapped in the cellar that summer rushed through my mind. Everyone stared at me, waiting for me to speak. Finally I was able to open my mouth. "It's dangerous," I croaked out. Aries let go of the door handle. She didn't look satisfied with my answer, but she didn't press for more details. The tour had concluded on a sour note, but I was the only one who seemed to notice. Mom had gone back inside the farmhouse, and the other guests and Bree were about to join her when a purple Jeep roared into the driveway.

Chapter 4

The Jeep belonged to Shay Clarke, the owner of the Campfire Junction campground. The campground's property shared a border with the farmhouse's land, thankfully several acres away from the farmhouse. Shay had recently moved back to town and had been a pain in my behind from day one. She constantly stopped by the farm to complain about some issue, real or imagined. She had not been pleased when she found out about my plan to turn the farmhouse into a B&B. Shay hadn't come right out and said it, but I believed she felt that my new B&B would be competition for her campground.

Shay hopped out of the Jeep, a smirk on her face. Her long, straight hair was bleached a bright blonde, but about two inches at the ends had been dyed blood red. She wore a face full of makeup, including thick black wings of mascara at the corners of her green eyes. She wore a low-cut yellow halter top and tight jeans. A thick roll of flab flared out from beneath the revealing top.

The guests had formed a loose group around Shay and her vehicle. Kathryn and Simon stood to my right, while Bree had taken a spot to my left. Shay grinned at each guest in turn. She finger-waved at Kathryn and Simon. Kathryn sucked in a breath and looked like she wanted to say something to Shay. Simon put a hand on her elbow, but Kathryn shook it off. Shay's gaze landed on Bree next. A look of pure disgust bloomed on her face.

Willing my voice to be pleasant, I took a deep breath and said, "Hi, Shay. What's up?"

Shay adjusted her clingy jeans on her hips with one hand and waved her cell phone with the other. "Just came to say hey," she said. She surveyed the guests fanned out around her in the driveway. "*All* of these people are going to go without cell phones for a *whole week?*" She pursed her lips in a pout and made a face like she smelled something nasty.

Bree leapt to my defense. "No one is forced to stay here," she said. "All of these people want to take a break from technology for a while. Staying at the B&B will be relaxing."

Shay rolled her eyes and laughed. "Whatever you say. I wouldn't be caught *dead* without my phone." She turned toward the guests, holding her phone up in the air in one hand like Lady Liberty's torch. The phone's case was coated with silver rhinestones that sparkled in the sunlight. "If you all come to *my* campground, just up the road, I wouldn't take your cell phones from you. In fact, you could have all the gadgets you want. We have a game room with all the latest virtual reality games, five big screen TVs, and a pool." She wriggled the hand holding the cell phone. "Doesn't that sound better than sleeping in some old farmhouse and staring at the walls for fun?"

Simon looked like he would follow Shay anywhere. He kept his gaze locked on her phone and I thought I saw a trickle of drool ooze from the side of his mouth. Kathryn elbowed him in the ribs and he shook his head as if coming out of a trance. Leo and Aries looked at each other and frowned. Dad and Kelsey looked disgusted. Ned Blankenberger stared at the large oak tree in the front yard, his attention no doubt riveted on whatever feathery creatures were hanging out in its branches.

Beside me Bree was vibrating like a tuning fork. I grasped her hand tighter. Shay turned to me and winked. "No need to set your trailer trash bodyguard on me, Rachel," she said.

Bree let out a growl deep in her throat. I stared at her, shocked. The normally mild-mannered Bree was simmering with rage.

"Why don't you run home and cry to your loser mama?" Shay taunted.

Bree's hand slipped out of mine and she lunged for Shay. Dad and Simon quickly stepped forward and held Bree back. Shay hadn't moved a muscle. She laughed as the two men hauled Bree toward the house, her lip curled back in a snarl.

Bree strained to break free from Dad and Simon. The two men planted their feet firmly in the gravel covering the driveway. Their biceps bulged from the effort it took to keep her away from Shay.

"If you don't shut up about my mother, I'll kill you!" Bree screamed, tears streaming down her cheeks.

Bree's outburst stunned all of the guests into silence. Shay laughed again. I opened my mouth to defend my employee when Mom darted out the front door of the farmhouse and rushed to my side.

"What's going on out here?" Mom asked. I heard a quaver in her voice and turned to look at her. Mom was rigid as a flag pole, arms straight down at her sides as if she were forcing herself not to move.

"Well, I have places to go and people to see," Shay said. She waved her cell phone in the air one more time, the bright sunlight reflecting off the glittery cell phone case. "Remember, if you get tired of watching the grass grow, you can always come stay at the Campfire Junction Campground just a half mile down the road." She hopped back into the Jeep and roared out of the driveway, stirring up a cloud of dust in her wake.

Waving a hand in front of my face to clear the air, I slowly counted to ten. My blood boiled at the little stunt Shay had pulled. Not only did she want to take away guests from my B&B, she wanted them to stay at *her* campground. I didn't want my guests to see me angry, though, so once I mentally counted to ten, I forced my lips into a smile and turned to face the group.

I decided my best strategy was humor. "Isn't she a hoot? She's such a kidder."

Dad was quick to agree with me. "You bet, Rache," he said. He and Simon had let go of Bree now that Shay had left. He strode over to me and clapped a hand on my shoulder. "Maybe someday she can get a chance to stay at the B&B and realize what *real* fun is." He turned to address the other guests. "We're the very first guests at this amazing new bed and breakfast, folks," he said. "Let's all be grateful we have a chance to enjoy this beautiful, tranquil place."

Dad's rousing speech had caused Leo and Aries to perk up noticeably. "Yeah," Leo shouted, raising one fist in the air. "I'm not going to let anyone bully me into feeling bad about disconnecting." Aries, standing next to him, nodded so hard her curly hair was a blur around her head.

"So, what are we waiting for?" Dad asked. "Let's get back to what we were doing."

The guests headed toward the house. I turned to Bree and put a hand on her shoulder to comfort her, but she shook off my hand. "Try not to let Shay get to you, Bree," I said.

Bree didn't respond. She let out a muffled sob and ran to her car. She tore out of the driveway and quickly disappeared from sight.

The only guest remaining outside was Mom. She had stopped holding herself so rigidly, but now she was trembling like a lost kitten. Her gaze was glued to the spot where Shay had parked her Jeep, as if the loathsome woman were still standing there.

"Mom, is everything alright?"

Mom bit her lip and pulled her gaze away from the driveway. She fixed her green eyes on me. "It's getting chilly, Rachel. You shouldn't be outside without a jacket." She turned on her heel and walked into the farmhouse, the screen door slapping shut behind her.

Even though Mom hadn't said it directly, I got the message: Mind your own business.

****

I sat on the front porch after all of the guests had dispersed, worrying about Bree. I kept one ear cocked, listening for the phone to ring, but it did not. I took a deep breath of the cool evening air and tried to relax, but my muscles were clenched tight. I closed my eyes and leaned back in the wicker rocking chair. A few moments later I heard the sound of a lawnmower. The sound grew louder and louder, until an ancient riding lawnmower bearing a tiny old man puttered into the driveway and stopped in front of the house. I opened my eyes and smiled, feeling some of my tension fall away.

"Ernie," I said. "How are you?"

Ernie Biddle was an elderly man who lived a few miles down the road. I paid him to mow the farm's sprawling lawn, a task I was glad I didn't have to take care of myself. Even when he didn't have to mow the lawn, he would ride his lawnmower over to the farm to visit, usually in the evenings.

"I'm good, missus," Ernie said.

I lost track of the number of times I told Ernie I wasn't married and that he could call me Rachel, not missus. He seemed to prefer the term missus, so I let him use it.

"Gonna rain later this week," Ernie said, casting his gaze up at the sky. "Wanna get the lawn mowed before that."

I agreed. The thick, lush green grass surrounding the farmhouse tended to shoot up after a spring storm. Ernie and I agreed he would show up to mow on Thursday evening. We chatted for a few more minutes after that, then Ernie puttered off back down the road. I stood up from the rocking chair. I was still worried about Bree, but I had to push my concerns about my employee aside and get back to running my B&B.

Chapter 5

The next morning, I woke up at 5:30 a.m. to prepare breakfast for the guests. When I got out of bed, Mom was fast asleep, one arm flung over her eyes. The sky was still dark as I dressed quietly, pulling on a pair of jeans and a light blue sleeveless cotton blouse. I pulled my hair away from my face into a high ponytail and left Mom snoring in my bed.

The farmhouse was cozy and still while all the guests slept upstairs. Outside birds tweeted, flying here and there among the branches of the oak tree in the front yard. I opened the red front door and let the early morning breeze blow in through the screen door. The scent of dewy earth and green grass wafted through the kitchen, chasing away the last traces of sleepiness and putting a little pep in my step.

I hummed as I pulled a carton of eggs from the refrigerator and placed it on the counter next to the stove. I returned to the fridge for a large hunk of Swiss cheese and a container of chopped ham. I pulled the cheese grater from its place in the cabinet above the stove and began rubbing the wedge of cheese over the large holes in the grater. The curls of white cheese dropping into the glass bowl quickly turned into a mini mountain.

The sound of the screen door opening stopped me midgrate. I twirled around to find Bree standing in the kitchen. She wore the same white polo shirt and khakis she had worn the day before, although today they looked rumpled and a little grubby. However, her hair looked like it had been combed and freshly woven into a French braid that hung down her back. Her eyes were bloodshot.

"Bree!" I said. Then, remembering my guests sleeping soundly upstairs, I lowered my voice. "What are you doing here?"

Bree stared down at the wooden floorboards and shuffled her feet. "I work here," she said. She lifted her head and looked at me. "Right?"

I took in a big breath, then blew it out slowly. Yesterday I hadn't been sure if Bree's taking off had meant she was just angry, or if she was quitting her job. Apparently it had been the former. I gazed at Bree for several moments. She looked so sad and lost. I didn't want to scold her, but I also didn't want her to think she could just take off whenever she felt like it. I wanted – no, needed – an assistant who was serious about her duties.

"I understand why you took off yesterday," I said, putting down the hunk of Swiss cheese. "However, that doesn't change the fact I really needed you to help out and you weren't here."

Bree sighed and nodded. "I know I let you down," she said. She clenched her fists at her sides. "But Shay just made me so mad with what she said about Mama."

I rushed to soothe Bree before she could work herself up all over again. "What Shay said was mean and vicious," I said. "If you can promise me you won't let your emotions interfere with your job again, I would be happy to have you keep working for me."

Bree's smile lit up the whole kitchen and I felt a big grin breaking out on my face, too. I enjoyed working with Bree and was happy she had returned.

"Thank you, Rachel," Bree said. "You won't be sorry." She scrubbed her hands at the sink, then pulled an apron from a drawer. "What would you like me to do first?"

I paused to think about what I would be serving for breakfast. Along with the ham-and-cheese omelets, I had planned to provide guests with home-baked bread slathered in butter and plump, tart raspberries. I scanned the countertops but didn't see any berries.

"Did you happen to pick any raspberries yesterday?" I asked.

Bree shook her head. "No. I was going to, but then Shay —"

I held up a hand. "Say no more."

"Do you want me to go pick the raspberries?" Bree asked, reaching behind her to untie the strings of her apron.

"No, no," I said. I glanced down at Shay's new white sneakers. "I don't want you to get your shoes dirty. Can you stay here and finish grating the cheese for the omelets?"

52

"No problem," Bree said, bustling over to the counter and picking up the wedge of cheese.

I rinsed the bits of cheese off my fingers then grabbed a large plastic pail from its spot next to the kitchen door. I didn't mind making a trip out to the garden myself, especially in the morning. I could take in the splendor of a country sunrise and watch the dark sky magically lighten over the fields.

I slipped my feet into a pair of old sneakers that I wore when working in the garden. I opened the screen door and closed it quietly behind me so I wouldn't make any noise and awaken the sleeping guests. Stepping down the stairs from the front porch I paused and took a deep breath. The smell of damp earth and growing things filled my nostrils and flooded my mind with memories of waking up early and walking to the garden with Grams. She had loved being outside early in the morning.

Swinging the empty pail by its handle, I crossed the large expanse of grass separating the house from the garden. Almost instantly my sneakers were soaked with dew. I could feel the moisture seeping into my socks. I would definitely have to shuck off this pair of socks and put on another pair when I got back to the house.

The raspberry bushes grew in a line along the section of the garden closest to the house. I picked all the berries I could in front, reveling in the sound of the first few berries plopping against the bottom of the pail. Eventually a layer of raspberries built up inside the pail. I stepped around the raspberry bushes, my sneakers sinking into the soft soil. Behind me was a line of thick, robust rhubarb plants, their large leaves brushing against my ankles as I picked raspberries.

"Yikes!" Windmilling my arms, I managed to keep myself from pitching face first onto the ground. I had stubbed my sneaker against something in the soft dirt. *I probably left one of my gardening tools behind again*, I thought. No matter how organized I was in every other aspect of running the farm, it seemed like I could never keep track of the tools I used when I worked in the garden. Just last week I had left a rake behind and had luckily stepped on the top of the handle, not the sharp tines.

I bent at the waist and brushed aside a large rhubarb leaf. Bree and the guests had picked all the rhubarb the day before. The guests had enjoyed the tangy rhubarb crumble I had made for dessert, and I was eager to make another of my favorite desserts, Grams' recipe for a rhubarb cake with a crunchy layer of cinnamon sugar on top. With thoughts of moist cake on my mind, I screamed when I saw a hand covered in garden soil poking out from underneath a rhubarb plant. I dropped the rhubarb leaf and stood. My scream had broken the stillness of the summer morning, but no one came running. While I was a little concerned that screaming didn't immediately equal help on the way, I was also glad no guests had heard me.

Taking a deep breath, I lifted the rhubarb leaf again. There was the hand, curled against the dirt as if the person had been ready to claw at something like a wild animal. My gaze traveled from the hand up the arm to the bare shoulder. The body, which was that of a woman, was wearing a slinky, strapless black dress. The dress was hiked up well past her hips, exposing a pair of lacy black thong panties. She wore black high heels on her feet, but one of the heels had broken off. A glob of matted straw was stuck to the bottom of the intact heel.

My first thought was that this woman had gotten drunk and passed out in my garden after a night on the town. But most people in the tiny town of Hillsville were in bed every night by ten o'clock, and there weren't any places here where a woman wouldn't be out of place wearing a little black dress and sky-high heels. Then my eyes spied great-grandma's antique gardening shears sticking out of the woman's back. OK, that was definitely a sign that this woman was dead, not drunk.

The woman's curly hair was piled on top of her head in an updo, but portions of the elaborate hairdo had come undone and trailed along the ground. Blonde strands with the tips dyed bright red. I only knew one person with hair that color. I pressed a hand to my mouth. Oh my gawd. Shay Clarke was dead in my garden.

I felt another scream bubbling up in my throat, but I gulped it down before it could once again shatter the stillness of the summer morning. In my haste to get out of the garden my foot kicked the pail of raspberries, scattering the bright red berries over the ground. A few bounced off Shay's bare legs and I stifled a moan.

I tripped over the pail and landed on my knees in the dirt next to Shay's body. Her head was turned toward me. Thick, sparkly silver eyeshadow coated her eyelids. She must have put on false eyelashes when she had gotten all dolled up because one of them was crawling over her right cheek like a spider, while the other had migrated onto her forehead. Her red lipstick had smeared around her mouth, making her look like a macabre clown. I launched myself to my feet and made a mad dash for the house.

I flew through the front door, shutting it behind me. Leaning against the door, my chest heaving, a terrifying thought hit me: What if the killer was still at the farm? I scrabbled for the lock and threw it into place.

"Rachel?" Bree stood in front of me, a large spoon in her hand. "Are you alright? What happened?"

I didn't reply. My body felt huge and out of control, like a Macy's Thanksgiving Day Parade balloon that had broken free of its holders. I stumbled through the kitchen to the phone hanging on the wall. It took five tries to punch in the numbers 9-1-1, but when I did, I was rewarded with the sound of a female dispatcher's voice coming through clearly on the line. "What is the address of your emergency?"

I recited the B&B's address. When the woman asked what my emergency was, I blurted out, "Murder."

"Ma'am? Did you say murder?"

I took a deep breath and focused my gaze on the bowl of shredded Swiss cheese sitting on the counter. It felt like days had passed since I had started preparing breakfast. A glance at the clock on the stove told me I had been outside about fifteen minutes.

"Ma'am, are you still there?"

"Yes, yes I am." Another calming breath. "I found a dead woman in my garden, underneath a rhubarb leaf."

I wasn't sure how important the rhubarb leaf was to the dispatcher, but I figured I would toss in that little extra detail for good measure. The woman on the other end of the line told me to stay put and that the police would be there shortly. She asked if she needed to stay on the line with me, but I told her I would be OK.

Bree pounced on me as soon as I hung up the phone. "Someone has been murdered?" she asked. "We have to help them." She tossed the spoon into the sink and was halfway out the door when I grabbed her by the back of her shirt and pulled her back into the house.

55

"You can't go out there," I said. Bree turned to look at me and I shook my head. "Shay is out there in the garden and it's too late to save her. She's dead."

Bree's hazel eyes widened and she dropped into a kitchen chair. "Shay? Dead?" she whispered. She stood up again and marched toward the door. "I can't leave her out there all alone," she said. "I can at least sit with her until the police come."

Before I could try to talk her out of leaving the house, I heard footsteps on the stairs. My heart pounded in my chest. What would I tell my guests?

Thankfully the first person down the stairs was Dad. He rubbed his eyes and yawned, but when he saw me standing stock-still in the middle of the kitchen, he rushed to my side. "Rachel, are you alright?" he asked. "What's the matter? Are you sick?" He glanced over at Bree, taking in her pale face and scared eyes. "What's going on?"

I shook my head. Dad held me in his arms and smoothed my hair with his hand the way he had when I was little and had a nightmare. "Whatever it is, it's going to be OK, honey," he said.

After a few minutes I stepped away from Dad's embrace. Bree took a seat at the kitchen table. I flopped into the chair next to her and stared up at the ceiling. The adrenaline had drained from my body, but my mind was just gearing up.

"Are you ready to tell me what happened?" Dad asked, sitting down across from us at the table.

I nodded and pulled my gaze away from the ceiling. "Yes." Deep breath. Best to go the direct route. Dad could handle it. "I went to the garden to pick raspberries to go with breakfast and found a dead body."

Dad's mouth formed the most perfect O shape I had ever seen. Before I could say more, the sound of a car pulling into the driveway caught my attention. I looked out the window and saw a police cruiser roll to a stop in the driveway. At just that moment I heard the sounds of several pairs of feet tromping down the stairs. I turned frightened eyes to Dad and Bree.

"The guests," I whispered. "There's a cop here to deal with a dead body. What am I going to do?"

"Leave it to me," Dad said, standing up quickly. "I can handle a few drowsy guests. I'll offer them some coffee and keep them occupied with my stand-up routine."

Dad's not-so-secret dream was to be a stand-up comedian. I wondered which would horrify my guests more—Dad's stand-up routine or a murdered corpse. My mind was too jumbled to think straight, so I decided Dad's routine would probably be less gruesome. Probably.

"Thanks." With an effort I heaved myself to my feet. Now that the adrenaline had subsided, I felt like I could sleep for days. Bree hurried to help Dad brew coffee and finish preparing breakfast.

I opened the front door to see an older man in a police uniform standing on the front steps. He was only a few inches taller than me, but several feet wider. Bits of egg yolk clung to his gray beard and jam stains decorated the front of his rumpled uniform shirt. I leaned forward and caught a whiff of blackberries. His face was twisted up into a scowl. I mustered a weak smile. "Good morning, officer," I said, stepping out onto the front porch.

"Good morning." He tugged his utility belt higher on his wide middle, only for it to once again slide under his overhanging belly. "My name is Officer Barnes. What's the trouble here?"

I thought the dispatcher would have already told him there was a dead body. I glanced behind me. Kathryn and Simon held steaming mugs of coffee in their hands. Aries and Leo were just walking into the kitchen. Leo's man bun was askew, tendrils of curly dark hair trailing over his left eye. He yawned and lazily brushed the hair behind his ear. Aries, dressed in sweatpants and a hot-pink tank top, gazed vacantly around the room with sleepy eyes. Before anyone could notice me talking to the police officer, I quietly closed the door behind me.

"I found a dead body," I whispered.

"What?" Officer Barnes's loud voice almost knocked me off my feet.

I leaned closer to the officer and in a slightly louder voice said, "I found a dead body in my garden."

I thought for sure this information would send the officer into immediate action. Instead, he leaned against the porch railing. "Are you sure?"

Was I *sure*? A shot of anger made me shake off my sluggishness and stand up straight. "Yes, I am sure."

Officer Barnes ran a hand over the short gray stubble on his scalp. "Awful strange to find a dead body around these parts. Maybe it's just an old scarecrow that fell down off his pole?"

I didn't dignify that question with a response. I turned on my heel and strode across the damp grass. The sun had risen, the sherbet-colored sky giving way to a crisp blue backdrop. Beads of dew still clung to the grass tips, sparkling in the early morning rays of the sun. Trusting Officer Barnes would follow me, I didn't look back as I walked toward the garden.

I stopped at the edge of the garden and steeled myself for what I already knew lay among the rhubarb plants. Officer Barnes stopped next to me, out of breath from the short walk. "Her body is over there," I said, pointing. "Under that large rhubarb leaf."

Officer Barnes walked gingerly through the moist soil and drew his baton from his utility belt. He used the baton to lift the rhubarb leaf and cursed under his breath. "There goes my chance at getting back to my early-bird breakfast at Mabel's Diner," he said.

Mabel's Diner was one of the two restaurants in Hillsville. Officer Barnes let the rhubarb leaf drop and stuck his baton back in its loop. He stepped out of the garden and pulled a small notebook from his pocket.

"Do you know the deceased?" he asked.

I relaxed a little bit. This was more like it. Officer Barnes came off as lazy and uncaring, but underneath it all he was a professional. I licked my dry lips. "Yes. Her name is —was— Shay Clarke. She owned the Campfire Junction Campground down the road."

Officer Barnes made a note on his pad. "She a friend of yours?" he asked.

"Ummm." I bit my lip. I didn't want to be unkind and say that my relationship with Shay was about as pleasant as a chronic yeast infection with a side of migraine, but I also wanted to be honest. I settled for a bland half-truth. "We knew each other, but we weren't friends."

That response seemed to satisfy the officer. He stepped back from the garden, turned his back on me, and muttered into his shoulder mic. "Techs are gonna be here soon to process the scene," he said. "Medical examiner will take the body, too."

The body. Shay had gone from a living, breathing human being to "the body" in the course of just a few hours. I stared down at the blonde hair with the tips dyed blood red and realized I knew very little about my neighbor. Was she married? I glanced at her hands. Her right hand was trapped under her body, but her left hand was splayed out in the rich black soil. No ring on her third finger. Did she have children? I didn't even know how old she was. I had assumed she was a few years younger than me, perhaps in her late twenties, but I really had no idea. A lump formed in my throat and I blinked away tears. No matter how loathsome Shay's behavior had been, she was still a person with friends and family who loved her.

"Ma'am?" Officer Barnes' voice broke into my morbid reverie. "You can wait in the house if you want. We can take it from here."

I looked up and saw several techs had arrived while I had been staring at Shay's body. I nodded and quickly stepped out of the way. Officer Barnes tipped his chin at me as I passed. I walked slowly at first, then burst into a run. I wanted to put as much distance as possible between myself and the dead body in my garden.

****

I watched as a swarm of people processed the crime scene in the garden, trampling the veggies I had so lovingly planted and tended. Then I chided myself for such a trivial thought. A woman had been murdered in cold blood.

The phone rang and I rushed to answer it. "Yesteryear B&B. How can I help you?"

"Hi, Rachel." The minute I heard Finn's voice I felt a tsunami of guilt crash over me. My last words to him from the day before echoed in my head: "I will call you. I promise." I hated not keeping my promises.

"You didn't call me back like you said you would." Finn's voice sounded hurt. Maybe my dark mood was clouding my perception, but I noticed his voice also seemed a bit whiny. I chalked it up to my rude early-morning surprise. Stumbling over a body – literally – first thing in the morning would definitely cast the rest of the day's events in a negative light.

"Finn, I am so sorry." I gazed out the window, continuing to watch the techs gathering evidence. Should I mention Shay's murder? Finn wasn't happy about me picking up and leaving Chicago. If he thought there was a murderer on the loose in my backyard, he would only use that as yet one more reason why I should sell the farmhouse and move back to the city. Of course, I could always argue that Chicago had far more murders than the tiny town of Hillsville.

"Do you have a few minutes?" Finn asked. I bit my bottom lip. Lately I was so busy I barely had time to brush my teeth. At the moment crime-scene techs were camped out in my garden and my guests were clumped together, buzzing like agitated bees as they ate their breakfasts. Now wasn't really a great time to have a heart-to-heart conversation with my former fiancé.

"Um." It wasn't the best answer, but it was the only answer I could come up with that wasn't an outright "No."

"I'm sorry to inconvenience you, Rachel." Finn's frosty voice must have iced over the phone lines from Chicago to Hillsville. "I thought that, as your *fiancé*, you would be able to spare me a little bit of your time. I guess I was wrong."

For the second time in less than twenty-four hours, Finn hung up on me. I held the phone in my hand, staring at it until the dial tone sounded. Dad came into the kitchen and frowned when he saw the phone dangling from my limp hand. He gently took the handset and hung it up.

"Rachel?" He put a hand on my shoulder. His touch was warm and reassuring. "The police said they are done processing the scene." He pointed out the window, where the medical examiner's van was pulling out of the driveway. "They have removed Shay's body."

A shudder rippled through me as Dad's words echoed in my head. *Shay's body. Shay's body. Shay's body.* A woman had been murdered at the farmhouse, the one place in the world where I had always felt safe and loved. As that realization dawned, anger replaced my fear. I watched the van as it turned right and kept my gaze riveted on it until it vanished from sight. I would not allow anyone to get away with murder at the farm. No matter what, I would find whoever had killed Shay.

****

I cleaned up the kitchen after breakfast, then headed upstairs to help Bree clean the guest rooms. I could hear Bree singing when I started climbing the stairs. She was singing a familiar oldie, but she was getting the lyrics completely wrong. I smiled to myself.

When I reached the upstairs landing, I saw that she had already cleaned Leo and Aries' room and was halfway through tidying up Ned's room. A wheeled cart with a pile of dirty sheets stood in the hallway. On the bottom of the cart were bottles of cleaning solution, rags, and a duster.

"Where do you want me to start?" I asked, poking my head into Ned's room. Bree had just gotten to the big finish of her song and I startled her midnote. She had been trying to wedge a pillow into a pillowcase and both items slipped from her fingers and fell to the floor.

"Sorry," I said. "I didn't mean to scare you. I thought you heard me coming up the stairs."

"It's OK," Bree said, bending over to pick up the pillow and pillowcase. She struggled to hold the pillowcase open while shoving the pillow inside, so I stepped across the room and took the pillowcase from her. Holding it open, I helped her guide the pillow inside. "Thanks," she said, arranging the pillow neatly next to its mate at the head of the bed. "I'm done in here, so you can help me work on the Green Apple room."

The Green Apple room was where Simon and Kathryn were staying. I thought about the mismatched couple as we stepped out of Ned's room and closed the door behind us. I hoped they were enjoying their anniversary vacation. The two seemed like opposites in every way, yet they had still managed to get through twenty-five years together. That filled me with hope. If two people as different as Simon and Kathryn could make it, perhaps there was a chance for me to live happily ever after.

"Can you?"

I had been woolgathering and had completely missed what Bree had said. "Can I what?"

"Can you clean the bathroom while I work on stripping the bed and vacuuming out here?"

"Sure." I retreated to the hallway to pluck various bottles of cleaning solution and a few clean rags from the cart, stepping over a pile of blankets and a pillow spread out on the floor of the guest room. I gasped when I saw the bathroom.

"What on earth happened in here?" I said.

Bree stopped pulling the sheets from the bed and peeked over my shoulder into the bathroom. "Wow. It looks like they used every tissue in the storage closet."

"And then some," I murmured, taking in the piles of crumpled tissue covering the floor of the small bathroom. A mound of tissues overflowed from the wastebasket next to the toilet, and there were yet more used tissues filling the sink. A box of Benadryl perched on the edge of the sink, partially covered by tissues.

Bree wrinkled her nose. "Eeeww. That's a lot of snot," she said.

I nodded slowly. I didn't look forward to plucking all of those tissues out of the sink with my bare hands. I placed the cleaning supplies on the closed toilet lid and went back to the cart to grab a pair of plastic gloves and a large garbage bag. I slipped on the gloves and shook open the garbage bag. The gust of wind produced from snapping the bag open blew several tissues around the room like tumbleweeds. Quickly I began grabbing handfuls of tissues and stuffing them into the bag. Best to get unpleasant jobs done with quickly, Grams always said, and I agreed.

****

A few minutes before noon I heard footsteps tromping down the stairs. "Hello?" Ned called out. "Anyone here?"

"In the kitchen," I called back. Ned walked into the kitchen rubbing his eyes and yawning. Underneath his dark blue robe, he wore a white T-shirt and a pair of white cotton pajama pants covered with pink flamingos. I couldn't help but smile at the pink flamingos, but the smile fell from my lips when I realized Ned had slept through the grisly discovery of Shay's body and all that had come after. Should I tell him what had happened?

"Would you like some breakfast?" I asked, glancing at the clock. Guests were on their own for lunch, free to take the prepared sandwiches and salad from the refrigerator, but Ned had slept through breakfast. Plus, after what had happened to Shay, I wanted to do something kind for someone else, my small attempt to erase some of the horror her murder had left behind.

"Some scrambled eggs with cheese would be great, if it's no trouble," Ned said.

"No problem." I smiled brightly and pointed at the kitchen table. "Have a seat and I can whip up your breakfast in just a few minutes."

I grabbed a couple of eggs from the refrigerator, along with some cream and shredded cheese. "How did things go last night with the owls?"

Before Ned could reply, Mom, Kathryn, and Aries came into the kitchen through the front door. The three women were talking in low voices as they entered the room. I caught the words "Shay" and "murder." They stopped talking when they saw Ned seated at the table.

"Don't mind us," I said, cracking the eggs into a bowl. I whisked them quickly, added salt and pepper, then poured the liquid into the pan on the stove. "I'm just making some eggs for Ned. Would anyone else like anything?"

Mom shook her head. "No, thanks. We all got hungry at the same time and thought we would come in for some lunch."

"No problem," I said. "Did you want something in particular?"

Kathryn opened the refrigerator door. "I thought I saw a large bowl of salad in here earlier," she said. She pulled a covered glass bowl from the refrigerator. While the others fixed a light lunch, Ned began talking about his night of birdwatching.

"Last night was incredible," Ned said, an enraptured look on his face. I placed a plate of scrambled eggs covered with melted cheddar cheese in front of him. "Do you have any hot sauce?" Ned asked. "I like my food spicy." I removed a small container of Tabasco sauce from a caddy in the middle of the kitchen table. "Thanks." Ned twisted the cap off the hot sauce and dumped half the bottle onto his eggs. I grimaced. The soft yellow eggs looked like they were drowning in hot sauce. Ned shoveled a forkful of eggs into his mouth and proceeded to relay every tiny detail of his owl adventures from the night before. I listened with one ear while I washed the dishes. Mom, Kathryn, and Aries took their salads and disappeared into the dining room, leaving Ned and I alone.

As Ned prattled on, it hit me: Ned had been outside last night. Could he have seen something related to Shay's murder? "What time did you get in last night?" I tried to keep my tone casual, although I think I could have shrieked the question at Ned and he wouldn't have noticed in his dreamy state, rhapsodizing about owls.

Ned stopped chewing and thought for a moment. "I wasn't exactly watching the clock," he said. He tilted his chin up toward the ceiling and pursed his lips. "Based on the position of the moon when I got back, I would say it was sometime around two a.m."

Two a.m. I had gone out to the garden between 5:30 and 6:00 and discovered Shay's body. The techs had said they didn't think Shay had been dead long before I found her body. I shivered, even though my hands were plunged deep into hot soapy water.

Ned resumed his talk about owls. "The last owl I spotted was a barred owl in that huge black ash tree. I heard him before I saw him. He was magnificent."

I knew which tree Ned was referring to. That tree was just a yard or so away from the garden where I had found Shay's body. Another shiver passed through me.

"I spotted him high among the branches," Ned said proudly. "I called out 'I see you!'" Ned laughed, his mouth open wide. A blob of sauce-drenched egg landed on the sleeve of his robe, but he didn't notice.

I glanced at Ned's plate. He had polished off almost the entire mound of eggs, along with nearly half a bottle of Tabasco sauce. He scooped up the last bite of scrambled eggs and stuck it in his mouth. The fork clattered to the plate and he wiped his lips with a napkin.

"Are you sure you can handle all of that hot sauce?" I asked, removing the plate from the table and adding it to the other dishes in the sink.

Ned leaned back in his chair and patted his abdomen. "Back in college they used to call me 'Iron-gut Blankenberger,'" he bragged. "I could eat stuff that would melt the paint off an Oldsmobile and never have a problem." He let out a small belch. "Excuse me."

I swiped at the dirty plate with a sponge. "So, what's on your agenda for today?" I asked.

"I'm going to work on my sketches of that black ash tree," Ned said. "I want to include it in some of my owl sketches and I want to make sure I capture its true majesty and beauty." Ned pushed away from the table and cinched his robe tighter. "Thanks again for breakfast," he said.

"You're welcome," I replied.

Ned headed toward the staircase just as Mom, Kathryn, and Aries emerged from the dining room. There was a bit of a traffic jam and Ned stepped aside so the three women could enter the kitchen. They handed me their bowls and forks. I waved away their offer to wash their own dishes.

"I can handle everything in here," I said. I finished washing the dishes and wiped down the counters. Satisfied that the kitchen was clean, I changed into a pair of shorts and a T-shirt. I was going to lead my guests on a hike through the woods. I couldn't wait to lead everyone through the leafy paradise that stretched behind the farmhouse.

Chapter 6

The guests taking part in the hike had gathered on the front porch. Kathryn sat in one of the rocking chairs, Simon next to her. They were both chatting with Dad, who was leaning casually against the porch railing. Leo and Aries were poring over a copy of a tree identification book.

Mom was not the hiking type, so she wouldn't be joining us. Ned was upstairs drawing. Kelsey had chosen to stay at the farmhouse and read one of Grams' tattered old romance novels.

Aries and Leo led the pack. This morning their eyes were bright, their cheeks pink with excitement. Leo's man bun looked freshly done, no stray wisps floating around his face. Aries bounced up and down in expectation. She stashed the tree identification book in a mesh sack she carried on her back. Packages of trail mix and bottles of water poked through the holes in the sack.

Behind the brother-sister duo were Kathryn and Simon. As always, Kathryn looked expertly turned out. She wore an olive-green T-shirt with a pair of crisp khaki shorts. Thick socks and sturdy walking shoes adorned her feet. She looked like a model in a camping supplies catalog. Simon, on the other hand, looked like he had rooted around in the bottom of his duffel bag and pulled out a ratty T-shirt and a pair of cutoff jeans shorts. His yellowed socks and holey sneakers made me wonder, yet again, at the secret of this mismatched couple's longevity.

Dad and I brought up the rear. I wanted to keep an eye on all of my guests. If anyone fell behind or looked like the activity was too much, I wanted to be there to offer assistance. Before we left the house, I had stashed a small first aid kit, a small portable radio, and several bottles of water into a backpack. Always be prepared, I say.

The walking trail through the woods was nothing more than a deer trail. All around us the plants and animals were bursting out in their spring splendor. I took in a deep breath of the sweet, clean air. A rabbit darted across the path in front of me and overhead birds called to each other. The rest of the world seemed to fade farther and farther away with each step we took into the woods.

I encouraged Dad to walk ahead of me and mingle with the other guests, but he stayed at my side. "I want to make sure you're OK," Dad said. "Finding a dead body in your garden isn't an everyday occurrence."

"No, it's not," I said, gently pushing aside a tree branch. "Thank goodness."

"If you need—"

A loud noise interrupted Dad midsentence, a high-pitched sound that echoed off the trees. I stopped and looked around. Aries and Leo were still in the lead, although they had stopped to rest on a fallen log. They were pointing and exclaiming over a patch of wildflowers growing next to the log, but they were too far away for their exact words to reach me. The sound came again, but the pair was too engrossed in their excitement over the flowers to notice.

I spied Simon trudging along on the trail. He stared straight ahead and seemed oblivious to the beauty that surrounded him. His face was a grim mask, as if he were on a death march and not a nature hike.

That left Kathryn unaccounted for. I looked to my right and saw her standing slightly off the trail. She caught my gaze and gestured wildly for me to approach as yet another high-pitched sound reverberated off the trees.

I raced to Kathryn's side, my hand instinctively reaching into my pack for the radio. Kathryn's face was red and she clutched her abdomen with her left hand. Her right hand was clamped firmly over her mouth. Surely, she must be sick.

"What's wrong?" I asked when I reached Kathryn's side. "Are you ill?"

Kathryn shook her head. Her hand fell away from her mouth and the loudest hiccup I had ever heard almost blasted me off my feet.

"I have the – *hicc* – hiccups," she said.

A wave of relief washed over me. I let go of the radio and smiled. "Hiccups are no big—"

"HICC!" Another mammoth hiccup overtook Kathryn's body.

Well, I could be wrong.

"Water," Kathryn gasped.

Of course. Many times when I had the hiccups I would drink water to make them go away. An easy fix. I swung my pack to the ground, unzipped it, and withdrew a water bottle. "Here you go," I said, handing Kathryn the water bottle.

She shook her head and let loose another turbo hiccup. "You – *hicc* – have to hold it – *hicc* –while I drink it."

By this time Dad had rounded up the other guests and brought them to where Kathryn and I stood. They gathered around us like a group of curious cows. Feeling somewhat foolish, I unscrewed the cap on the bottle. Before I could bring the bottle to her lips, Kathryn's hands shot straight up in the air, almost knocking the bottle from my hand. Alarmed, I spun around on my heel. I fully expected to see a homicidal maniac, armed to the teeth, but the only thing behind me was a sparrow hopping on a tree stump. My sudden movement startled the little bird, sending it flying off to a bush farther up the trail.

"What's going on?" Simon asked. "Is she sick or something?"

"Kathryn has the hiccups," I said, as the loudest hiccup yet came out of Kathryn, bouncing off the trees and scaring the poor sparrow away from the bush in search of a safer, saner location. Kathryn's arms were still in the air.

"This is how – *hicc* – I get rid of my – *hicc* – hiccups," Kathryn said. "Please. *Hicc*. Hold the water bottle – *hicc* – while I – *hicc* – drink it."

Kathryn looked miserable. With every hiccup her body seized up. Quickly I held the bottle to her lips. She kept her hands in the air and drank slowly from the water bottle. About halfway through the bottle her body relaxed and she dropped her hands to her sides. "Thanks," she said, panting. She rubbed at the water dripping down her chin. Wet spots gathered on her T-shirt.

"Do you want to rest for a minute?" I asked.

Kathryn shook her head. "I'm OK," she said, a wobble in her normally strong voice. "I'll just have to take it slow for a while."

"No problem. You can walk in the back with me."

Simon watched as Kathryn adjusted her fanny pack and brushed pieces of tree bark off her shorts. "What the heck?" he muttered, shaking his head. "I've never seen anything like that in my life."

I silently agreed. Not only were Kathryn's hiccups severe, but her method for getting rid of them was unique. I was just glad it was over.

****

That evening after dinner, I stood in front of the kitchen sink, up to my elbows in soap suds. Bree had had to go home early to tend to her mother, and I had told her I would tackle the dishes on my own. I was scrubbing plates when I heard someone cough. When I turned around, suds dripping from my fingertips, I saw Kathryn standing in the doorway to the kitchen. "Is everything alright?" I asked. Even though all of my guests seemed happy, I still worried that the Yesteryear B&B wouldn't live up to their expectations. I had tried to brush aside the nagging worries, but an undercurrent of unease still buzzed just below the surface.

"Do you need any help?" Kathryn asked. She was dressed to the nines in a sleeveless black blouse covered in large pink poppies. The designer jeans she wore fit her slim hips as if they had been made just for her.

Although her question shocked me, I managed to keep my expression pleasant as I accepted her offer. Based on everything I had observed about Kathryn, she would have been the last person I would have expected to offer to get her hands dirty. "Would you like an apron?" I asked. I didn't want to be blamed for any stains on her beautiful clothing.

"Yes, please."

I dried my hands on a kitchen towel and reached into a nearby drawer to extract a couple of Grams' homemade aprons for Kathryn to choose from. She picked a full-length white apron Grams had hand embroidered with sprays of small pink roses. "I like this one."

"You have great taste," I said, watching Kathryn slip the apron over her head. She turned her back to me so I could tie the apron strings. "I loved this apron when I was a little girl. Sometimes

69

Grams would let me wear it, but she always worried about me tripping over it because I was so short." I cast my gaze over Kathryn. With her chic, sleek blonde hair and perfectly applied makeup, she looked like a model for high-end kitchen appliances. With a laugh, I added, "In reality, I think she was more worried I would step on it and rip it. But I never did."

Kathryn smiled. "You must have been very close to your grandmother."

I turned back to the dirty dishes in the sink. I scrubbed at a pan to keep myself from crying. Even though it had been almost seven months since Grams had passed, reliving the wonderful memories we had shared could still bring tears to my eyes. Even though they were often tears of happiness, I still didn't want to turn on the waterworks in front of a guest. I finished scrubbing the pan and handed it to Kathryn, who plucked a fresh dishtowel from the pile next to the sink. She began drying the pan, waiting for my response. I decided to change the subject and get her talking instead. "So how are you enjoying your stay at the B&B? Is it like a second honeymoon for you and Simon?"

Kathryn's face clouded over and I worried I had said the wrong thing. Her expression cleared quickly, though, and she placed the dry pan on the counter and accepted a handful of silverware to dry. "I haven't done the dishes since I was a little girl," she said, looking down at the fork she was drying as if she didn't recognize what it was. "At home we have a maid take care of all the kitchen chores."

"Sounds nice," I said, glancing down at the yellow rubber gloves I wore on my hands. "Where do you live?"

Kathryn gazed out the window while she worked on drying a spoon. "Outside of Boulder."

"Colorado is such a beautiful state," I said. "I went to Denver for a restaurant owner's convention a few years back and loved it."

Kathryn nodded but didn't elaborate. She may have been willing to help in the kitchen, but she wasn't turning out to be a sparkling conversationalist. I cast about in my mind for some topic that might get Kathryn talking. I noticed she wore a silver charm bracelet on one slim wrist. Three silver hearts dangled from the bracelet, each with a different-colored stone within the heart. Presumably birthstones, one for each child. I hadn't met a mother yet who didn't want to brag about her kids, so I figured asking about them would be a sure way to give Kathryn plenty to talk about.

"You must have three kids, right?" I asked, looking down at the bracelet.

Kathryn's fist tightened around the dripping glass I had just handed her. I watched her knuckles turn white and worried the glass would shatter in her hand. Before I could say anything or remove the glass from her grip, she quickly dried it and placed it in the cupboard. "I have two children living at home," she said. "My oldest son is grown and out of the house."

"Is he in school?"

Kathryn shook her head. "No." I waited for her to say more, but she kept her focus on drying the bowl I handed her.

OooOK. The oldest son must be a sore topic for Kathryn. Perhaps he had dropped out of college and she didn't want to admit it. Or maybe he was working a job she didn't think was good enough and she didn't want to tell me what it was, thinking it might injure her perfectly cultivated image. It did not matter to me what her son did for a living or the choices he had made for his life, but Kathryn seemed like a woman who put a lot of effort into appearing perfect. I could see how having a son who didn't live up to her high standards could easily be a source of frustration for her.

"What about the other two kids?" I asked. A smile flickered across Kathryn's lips and I let out a little sigh of relief. Finally. A topic I didn't have to tiptoe around.

"My son, Cole, is fifteen years old, and my daughter, Jenna, is thirteen," Kathryn said. I listened intently as she told me about Cole's mastery of the cello and Jenna's love for horseback riding.

"Sounds like you have some pretty great kids," I said. I had finished washing the dishes and was rinsing out the sink.

"I do," Kathryn said. "It is a wonderful feeling to be able to give your children access to such esteemed hobbies. Growing up, my family didn't have much money, so I want to give my kids all the things I never had."

"Your husband must be just as proud of them as you are," I said.

Kathryn untied the strings of the apron and lifted it over her head, a faraway look on her face. "My husband usually doesn't have time to attend Cole's recitals or Jenna's competitions," she said. "He travels a lot for work."

I rinsed out the sponge and placed it in a basket next to the sink. "Simon travels a lot?" I asked. As a brewery owner, I guess it made sense that he would always be on the lookout for new beers.

"Simon?" Kathryn looked confused for a moment, then her expression cleared. "Oh, yes, Simon. He travels constantly." She laughed lightly. "Not much I can do about it."

Something about Kathryn's reply didn't feel quite right, but I shrugged it off. "Looks like we're just about done in here," I said. "I really appreciate your help."

"You're welcome," Kathryn said. She turned so I could untie the apron strings, then she lifted the apron over her head and handed it back to me. I folded it carefully.

I lingered in the kitchen, running the broom over the floor. I moved slowly through the living room, adjusting throw pillows no one had disturbed, straightening picture frames that weren't crooked. The old farmhouse was quiet except for the soft creak of wood settling. At ten o'clock I locked the front door. My sock-clad feet shuffled on the old floorboards as I crept past the nightlight by the stairs. The shadows inside the old farmhouse surrounded me, and I drew strength from their comfort and familiarity.

When I got to my bedroom, the door was half-closed. A sliver of light spilled out, casting a golden blade across the floor. I stood in front of the door for several seconds, my hand on the knob, wishing I didn't have to enter. Taking a deep breath, I pushed the door open and stepped into the room.

Mom sat propped up in bed reading a paperback novel. She looked up as I entered, smiled, then turned her attention back to her book. "Long day?" she asked, turning a page.

"Yes," I said, pulling a pair of shorts and a tank top from the dresser drawer. I quickly pulled on my pajamas. "I love it, though." I went into the bathroom to brush my teeth.

"You really don't have a cell phone?" Mom asked, flipping another page in her book. She asked the question like it was idle chitchat, and not the third time she had asked me that question since she had arrived at the farm.

"Nope," I said through a mouthful of minty toothpaste. "I gave it up after I decided to make the B&B tech free. I wanted to see what it was like. Honestly, it was a relief."

"Hmm." Mom laid the open book on her chest. "You know, most people don't voluntarily live like old-time pioneers."

I rinsed my toothbrush and placed it back in the cup. I opened up a container of moisturizing cream and rubbed a dollop of it over my face and down my neck. "And most people are miserable, checking their screens every five seconds," I replied. "I'm not."

Mom's lips tightened, but she didn't argue. Her eyes followed me as I walked from the bathroom to the cot set up in the corner of the room. I slipped under the covers and pulled one of Grams' quilts—a scrap quilt that was my absolute favorite—up to my chin. The small room suddenly felt claustrophobic.

Mom slapped her book shut. "You left a thriving restaurant to play house in the middle of nowhere," she said. "Not to mention a wonderful man who wanted to marry you. Forgive me for being curious."

I lay on my back on the cot, staring up at the ceiling. "You know why I left Chicago, Mom. I couldn't sell Grams' farmhouse. I have too many happy memories here." I was silent for several moments, trying to put into words how I felt about the house. "I feel like Grams' spirit is here with me. I can't turn my back on that."

"Oh, Rachel." Mom slid her book onto the bedside table. "Must you always let your feelings boss you around?" She clicked off the light. "Can't you be practical?"

I felt tears sting my eyes. Why couldn't Mom understand how important Grams' house was to me? "I am being practical," I said, managing to keep my voice from wobbling. "I have a waitlist a mile long for the B&B. People can't wait to come here and unplug from their devices. The farmhouse isn't just a haven for me. It's a place for my guests to go to get away from the rest of the world for a while."

Mom didn't reply. Only when her breathing deepened and she let out a small snore did I realize she had fallen asleep in the middle of our conversation. In the silence that followed, I felt the weight of our differences stacked between us like old boxes no one wanted to open.

****

I tried to let my body relax and fall into a deep sleep, but Mom's snores filled the dark bedroom within minutes. I tossed and turned on the cot, which was about as comfortable as trying to sleep on a sheet-covered rock. After lying awake for a couple of hours, I decided to take my blanket and pillow into the living room and sleep on the couch. I had just gotten settled when a voice floated to me through the darkness.

"Rache?"

"Yeah, Dad?"

A sliver of moonlight beamed through the window and I saw Dad standing in the doorway, dressed in a pair of cotton pajama pants and a white T-shirt. "Can I ask you for a favor?"

I sat up on the couch. "Sure. What do you need?"

Dad walked into the living room and perched on the edge of the couch. "How about you let dear old dad have his cell phone for just a minute?" he said, clapping a hand on my shoulder.

I collapsed back against the pillow and let out a sigh. "Dad, you know that's against the rules," I said.

"I know, I know," Dad rushed to reassure me. "But can't you bend the rules just a little bit? I just want to read one story on one news site. I promise it won't take long."

I stared at the darkened ceiling, watching the shadows dance in the corners. "Dad, if I let you look at your phone, what will the other guests say?"

"That's the beauty of it," Dad said. "No one needs to know. It can be just between us."

I sat up, punched my pillow, then laid back down. "I'm sorry. I can't open the safe for you."

Dad stood up from the couch. "Well, you can't blame a guy for trying, can you?" He bent over and kissed me on the forehead. "Nighty-night, Rachel. Sweet dreams."

I listened to Dad's footsteps on the stairs, then heard the door to his room softly open and close. I shut my eyes and let my body sink into the couch. Even Grams' saggy old couch was an improvement over that miserable cot. I felt myself drifting into the depths of sleep when a voice called out to me. Had Dad come back?

"Hey." The voice was coarser, definitely not Dad's. I sat straight up on the couch.

"Who's there?" I asked, my voice trembling.

"It's me, Simon." Simon stepped into the living room and I quickly pulled the blanket up to my chin. Although I wasn't wearing anything revealing, I still felt exposed wearing my pajamas in front of a man I didn't really know.

"What do you want?" I asked. My tone came out ruder than I would have liked, but Simon deserved it, sneaking up on me in the middle of the night. What was he doing down here anyway?

"Listen," Simon said, strolling into the room and standing over me on the couch. He reached into the pocket of his sweatpants and pulled out a wrinkled twenty-dollar bill. "How about we quit playing this silly little game?" He wiggled the money at me, but I kept my hands under the blanket. "I get to look at my phone and you make a couple bucks. What do you say?"

I shook my head. I watched Simon's face twist into an angry expression. The fleeting look passed quickly, though, and I didn't know if it had been a trick of the moonlight.

Simon thrust the money at me once more. "No one needs to know. It can be just between us."

The exact words Dad had uttered a few minutes ago, but this time the tone was harsh and demanding.

"I'm afraid I can't do that," I said, willing my voice to be strong. Simon stood next to the couch for several moments, then turned and strode out of the living room. I listened to him stomp up the stairs, hoping the noise wouldn't wake up any of the other guests. I spent another hour staring at the flickering shadows on the ceiling, then finally fell into an uneasy sleep.

Chapter 7

After breakfast the next morning I made a trip into town to visit the post office, a small stone building located on Main Street. I remembered Grams taking me to the post office when I was a child. The postmistress, Miss Millie, had always been one of my favorite people to visit. When I had moved back to town, I had been delighted to find out Miss Millie was still ruling the Hillsville post office with her iron fist and love for local gossip. If anyone could tell me who would have wanted to kill Shay, it would be Miss Millie. The bell over the door dinged when I stepped into the small building.

"Good morning," Miss Millie called out. She was a tiny woman with tight gray curls, almost like a helmet clinging to her head. She stood on a milk crate in order to see over the counter.

"Good morning," I replied. I stopped in front of a rack of greeting cards. A friend of mine in Chicago was having a birthday and I wanted to send her a special card. I picked up a card with a dog on the front. I would ease my way into asking Miss Millie what she knew about Shay. "How are you today, Miss Millie?"

Miss Millie patted her gray curls. "Been better. My arthritis in my right knee is acting up."

I clucked my tongue in sympathy. "That's too bad."

"Well, I guess I shouldn't complain," Miss Millie said. She peered at me over her bifocals. "Sounds like there's been all sorts of commotion over at your place." She stared at me expectantly, no doubt wanting juicy gossip about Shay's murder.

"Yes," I said, opening the card to read what was written inside. "I guess you heard about Shay?"

Miss Millie's short frame was vibrating with the anticipation of a big piece of gossip. "It's all anyone's talking about," Miss Millie said. She leaned across the counter. "I heard you were the one who found the body."

I nodded and gulped. The image of Shay's body, a pair of antique gardening shears sticking up out of her back, filled my mind. I fought the nausea, intent on finding out more about who might want to kill Shay.

"Do you have any idea who would want to hurt Shay?" I asked.

Miss Millie clasped her hands in front of her on the counter, a wicked gleam in her eye. "There was surely no love lost between Shay and Darlonna Crowder," she said.

"Oh?" I dropped the card with the dog on it back in its slot and casually lifted out a card with two cats and a baby on the front. I didn't want Miss Millie to see how anxious I was for any scrap of a clue as to who could have killed Shay. "What happened between them?"

"Darlonna had an accident at Shay's campground and she sued." Miss Millie shook her head, frowning. Her tight curls didn't move. "Darlonna lost and was real bitter about it. Heard they had a big shouting match in front of the Corner Market not too long ago."

I thought about asking Miss Millie for more information on Darlonna, but I didn't want to arouse her suspicions. Knowing Miss Millie's penchant for gossip, she would be on the phone with Darlonna as soon as I walked out the door. I would figure out a way to get in touch with Darlonna myself.

"It's too bad that boy of Shay's is going to have to live his life without a mama," Miss Millie said, filling the silence. She wiped an invisible speck of dust off the shiny counter.

My head snapped up. "Shay had a son?" I asked.

Miss Millie nodded. "She sure did. His name is Carter. In the same grade as one of my great-nephews. Only about fourteen years old."

I felt terrible for that young man. Did I have what I needed to put together a casserole to take to Carter? I mentally ran through the items in my kitchen. I could make time to swing by the campground and offer my condolences, along with something to fill his belly.

"Was Shay married?" I asked. If so, I would need to make enough food for two hungry males.

Miss Millie shook her head. "No, but she did have a no-good boyfriend named Bobby." Miss Millie's lips pinched together in disapproval. "He works over at Skyler Industries."

Skyler Industries. The same factory where Bree had worked for a few short months.

"I'm so glad you decided to give Bree Foster a second chance," Miss Millie said. I jumped, wondering if the aging postmistress had read my mind.

"What do you mean?" I asked, turning toward the counter. Miss Millie's face registered her surprise. She opened her mouth to respond, but the bell over the door dinged and an elderly woman entered the post office. The woman's eyes lit up when she saw Miss Millie and she rushed forward to place two large cardboard boxes on the counter.

While Miss Millie and the elderly woman chatted, worst-case scenarios about Bree started crowding into my mind. I felt itchy with impatience to find out from Miss Millie what had happened. Had Bree perhaps been in trouble with the law for stealing? An employee with sticky fingers at the B&B would be disastrous. Or maybe she had embezzled from a previous employer. But Bree seemed so honest and open. What deep, dark secret could she be hiding?

Finally, the elderly woman left, waving at me on the way out. I returned the wave, feeling weak with worry about what Miss Millie would divulge about Bree. Miss Millie turned back to me. I plucked a card with a picture of a grinning Golden Retriever out of the rack and placed it on the counter. "I also need a book of stamps, please," I said. I was dying to hear more about Bree, but didn't want to appear too anxious. By the way Miss Millie was eyeing me, a slight smile on her lips, I didn't think I was hiding my anxiety too well. Miss Millie pulled a book of stamps from under the counter and placed it next to the greeting card.

"Oh, dear. You don't know, do you?" Miss Millie's voice was low and sad, but her eyes lit up. I could tell she was looking forward to filling me in on all the juicy details. "Bree used to work at Skyler Industries," Miss Millie said. I felt my anxiety ratchet down a few notches. That wasn't news to me. Miss Millie continued, "Bree worked there for four months." I let out a small breath, releasing more of my pent-up worry. That also wasn't news. Miss Millie noticed my reaction, then went in for the kill. She pitched her voice so low I had to lean across the counter to hear what she said next.

"She threatened to kill a supervisor," Miss Millie said. I couldn't keep the shocked expression off my face. Miss Millie looked quite pleased. "Yes, it's true," she said, nodding authoritatively.

"Why on earth would Bree do something like that?" I asked. I pictured Bree telling me about how she took care of her mother and her secret desire to one day go to nursing school. I couldn't imagine her squishing a fly, let alone killing another human being.

"Bree was in the employee break room when she went off on the supervisor and threatened him," Miss Millie said. Miss Millie looked pleased, but her smile dimmed a bit when I pushed back.

"Where did you hear this story?" I asked. Even though I hadn't known Bree for very long, I didn't want to rush to judgment or be pulled in by gossip.

Miss Millie stood up straight on her plastic milk crate and looked me straight in the eye. "I don't divulge my sources," she said primly, folding her hands on the counter in front of her. "Suffice it to say that I heard this story from a *very* reputable source, someone who works at the factory and heard about it firsthand."

I realized with a sinking feeling in my stomach that what Miss Millie had described was the same thing that had happened between Bree and Shay. Shay had definitely been the aggressor, but Bree still lost her temper and threatened her. It was not a good sign that Bree had a history of threatening people. I wondered if I had unknowingly brought a killer into the B&B. Could Bree have murdered Shay and left her body in the garden?

I didn't want to suspect Bree. I had felt an immediate connection and kinship to the young woman. The image of Bree as a doting, loving daughter who someday wanted to be a nurse and take care of others didn't jibe with the vision Miss Millie was painting of her as a violent person. Although I didn't want to believe Bree was capable of harming anyone, let alone murder, I couldn't shake the feeling that something just didn't fit.

I paid for the card and the book of stamps, said goodbye to Miss Millie, and headed for my car. Miss Millie had given me a lot of information about Bree's past, and most of it I didn't even want to consider, let alone believe.

****

When I got back to the farmhouse after my visit with Miss Millie, I decided to again ask Bree about why she had been fired from Skyler Industries. The two of us were folding sheets. We were the only ones around at the moment. Dad and Kelsey had decided to take a bike ride. Aries and Leo were in the barn petting the cats. Ned was sleeping late after another night out with the owls. I wasn't sure where Kathryn and Simon had gotten off to.

I was nervous about bringing up the topic of what had happened at the factory with Bree, but I felt it was important. Bree told me she had been questioned by the police. Everyone at the B&B had witnessed her threatening Shay, so it wasn't a secret. I thought it would be in her best interest to tell me about what had happened to get her fired from her job at the factory.

I decided to start our conversation with a neutral topic. "Do you know a woman named Darlonna Crowder?" I asked, folding a pillowcase and adding it to a stack of bed linens.

Bree's eyes lit up. "I love Miss Darlonna!" she said, bending in front of the dryer to take out another load of warm linens. She placed the pile on the folding table. "I was friends with her granddaughter, Amber, in school. Sometimes I would go over to Darlonna's house with Amber."

This was excellent news. If Bree was close to Darlonna, that would give me an excuse to pay her a visit and ask her a few questions. Such as *Did you happen to kill a woman in my garden and leave her dead body under a rhubarb leaf?*

"Do you think we could pay Darlonna a visit?" I asked.

Bree looked at me curiously. "Why?"

"I want to talk to her about Shay. I heard the two of them had a history together."

"Sure, we can go visit," Bree said, folding a pillowcase. "I'd love to see her again."

Several minutes passed in silence as we focused on our shared task. Finally, I cleared my throat and jumped right in. "I know it's not really my business, but I was wondering why you left your job at Skyler Industries. Did something happen?" *Like, did you threaten to kill your supervisor?* I wanted to add, but wisely kept my mouth shut.

Bree's smile bent into a frown, marring her lovely features. "I don't want to talk about it," she muttered, keeping her head down as she folded a fitted sheet.

I struggled to find a gentle way of saying what I knew, but I couldn't, so I just said it. "I heard you threatened to kill your supervisor. Is that true?"

Bree stopped folding the fitted sheet and laid it on the table. She closed her eyes. "Who told you?" she asked.

I didn't want to get Miss Millie in trouble. "I heard it around town," I said. "So, it's true? Bree, why would you say something like that?"

Bree opened her eyes and finished folding the fitted sheet. "I don't want to talk about it," she said again. She kept her head down and wouldn't look at me.

I sighed and dumped another pile of dirty sheets into the washing machine. I added laundry soap and turned on the machine. I watched Bree as I listened to the water filling the tub. Her expression was troubled as she folded a stack of towels. I still could not believe Bree was a killer. But could I be wrong?

Ned stuck his head into the laundry room. His long brown ponytail was draped over his shoulder. He lifted his Bird Nerd hat up and down on his head so fast it looked like a blur over his balding scalp.

"Is something wrong?" I asked.

Ned nodded and clapped his hat back on his head. "Did one of you happen to knock over my sketchbooks while you were cleaning?" he asked.

Bree and I both shook our heads. Since Ned slept late, we hadn't even gotten around to cleaning his room today.

Ned let out a breath. "My sketchbooks were open and on the floor. The pages were bent." Ned winced, as if just the thought of crinkled pages in his sketchbooks caused him physical pain. "My best camera wasn't where I left it, either. I put it on the dresser last night, but after I got out of the shower it was on the bed."

"We haven't been in your room since we cleaned it yesterday morning, Mr. Blankenberger," Bree said.

Ned shook his head, causing his braid to sway over his shoulder. "I'm always so careful with my gear," he muttered, turning and heading back toward the stairs.

I finished folding the last towel and added it on top of the stack on the folding table. I quickly dismissed Ned's questions about his sketchbook and camera. He usually had his head in the clouds, thinking about birds. It wasn't difficult to believe he had accidentally knocked over his sketchbooks and moved his camera, then forgot all about it. Besides, I had bigger problems, like what secrets my mother, and now my employee, were hiding from me.

Chapter 8

Bree, unusually subdued after our tense conversation about her job at the factory, offered to clean the living room. While Bree started up the vacuum, I quickly put together a casserole to take to Shay's son, Carter.

I poked my head into the living room. "I'm going to offer my condolences to Shay's son and take him something to eat." I showed her the foil-covered casserole dish.

Bree nodded, keeping her gaze glued to the carpet. I hated to see Bree upset. I wanted to make things better between us, but I didn't know how. I vowed to smooth things over between us when I returned.

I got into my car and drove down the road to the campground. It was my first time visiting Campfire Junction. I had driven past the entrance numerous times, but that was as close as I had gotten. I had been too busy getting the B&B up and running and handling my grief about Grams to devote that much time to thinking about the neighbors.

I turned into the entrance of the campground. My car shimmied and shook as I drove over the rutted drive. I tried to steer around the crater-sized potholes, but to do so I ran the risk of driving off the road completely and into the campsites. Instead, I slowed down, but even at a crawl I felt like my fillings were going to shake right out of my teeth.

Bree had told me that Shay and her family lived in a mobile home at the campgrounds, near the clubhouse and pool. I stopped the car in front of a dingy white mobile home with peeling dark brown trim. The trailer had definitely seen better days. A leaky air conditioning unit stuck out of a front window, dripping water onto the ground and making a mud puddle below. A large rust stain cascaded down the side of the trailer under the A/C unit. A small wooden porch had been tacked onto the trailer by the front door. I climbed the rickety stairs and prayed they held together long enough for me to reach the small landing. My heart skittered a bit when I heard the sound of a plastic bottle clattering along the sidewalk, blown by a sudden gust of wind.

Adjusting my purse strap over one shoulder, I balanced the casserole dish in my left hand so I could knock with my right. Before I could even make a fist, the sound of gunshots ripped through the air around me. Instinctively I went down into a crouch, throwing my right arm over my head while tucking the casserole dish under my left arm. I clung to the glass dish as if it were a life preserver.

The shooting stopped and I could hear men's voices. It sounded like they were coming from inside the trailer. I remained in a crouch, but I did drop my right arm to my side. A cell phone ring tone sounded inside the trailer. "Hey, man," said a voice. "Yeah, just playing video games."

I breathed a sigh of relief. Feeling foolish, I hoisted myself back to a standing position. The aluminum foil on the casserole dish had slipped sideways, so I righted it, tucking the foil around the smooth edges of the glass dish as I composed myself. I lifted my hand and knocked loudly on the door. I didn't hear a response, so I knocked again.

"Come in." I turned the knob and tried to push the door open. Something was blocking the door. I pushed a little harder and managed to create an opening large enough to slip through, but only if I turned sideways and sucked in my breath. A teenage boy was sprawled on the floor in the living room in front of a big screen TV. He had paused the game and was slouched against the couch, his cell phone pressed to his ear.

The house was a mess. A mountain of clothes and shoes was piled up by the front door, which was what had blocked my entry. Paper plates with stale pizza crusts on them, discarded containers of energy drinks on their sides, and empty candy bar wrappers covered the remaining floor space. The place smelled of dirty socks and body odor. The young man, who I took to be Shay's son, Carter, saw me and mumbled something into the phone. He poked the screen to end the call and looked up at me. He didn't even make a move to get up.

Not sure what to do, I hovered in the doorway. Finally Carter said, "Shut the door. The A/C is on. Mom will have a fit." He stopped talking and looked pained.

I shut the door behind me. "My name is Rachel Kent. I own the B&B down the road?" Not sure why that came out as a question. Of course I knew I owned the B&B down the road.

"Yeah. I heard about you."

"I want to tell you how sorry I am about your mother's . . . passing."

Carter paused the game. A hank of greasy hair flopped over one eye and he brushed it aside, only for it to fall back into his face. He wore a gray hoodie with stains on it and a pair of wrinkled camo pajama pants. He looked like he had slept in his clothes. My heart broke for him. He was only fourteen years old, still a child, really. And he had just lost his mother.

Carter's face grew hard as I stared at him. He might be a young boy, but in his mind, he was a man. He didn't look like he enjoyed a stranger barging into his house to pity him. I hoisted the casserole dish a little higher. "I brought a casserole. I thought you might be hungry."

Carter's eyes lit up when he saw the glass dish topped with foil. He didn't move, though, just waved a hand toward the kitchen.

I stepped around the piles of clothes, shoes, and stacks of empty TV dinner trays, some with food crusted on them. I almost went down after getting my feet tangled in the straps of an empty backpack splayed across the floor in the kitchen doorway, but managed to right myself just in time.

I heard Carter snicker behind me. I didn't turn around. Instead, I put the casserole dish down on the counter. "Would you like me to heat some up for you?" I didn't wait for a response. I started opening drawers searching for a spoon. I managed to find one clean spoon lodged in the back of a jumbled drawer. Either Shay hadn't been a very organized housekeeper or, in the space of a few days, Carter had turned feral. In my search for something to put the casserole on, I got lucky, finding a stack of clean plates in a cabinet above the stove. Judging by the piles of used paper plates in the kitchen and on the living room floor, they were Carter's preference.

Lifting off the aluminum foil, I scooped a generous helping of casserole onto a plate. I searched for a paper towel to cover the plate, but couldn't find one. There were no more paper plates left either. I decided splatters in the microwave were the least of Carter's problems and plunked the plate down on the glass turntable. I set the timer and turned around.

Carter stood right behind me. I let out a sharp yip but tried to mask it with a cough. Carter didn't seem to care. He lifted the foil off the casserole dish. "Are these potatoes?"

Before I could think, I blurted out, "Yes. Funeral Potatoes." I mentally kicked myself with the same foot I had just pulled out of my mouth. "I mean, uh, cheesy potatoes."

The microwave timer dinged. Carter opened the door and pulled out the plate. I handed him the spoon I had been holding and he eagerly dipped it into the mound of casserole. "Thanks," he said, heading back to the couch.

"You're welcome," I said.

"Are you that lady that steals people's cell phones?" Carter asked, his mouth full of cheesy potato casserole.

"What? No. Who told you that?"

Carter shoveled the last bite of casserole into his mouth and put the plate down next to a crooked tower of empty TV dinner trays. I resisted the impulse to pick up the plate and take it to the kitchen. I wasn't this boy's maid.

"Mom did. She said you charge people a bunch of money to stay at your house and then steal their cell phones." He shuddered. "Sounds horrible."

"I do not steal anything from anyone," I said, trying to keep my voice even. "People – grown adults with minds and wills of their own – come to my bed and breakfast to enjoy some quiet time without their phones."

Carter looked dubious. My gaze swept over the dirty living room. "Is your father here?"

I wasn't prepared for the eruption my question caused. Carter shot up off the couch faster than I ever could have imagined. I took a big step back, my hand on the doorknob in case I had to make a run for it.

"My father is an asshole!" Carter screamed, his face turning bright red. His hands balled into fists at his sides. "He went to prison when I was a baby and I haven't heard a word from him since."

I could see tears pooling in Carter's eyes. He rubbed a clenched fist over first one eye, then the other. My heart broke for him all over again.

"I'm sorry to hear that." I kept my tone soft. "Are you staying here alone?"

Carter pulled in deep breaths, almost panting in an effort to keep his anger in check. "Not really. Mom's boyfriend, Bobby, lives here. He's at work right now."

"Oh." Carter didn't sound all that thrilled when he mentioned Shay's boyfriend.

Carter plopped onto the floor, resting his back against the couch. He grabbed the game controller and took the video game he had been playing off pause. The loud sounds of shooting and men's voices filled the trailer, overwhelming the small space. I resisted the impulse to clap my hands over my ears.

"I'll let you get back to your game," I said, pulling open the trailer's front door. Carter didn't even respond. He kept his gaze riveted on the screen as I backed quickly out of the door, almost falling down the wooden steps in my haste to get back to the car.

I pulled open the car door and sat in the front seat. I lowered my head down to the steering wheel and groaned. As much as I hadn't liked Shay, seeing her son without his mother was almost too much to bear. The condition of the trailer made me wonder if I should do more. One casserole wasn't going to help that boy or heal his hurt. But I didn't think Carter would be too happy with me barging into his life and acting like his nanny.

I lifted my head, pushed back my hair, and put the car in gear. Carter had Bobby to look out for him now. I had to remember my mission – to find Shay's killer. I would help Carter later.

Chapter 9

When I arrived back at the farmhouse, Bree was placing a pile of clean dishtowels in the drawer next to the kitchen sink. I wanted to ask if she could make a trip into town with me to talk to Darlonna, but tension still hung in the air between us and I wasn't sure what to say. I decided to go the simplest route and offer a sincere apology.

"I'm sorry I pried into your past," I said. "You have been a wonderful employee. It's none of my business what happened at your last job."

Bree kept her back to me. She placed the last dishtowel in the drawer and pushed it shut. She turned to face me, her large hazel eyes filled with pain. "I'm sorry, I just can't talk about it," she said.

"I believe you," I said. Bree looked so young and vulnerable. I wanted to ease her suffering, but I had no idea how.

"Do you want to take a break and visit Darlonna?" I asked.

"That would be great," Bree said, smiling at me. We got into my car and I drove into downtown Hillsville.

"That's her house over there," Bree said, pointing to a small house on the corner of Elm and Oak Streets.

I parked in front of the house. Bree and I stepped out of the car and climbed the cement stairs leading to the house. After I rapped on the door a few times, we huddled together on the top step and waited for someone to answer the door.

"What do you want?" demanded a thick, raspy voice from inside the house.

"Hi, Darlonna, it's Bree Foster."

The door opened a crack and a heavily wrinkled face appeared. One watery green eye caught sight of Bree and the door opened all the way. "Bree, honey, how you been?" Darlonna wrapped a thin arm around Bree's waist and squeezed her tight. She gazed at me and scowled. "Who are you?"

"I'm Rachel Kent. I recently moved into my grandmother's old farmhouse and turned it into a B&B."

Darlonna's scowl deepened. "You that woman what steals people's phones? Shame on you!"

What was with people? How could they not grasp the concept of other people *wanting* to go without their cell phones for a few days?

I decided to kill Darlonna with kindness. I smiled at the cranky old woman. "Actually, ma'am, my guests stay at the farmhouse for the pleasure of unplugging from their phones for a while."

"Hmmpf." Darlonna didn't look convinced. She stepped aside and gestured for us to enter the trailer. She wore a heavy gray boot on one foot. Her movements were slow and deliberate.

Bree sat down on one side of a floral print sofa. The springs had given out on the other side and the cushion sagged, so I chose to sit in a wooden rocking chair next to the couch. Darlonna maneuvered herself into a worn recliner across from us, being careful not to jostle her booted foot. She picked up her cell phone and waggled it at me.

"Don't go trying to steal my phone," she warned. "I gotta play my online slots or my heart will stop."

I didn't quite get the connection between online gambling and Darlonna's heart health, so I just nodded. From the looks of the trailer, Darlonna either didn't win very often or kept all her online casino winnings stashed under her mattress.

"What brings you to visit this old lady?" Darlonna asked, directing her question at Bree.

Bree looked to me. She was good at chitchat, but apparently her social skills didn't include interrogating grouchy old ladies during a murder investigation.

"Well, Darlonna, we want to talk to you about Shay Clarke," I said.

Darlonna turned her watery eyes on me. "Don't say that woman's name in this house," she hissed, lurching forward in her recliner.

I scrunched back in the rocking chair, terrified by the hatred blazing in the older woman's eyes.

Bree rushed to console Darlonna, assuring her we weren't friends of Shay. "We're here because Rachel found Shay's body and we want to find out who killed her."

Darlonna leaned back in the recliner, a satisfied grin on her face. She looked like the cat that ate the canary, with yellow feathers still fluttering around its mouth. "So, you got the pleasure of finding her body?" she asked me.

I shivered, then gulped loudly. "Well, it wasn't exactly a pleasure," I said. "But, yes, I was the one who found her body."

"It would have been a pleasure for me," Darlonna said. She pointed at her booted foot. "Because of that miserable woman I have had to have three surgeries on my foot. Doc said I may never walk right again."

"What happened?" Bree asked, her voice barely above a whisper.

Darlonna settled back in her recliner and launched into her story. "One weekend about five months ago I took my grandkids to that godawful hole she calls a campground." She shook her head sorrowfully. "Back when her parents owned Campfire Junction it was a beautiful place, perfect for families." She scowled and tapped the gray boot with one finger. "Safe back then, too. But not anymore. The pool had one of them big fancy waterslides and the grandkids convinced me to go down it." She grimaced. "That thing was a deathtrap, but I didn't know it. I went down the slide and was having a pretty good time until the whole thing fell apart. Dumped me half on the ground, half in the water. Broke my foot in three places." She scowled down at the gray boot. "Ain't been the same since."

"That's terrible," I said. "What did Shay do about it?"

Darlonna winced when I said Shay's name, as if it caused her physical pain. "Nothin', except she accused me of damaging her property!" Darlonna whacked the arm of her recliner with her fist. "I told her I would see her in court, and I filed a lawsuit the very next day." Darlonna fell silent. I watched her shoulders rise and fall as she took deep breaths, trying to calm her anger. "My attorney thought I had a solid case, and I did, too, but Shay managed to win on some sort of paperwork snafu. The judge called it a 'technicality.' Whatever that means." Darlonna's face turned red. "What it means for me is that I was on the hook for paying all of my medical bills, as well as that snake's court costs."

Darlonna fell silent. The only sound in the small house was the loud ticking of the clock hanging on the wall.

"I'm so sorry that happened to you, Darlonna," Bree said. She stood up from the couch and rushed over to the recliner to wrap Darlonna in a hug. "You didn't deserve to be treated that way."

Darlonna patted Bree's arm. "You're a good girl, Bree," she said. "Your mama raised you right."

Bree stepped back from the recliner and returned to her seat on the couch. I guessed I was the bad cop in this conversation, while Bree got to play the sympathetic good cop. Oh, well.

"We heard that you and Shay had a very public feud going," I said, trying to keep my tone light.

"Yes, indeed," Darlonna said. "I saw that sorry excuse for a human being one day coming out of the grocery store and I couldn't keep my thoughts to myself. I let her have it, right there in front of God and everybody in town."

"And what did Shay say?" I asked.

Darlonna's thin body quivered with rage. "She laughed in my face," she said in a quiet voice. "Told me I was a loser."

Ouch. I exchanged a look with Bree. Those were some pretty harsh words, certainly enough to make someone react with anger. I glanced at Darlonna's boot. But would an elderly woman with an injured foot be able to chase down a much younger woman and plunge a pair of antique gardening shears into her back?

"I'm not sad that woman's dead," Darlonna said. She stared first at Bree, then at me. "Whatever happened to her, she deserved every bit of it."

Yikes. Darlonna's penetrating stare turned my blood to ice in my veins. This was a woman who had been seriously scorned.

"Do you know anyone else who might have wanted to hurt Shay?" I asked, hoping to redirect Darlonna's anger.

Darlonna pursed her lips in thought, tapping the arm of her chair with her index finger. A smile lit up her face. "I sure do," she said. She began poking at her phone screen. When she found what she wanted, she turned the phone toward Bree and I. "This is Shay's ex-husband, Dwight Sampson," Darlonna said.

Bree and I looked at the phone. The mugshot of a large man with a long, thick beard and a menacing scowl filled the small screen. "He was arrested for armed robbery," Darlonna said. "Heard he got out of the joint and that he's back in Hillsville. My sister's boy said he saw Dwight and Shay arguing downtown." Darlonna turned the phone back around and looked at Dwight's mugshot. "Not a guy I'd want to tangle with."

I shivered. I agreed with Darlonna. Dwight looked like he could snap someone in two with just one hand.

Her anger spent, Darlonna's body sagged and she drooped in her recliner. Bree noticed and quickly stood up.

"We're going to let you rest now, Miss Darlonna," she said. She wrapped the woman in another gentle hug and grabbed my elbow, pulling me out of the rocking chair. "Thank you for talking to us. You take care of yourself now."

"Thank you, Bree," Darlonna said, picking up her cell phone. "You come back anytime you like." She gave me a harsh look and I realized I wasn't included in that invitation for a future visit. "And say hi to your mama for me."

"I will," Bree said, following me out the front door and down the steps.

We got back into my car and I let out a breath. "Wow, that was intense," I said, turning on the car and backing out of the short driveway. "She certainly has a lot of resentment toward Shay."

"Do you blame her?" Bree asked. "After what Shay put her through?"

"No, I don't blame her," I said. "But do you think she could have killed Shay?"

Bree hooted with laughter. "That frail old woman with an injured foot?" she asked. "What did she do, knock Shay over with her boot so she could stab her with some shears?" She laughed again.

"You're right," I said, trying to imagine Darlonna chasing after Shay and killing her in Grams' garden. The image didn't make sense. "Could Darlonna have paid someone to kill Shay?"

Bree thought, then shook her head slowly. "I don't think so. She said she had to pay for her medical bills and Shay's court costs. That wouldn't leave a lot left over for paying someone to kill Shay."

I nodded. Plus, there was Darlonna's online gambling habit. My guess was she saved every spare penny for that, but I didn't voice my opinion out loud for fear of offending Bree. Instead, I changed the subject to Bree's favorite country singer, and she chatted about her favorite songs all the way to the farmhouse.

Chapter 10

I was mopping the mudroom floor that afternoon when Leo and Aries dashed across the wide yard, onto the front porch, and through the front door. Leo wore a pair of baggy neon pink swim trunks. Aries was dressed in a black one-piece bathing suit. They were both out of breath from their sprint across the yard. My antennae went up, searching for a reason they would have to run to the house. Had someone been injured? Had they spotted a poisonous snake floating around with them in the pond?

"We found this," Leo said. With one hand he pushed a clump of curly wet hair out of his face, and extended his other hand toward me. "It's a cell phone."

I took the phone from Leo's outstretched hand. The phone had been smashed, the glass front cracked and shattered. Mud dripped from the phone case onto the freshly mopped floor.

"We found it in the pond while we were swimming," Leo explained.

No kidding. I held the phone between my thumb and index fingers and rushed to stand over the trashcan. I studied the dripping phone and felt a jolt of fear in my gut. Even though it was badly damaged and filthy, I still recognized Shay's distinctive sparkly phone case immediately.

"Would you hand me some paper towels, please?" I gestured at the roll on the counter and Aries tore off several sheets. I thanked her, took the paper towels, and swaddled the cell phone in them.

What would Shay's phone be doing in the pond? I wondered. Shay had not looked wet when I found her body in the garden. She certainly hadn't been dressed for a late-night swim, either. I thought back to Shay standing next to her Jeep in the farmhouse's driveway, wiggling her phone and taunting my guests. She had made a comment about not being caught dead without her phone. A shiver raced down my spine. Well, Shay had been wrong. She had most definitely been caught dead without her phone.

"What are you going to do with it?" Aries asked. She stared at me, her brown eyes wide. She wrapped her arms around herself and started to shiver.

My hospitality training kicked in and I hurried into the bathroom for two fluffy towels. I handed one to each of the twins. They had left their own towels back at the pond when they made the mad dash to the farmhouse.

"Thanks," they said in unison. Aries draped her towel around her shoulders. Leo wrapped his around his waist.

I cradled Shay's paper towel-swaddled cell phone in my hands and debated Aries' question. What was I going to do with it? There was only one logical choice. "I'm going to give this to the police," I said, striding over to the wall phone in the kitchen.

Dad and Kelsey sat at the round kitchen table with Kathryn and Simon, glasses of iced tea in front of them. The four of them looked up as I passed on my way to the phone. Dad glanced at the wad of paper towels in my hand and raised his eyebrows. I held up a finger to signal I needed a minute, then lifted the phone off the hook. I dialed the phone number for the local police department that I had scribbled onto the pad attached to the wall next to the phone. I hadn't quite memorized the number yet, but I was well on my way. My call was answered quickly by a brusque woman's voice. I explained why I was calling and the woman said she would transfer me to Police Chief Potts. I had expected to speak with Officer Barnes. I had never spoken with the Police Chief before.

"Potts."

Potts' voice was deep and masculine in my ear. I was tongue tied for several moments, then my fingers tightened around the paper towels and I remembered why I was calling.

"I found Shay Clarke's cell phone," I said.

"Where?" Potts' voice held a hint of urgency.

"A couple of my guests pulled it out of the pond in my backyard."

Potts let out a breath. "What kind of shape is it in?"

"Well, it's not pretty," I said. "It has been smashed and it's covered in mud."

"That doesn't mean we can't get any information from it," Potts said. "The forensics guys can do a lot with damaged cell phones."

I felt a surge of hope in my chest. Maybe we could still get to the bottom of this mystery and find Shay's killer.

"When can you come pick it up?" I asked. I cast a quick glance over my shoulder. Everyone at the table was listening to my side of the conversation.

"I can't come until sometime tomorrow," Potts said. "I want to pick that cell phone up myself so I can make sure nothing happens to it. Can you put it someplace safe until then?"

I twisted my lips and thought for a minute. "Absolutely," I said. "I will put it in my safe. It will be here and waiting for you when you arrive." I hung up and turned around.

"You found Shay's cell phone?" Kelsey asked. "Where was it?"

Aries and Leo had gone upstairs to change out of their wet swimsuits, so I quickly explained how and where they had found the phone. I unwrapped the phone and showed it to the assembled group.

"Looks like it got stomped on," Dad commented, gazing down at the phone in my hand. "Wonder how it ended up in the pond?"

Silence greeted Dad's question. No one wanted to speculate as to how Shay's phone had ended up at the mucky bottom of the farm's pond. Everyone at the table watched as I rewrapped the cell phone in the paper towels. I went into the mudroom to place the phone in the safe. I made sure the safe was securely locked before walking away. I hoped Shay's phone would yield an important clue about who might have wanted her dead. That way the police could arrest the killer and life at the farm could get back to normal.

Chapter 11

With Shay's phone safely tucked away, I took inventory of the contents of the cupboards and refrigerator. It looked like I needed to pick up a few items in town. I tasked Bree with handling any guest issues that might arise in my absence, then got into my car and drove to the one grocery store in Hillsville, the Corner Basket. Although it was a small-town grocery store, it did have a fully-stocked meat counter, as well as a butcher named Marvin. A short, middle-aged man with a slight paunch and glasses, Marvin was always quick with a joke and a smile. Even on my worst days, Marvin could say something to lift my mood and make me laugh. Since I had never before had a day when I had found a dead body in my garden and my mom and employee were hiding deep, dark secrets they refused to reveal, today would be a real test of Marvin's ability to cheer me up.

I entered through the automatic doors and grabbed a cart. As I pushed the cart forward, I held my breath, wondering if I would be unlucky enough to get stuck with one of the many carts with wonky wheels that wanted to go in every direction but straight. I let out a huge sigh of relief. I had managed to select – on the first try – one of the three carts in the store that had fully functional wheels. I took that as a good omen.

I hummed a little to myself as I steered the cart toward the meat counter, stopping along the way to pick up a few items on my list and to take a closer look at other items that caught my eye. I turned left toward the meat counter, anticipating that first glimpse of Marvin's cheerful smile.

The man behind the counter was definitely *not* Marvin. The man reaching into the glass counter to pull out a large slab of steak for a customer was a big guy, easily six foot five and at least three hundred pounds. A huge white apron covered his bulk. Underneath the apron he wore jeans and a black T-shirt. His biceps flexed with even the tiniest movement. I tried not to stare, but I couldn't help myself. The man's upper arms were as big around as my thigh and covered with tattoos. His long, thin brown hair was pulled back in a ponytail. A hairnet spread over the top of his head, reminding me of the lunch ladies in the elementary school cafeteria. But this guy was no lunch lady. Instead, he looked like he ate lunch ladies for breakfast.

I wheeled my cart toward the meat counter. The customer standing there placed the parcel of steak in his cart and smiled at me before resuming his shopping. The man behind the meat counter grinned at me. He wore a nametag that read *Dwight*.

"Good morning," he said. "What can I do for you today?"

I stood on my tippy-toes so I could see through the large glass window separating the meat counter from the back room where they cut meat. No one was in the room, but I still held out hope that Marvin was there. I glanced at my watch: eleven o'clock. A little early for lunch, but maybe Marvin had to run an errand. My mind was churning up reasons for Marvin's absence as fast as I could process them.

Dwight's smile faltered a little. "Ma'am? What would you like?"

I tried to rein in my wild thoughts. "Is Marvin around today?" I kept my voice casual. I didn't want to offend this man. After all, it wasn't his fault my favorite butcher was nowhere in sight.

Dwight shook his head. "Marvin's last day was yesterday. Said he was moving to Miami to be closer to his grandkids." He clapped his hands together heartily. "I'm here to help you with whatever you need. My name is Dwight Sampson." He reached for a large knife on the counter next to him and lifted it in the air.

Instantly my mind stopped cranking out reasons for Marvin's absence and instead put two and two together. Dwight Sampson, Shay's ex-husband who had just been released from prison? I gulped and stared at him brandishing the bloody knife. He took a step toward me, and that was all I needed to see. Survival mode kicked in and I let out a squeak, pushing my cart as fast as I could in the opposite direction.

I heard pounding footsteps behind me. "Come back!" Dwight bellowed.

I put on a burst of speed, steering my shopping cart like a NASCAR driver. A toddler sitting in a cart clutching a sucker in his grimy fist stared as I zoomed past. I took a hard left and headed toward the exit. Dwight wouldn't chase me into the parking lot, would he?

An elderly man in a motorized scooter blocked the aisle on the right. I steered to the left, but a woman with four children sorting through a bin of green beans blocked that escape route. I turned left down a side aisle, where an employee was stocking shelves. A pallet and several open boxes blocked the way. I turned to flee back the way I had come, only to encounter Dwight, still carrying the knife. His face was red with exertion and his enormous chest heaved. His hairnet had come loose and was askew over his right ear. I crouched behind my shopping cart, ready to use it as a weapon however I could. It felt like using a toothpick to defend myself against a Great White shark, but it was better than nothing.

"Don't come near me!" I shouted. I pulled an extra-large can of hominy off the shelf and lifted it over my head. "I know how to use this!"

Dwight's gaze shifted from my face to the can of hominy. "Hey, lady, take it easy," he said.

"I'll take it easy when you put down that knife," I retorted.

Dwight stared at the knife he clutched in his hand as if he had never seen it before. "Oh, man," he said, panicked. "I'm not supposed to take this thing out of the back room." Before I could say another word, Dwight turned and ran back to the meat counter. I slowly lowered my shaking arm, still clutching the can of hominy. The employee doing the stocking stared at me with his mouth open.

Within a few minutes Dwight had returned without the knife, still drying his freshly washed hands with a striped towel. He had removed the humongous white apron to reveal a black T-shirt with the logo of a heavy-metal band splashed across the front.

He held his empty hands out to me, the towel dangling limply. "See, I ain't gonna hurt ya."

I looked at him warily. Even without the knife Dwight was an imposing figure who could still do a great deal of bodily harm. I hefted the weight of the can of hominy, but Dwight didn't seem to notice. He continued to stare at me with a concerned look on his face. "Would you like me to call someone for you?" he asked when I still didn't utter a word.

The sincere expression in Dwight's eyes finally convinced me to return the can to the shelf. My nerves were rattled and my entire body was shaking. I opened my mouth and was surprised at the words that tumbled out: "I knew Shay."

Dwight sighed. "My break starts in about thirty minutes," he said. "Can we talk after that? I can meet you at the coffee shop at the front of the store."

Now that I knew Dwight wasn't trying to kill me, I didn't feel terrified. I was in a busy supermarket, after all. If we sat and talked at the coffee shop we would be in view of plenty of people. Dwight wouldn't try to hurt me in front of witnesses. Right?

"Let's do that," I said, nodding stiffly. Dwight stepped aside and I wheeled my cart past him, my head held high.

I spent the next fifteen minutes returning the perishable items in my cart to the shelves. I left the other items in the cart. After I finished talking with Dwight I would resume my shopping. I parked the cart near the small coffee shop area and ordered a green tea. I spent the rest of the time waiting for Dwight, slowly sipping hot tea and calming myself down.

When Dwight joined me at the coffee shop, he looked weary and sad. Even though I was still a little scared of him, my heart went out to the man. It couldn't be easy to be released from prison and return to a small town where everyone knew your past and loved nothing more than to dissect it with the neighbors. I remained watchful, but I kept reminding myself of the old adage that everyone deserves a second chance.

"Would you like a refill?" Dwight asked, pointing at my to-go cup of tea sitting in front of me on the small round table. I shook my head. "How about something to eat?" He gestured at the selection of pastries and muffins inside a glass case next to the counter. "No, thank you," I replied. The fact he thought of me before ordering for himself was chivalrous and touching and I felt my defenses ratchet down even further.

Dwight approached the woman standing at the register. I heard him order an extra-large coffee and a jumbo blueberry muffin. "Thanks, Yolanda," Dwight said, smiling as the woman handed him his order. He dropped a twenty-dollar bill in the tip jar, then brought his beverage and pastry over to the table and hoisted himself onto a tall stool.

I could feel my guard dropping, although I was doing my best to pick it back up again. Not only was Dwight friendly, he was super generous. I had seen far too many demanding, stingy tippers at the restaurants I had worked at over the years. To see someone make a genuine connection with an employee and be generous was refreshing. But then again, Dwight worked at the store so it made sense he would know the name of the woman working at the coffee shop. And he knew I was watching him. Perhaps he put the twenty-dollar bill in the tip jar only because he knew I was watching. I stopped myself from being so cynical. *Give the man a chance,* I thought.

Dwight took a big slug of the coffee and took a big bite out of the muffin. He smiled ruefully. "Sorry about my table manners," he said, shielding his full mouth with a large hand. "I love food."

I smiled in spite of my lingering misgivings. "It's OK," I said. "I'm a former chef and a current B&B owner. I like to see people enjoying their food."

Dwight's eyes lit up brighter than a little kid's on Christmas morning. "You were a chef?"

I nodded and finished off the last sip of my tea. "In Chicago. After years of toiling in other people's kitchens, I finally opened my own place." I set the empty container down on the table in front of me. "It was a dream come true."

"What happened?" Dwight asked. "How come you're here and not at your restaurant?"

I stared over Dwight's shoulder, wondering about how much I should tell him. I watched the automatic doors glide open so an elderly woman pushing a walker in front of her could enter. I pulled my gaze away from the front door and concentrated on Dwight. He looked like he was truly interested. I decided to go with the short and sweet version. "My grandmother passed away and I inherited her old farmhouse and all the land," I said. "I decided to leave the city and start a B&B here instead."

Dwight nodded. "The Yesteryear B&B, right?"

I nodded and winced, waiting for Dwight to ask about stolen cell phones.

Instead, Dwight heaved a huge sigh and a dreamy look came over his face. "That's the place that doesn't allow cell phones, right?"

"Yep, that's the one."

"Sounds like heaven."

I almost fell off my high stool. "Really?

Dwight nodded. "Heck, yeah. No cell phones, no rumors on social media about me. I wish I could live in a world like that."

Hmmmm. Maybe Dwight wasn't so bad after all.

Dwight crammed the rest of the blueberry muffin into his mouth, chewed quickly, then swallowed. "Look, I know there are all sorts of stories going around about me," he said. "Can I tell you my side of the story?"

Surprised by the abrupt change of topic, I nodded.

"I've always struggled with controlling my temper," Dwight said. "Me and Shay were both young and immature when we got married. I am the first to admit I wasn't ready for a wife or a child, but I ended up with both real fast." He wiped his massive fingers with a napkin. "We argued and fought a lot, and we weren't quiet about it, but I never laid a finger on Shay or, heaven forbid, my baby.

"When I went to prison, I blamed everyone but myself," Dwight continued. "I was bitter and angry, but then I started talking to the prison chaplain, Rick, and he helped me. I was all kinds of stubborn, but Rick didn't give up on me. I never realized how rotten I felt. Eventually I started to think differently about myself and my life. I realized the path I was on was only going to end in self-destruction. By the time I was released from prison I had learned new ways of dealing with my temper. I'm not perfect – far from it – and sometimes my anger still gets the better of me, but the worst thing I do these days is smack pillows at my house."

I laughed. "Poor pillows."

Dwight smiled and continued his story. "I came back to Hillsville because this is where I have a few family members who will still speak to me. Right now I'm staying with a cousin. A lot of people in my family turned their backs on me when I went to prison, and I can't say as I blame them. I wasn't a good person back then. But I know I'm not that person anymore. I've changed."

"What about Shay?" I asked.

"I knew I didn't want to get back together with Shay," Dwight said. "There were too many issues in our past, plus I just don't love her anymore. But I did want to meet with Shay to talk about working out an arrangement so I could see our son." Dwight scrubbed his hand over his face and sighed. "Shay was not about to work with me on that. She refused to let me see Carter and she also told me that she never gave Carter the letters I sent him from prison. That set my temper off big time, which is why me and Shay had a screaming match in public."

I watched Dwight's face as he talked about his son. I could see the love and the happiness thinking about his son caused, but I could also see the hurt and pain when Dwight talked about how long it had been since he had seen his son and how Shay had wanted to keep Carter away from him.

Dwight pulled his cell phone from his pocket and glanced at the display. "I gotta get back to work," he said. He stretched his hand across the table and I extended mine. His grip was firm and warm. I let go of his hand and reached for my empty cup, but Dwight beat me to it. "I got it," he said, stuffing my cup into his empty coffee cup.

"Thank you," I said. I lifted my purse from the back of my chair. Something was still bothering me, though. I decided that since he had been so open and honest about everything else, he wouldn't mind answering my question. Dwight was cleaning up his side of the table, scraping the crumbs from the tabletop onto his huge palm.

"Why did you put such a big tip in the tip jar?" I asked. Dwight paused, confused, then after a beat seemed to realize what I was talking about.

"I know Yolanda has been going through a tough time lately," Dwight said. "Her old man left and she has a sick little girl at home. People here have tried to give her a few bucks, but she refuses the money. Says she doesn't want to be a charity case." He shrugged. "I figured she couldn't refuse a tip."

"That's very kind of you," I said.

Dwight turned and deposited the trash in the can nearby. "We all gotta look out for each other," he said. He waved at me. "See you around, Rachel."

I watched as Dwight walked down the main aisle, then turned left toward the deli counter. I believed Dwight was sincere in everything he had told me, but I also wondered what he would do in order to reunite with his son. Dwight admitted he had anger management issues. Would he murder Shay if she stood in the way of him seeing his son?

Although I was physically and emotionally exhausted after my encounter with Dwight, I still had shopping to do. I dragged myself through the store, pulling items off the shelf and putting them in my cart. I was running behind when I finally pushed the cart, laden with reusable shopping bags, out to the parking lot to load them into the back of the car.

A drop of rain landed on my arm as I placed the last bag in the backseat. A bank of thick dark clouds loomed over the roof of the grocery store. A spring thunderstorm was brewing, and I wanted to be home before it hit. I drove quickly out of the parking lot, but within seconds the winds kicked in and the sky opened up.

Chapter 12

About five miles from the farmhouse, I heard what sounded like a gunshot. My heart leapt into my throat and I swiveled my head from side to side, looking for a gunman. But there was no one in sight on the empty stretch of road. Rain poured down in sheets and the wind whipped tree branches, causing them to thrash against the forbidding gray sky. Then I heard the dreaded *floppity-floppity-floppity* sound of a blown-out tire and felt the car wobble and bump. I eased the car over to the side of the road.

I leaned my head against the car window, begging myself not to burst into tears. A jagged streak of lightning split the sky and filled the inside of the car with an eerie, flickering glow. A clap of thunder soon followed, vibrating through my body. I didn't carry a cell phone with me, so I couldn't call for help. I felt like a sitting duck who was going to get her goose cooked if I sat in the car in a lightning storm. I smiled to myself at the mixed metaphor and felt a smidge better. Ned would have swooned at the mention of not one but two kinds of birds. The rain started coming down even harder, drumming on the car roof so loudly I couldn't even hear myself think.

A knock on the driver's side window next to my ear almost stopped my heart. I pulled away from the window. A man stood next to my car. His clothes were quickly soaking up the rain and the sparse hair on his head was already plastered to his scalp. He made a motion for me to roll down the window, but I hesitated. Who was this guy? What if he was a knife-wielding serial killer on the hunt for vulnerable women? After all, who else but a madman would be standing around outside in weather like this?

I glanced behind my car and saw an older model minivan parked behind me. I had been so wrapped up in my thoughts that I hadn't noticed headlights, and the rain was so loud I wouldn't have heard an F18 jet land on top of my car. I groaned. All the really serious murderers drove around in vans, right? But then I caught a glimpse of movement through the van's windshield. It looked like a little boy monkeying around in the front seat. Did serial killers travel with kids? The man knocked at my car window again so I powered the window down a crack in an effort to keep the inside of my car from getting drenched.

"Do you need help?" the man asked. He looked to be in his late thirties, a bit pudgy around the middle but his arms were strong and muscular. His clear blue eyes gazed at me with concern.

"I have a flat tire," I said.

"Do you have a spare?" he asked. I nodded. "Would you like me to change the tire for you?"

I stared at the man, amazed. I thought I had just seen Noah float by on his ark, and this guy wanted to change a flat tire on my car? How could I refuse? "I would really appreciate that."

"Go ahead and pop the trunk and I'll get started." I rolled up the window and pushed the button to open the trunk. The man rapped on the window with his knuckles and I lowered the window again, still trying to keep the driving rain out of the car. "You can go ahead and sit in the van if you want," he said, pointing at the vehicle. "I warn you, though, my two boys are in there and they just might drive you crazy."

"I think I'll take that chance," I said. I opened the car door and dashed toward the van, tugging open the side door. I jumped into the backseat and sat next to a little boy with hair the color of paprika.

"Hi, I'm Jason," the little boy said.

"And I'm Mason!" said another little boy, shooting up from the back area of the van. He vaulted over the seat and landed in a heap next to his brother. He quickly unrolled himself. "I'm the oldest," he said, sticking his tongue out at Jason.

"I'm Rachel Kent, and I'm an only child," I replied. "It's very nice to meet both of you."

"Our daddy likes to help people," Jason said.

I gazed out the van window. The man had pulled the jack from the trunk and had lifted the car several feet off the ground. He was using a tire iron to remove the lug nuts. Rain continued to pour from the sky in buckets. The man's clothes were sopping wet and every few minutes he swiped his forearm across his face to remove the droplets of moisture. His strong, muscular arms pulled the blown tire from the car. As he shifted his weight to put on the spare, I couldn't help noticing the way his wet jeans clung to his backside.

"Wanna play a game?" Jason's squeaky voice interrupted my thoughts and made me jump guiltily. An absolute stranger had gone out of his way to help me in my time of need, and all I could do was ogle his backside? Keeping the kids entertained would be a much better use of my time. I cast one last look at the man then turned my attention to the boys.

"Sure. What game would you like to play?"

The boys kept me entertained for the next fifteen minutes with their wacky games and hijinks. Suddenly, in the middle of reenacting a sword fight the two boys had seen on TV, only using plastic drinking straws instead of swords, Mason turned to me and said, "Our dad's a widower."

The matter-of-fact statement shocked me. I stuttered for several seconds, unsure of what to say. Mason continued to stare at me, so I had to say something. "I'm sorry to hear that," I said. It sounded lame to my ears, but it was the best I could do after having such a weighty fact thrown at me with no warning.

"Widder means he ain't married no more," Jason added, as if he thought I might be confused about the definition of the word.

"Yes, that's true," I said, still uncertain about what to say to two little boys whose mother had passed away.

Then, as suddenly as the thought had occurred to Mason, it was gone. "Let's play dinosaurs!" he shouted. "I want to be a T. Rex!"

"No fair," Jason howled. "You were a T. Rex last time. I want to be the T. Rex!"

Jason's bright red hair stuck up in clumps around his head and his little chin quivered. Mason balled his hands into fists and puffed out his chest. Trying to prevent a sibling squabble, I quickly jumped in to offer a solution. "How about you *both* be a T. Rex?" I asked.

The boys nodded, finding that idea acceptable. I let out a sigh and leaned back against the seat. Just as the boys were about to each act out their version of the king of dinosaurs, Kurtis opened the driver's side door and hopped into the van.

"Whew!" he said, pulling a towel from underneath his seat. "I don't think it's ever going to stop raining." He rubbed the towel over his head and down his arms. "Your spare tire is on. You can drive around on it for a little bit, but it's best if you get a new tire as soon as possible."

"Thank you," I said, leaning forward and extending my hand. "I'm Rachel Kent, by the way."

The man draped the wet towel over the center console and took my hand. "I'm Kurtis Tellke." His grip was warm and firm. I could feel callouses on his fingers, a sure sign of a man who worked with his hands for a living. "I own Kurtis' Garage," he said, letting go of my hand, his fingers brushing slowly against mine. "I could take care of that tire for you if you want to stop in tomorrow."

"That would be great," I said. I instinctively reached for my purse, then realized I had left it in the car. "If you wait a few minutes, I would be happy to get my wallet and pay you for putting on the spare," I said. I shifted in my seat to open the van door, but Kurtis waved both hands in the air.

"Absolutely not," he said. "I won't take any money."

I started to protest, but Kurtis shook his head. "Folks help folks. That's what life is all about."

"Th-thank you," I stammered. Such humble generosity was unfamiliar to me, and I didn't know what else to say. "I really appreciate your help, Kurtis." Saying his name brought warmth to my face, and I worried I was blushing. I ducked my head to hide my pink cheeks.

"You're welcome."

I slid open the van door, waved at Jason and Mason, who energetically waved back, then dashed back to my car through the rain. I pulled open the driver's side door and slid behind the wheel. I turned the key in the ignition then looked up as Kurtis' van pulled alongside my car. He waved at me, then took off down the road. I watched as the van grew smaller and smaller, eventually disappearing into the driving rain.

****

Leo was sitting on the covered porch, watching the rain, when I pulled into the driveway. I was surprised to see him sitting alone, without his sister next to him. So far, the twins had spent all of their time at the farm together. Leo jumped up from the rocking chair when he saw me and bounded down the stairs to the car.

"Do you need some help?" he asked.

"Sure." I pulled open the car door and Leo reached inside to retrieve several of the bags. I grabbed the remaining bags and we dashed up the stairs through the rain.

"Go ahead and put the bags on the table," I said. Leo complied. I dropped the bags I held on the table, as well. Leo began pulling items from the bags and handing them to me so I could put them away.

We worked in companionable silence for several minutes, then Leo spoke. "I miss my phone," he whispered.

I put a package of yeast in the cupboard and shut the door. "That is perfectly normal," I said.

"No, you don't understand," Leo said, twisting one of the empty reusable bags in his hands. "I feel the same way I did when Nana Sanchez died – like a part of me is gone. I'm miserable without my phone." I opened my mouth to comment, but Leo rushed on. "It's not just my phone that I miss. I miss a Starbucks on every corner and lots of people." He hung his head. "Aries and I have been dreaming of living off the grid and now I can't even stand to think about it. I feel like a failure."

"You're allowed to change your plans," I said.

Leo snorted. "Not according to my sister." He ran a hand through his curly dark hair, damp from the rain, and let out a heavy sigh. "Aries would hate me if I told her how I feel."

"You don't have to be just like your sister or lock yourself into something you hate," I said gently. I placed a hand on Leo's shoulder. "I would know. I gave up the life I had built in Chicago, including a successful restaurant and an engagement, to come live here at the farm." I paused and decided I could be honest with Leo. "Sometimes I wonder about what might have been. But then I think about the joy I feel and how connected I am to Grams every single minute of the day. I wouldn't change that for anything."

Leo looked hopeful, but I could still see traces of doubt lingering in his dark brown eyes. "Everyone is different," I said. "Even twins. You need to find what makes you happy. And if that's Los Angeles, then that is where you should be." Leo shook his head and started to reply, but I stopped him. "And as your sister, Aries should love you and support you no matter what you decide."

"She'll be so angry and disappointed," Leo said.

"Maybe, maybe not. How about you tell her how you feel first?"

Leo nodded. "I guess I could do that."

He gave me a small, wobbly smile, one that didn't quite reach his eyes but was trying its best. I returned his smile and gave his shoulder a reassuring squeeze. Outside, the rain slowed to a soft patter, the sky beginning to lighten along the edges.

"Do you know what the other guests are up to?" I asked.

"A few people were talking about playing board games until the rain passes."

My emotional encounter with Dwight and the flat tire had really thrown me for a loop. A relaxing afternoon of board games sounded like heaven after what I had just been through.

"Let's join them," I said. "We'll take some tea with us. I'll bet everyone's thirsty." I opened the freezer compartment and removed a bowl filled with ice. I plunked the ice on a large tray and grabbed a handful of spoons. I opened the cupboard door where the glasses were kept and grabbed ten glasses. I arranged them in a circle around the bowl of ice then headed into the living room. Leo followed behind me toting the pitcher of tea, along with a small glass bowl of sugar cubes and a small plate piled high with lemon slices.

Shrieks of laughter greeted us as we stepped into the living room. Card tables and chairs were set up around the spacious room. Games were already in full swing at two tables. The table in the far corner near the fireplace held a Scrabble board. Around it sat Dad, Kelsey, and Bree. Kelsey hooted as Dad laid out his tiles, a look of intense concentration on his face.

"Laggy isn't a word," Kelsey said, peering down at the tiles Dad had laid on the board.

"Is too," Dad said.

"Use it in a sentence."

Dad paused and tapped his index finger against his chin. "I didn't get any sleep last night and today I feel laggy."

Kelsey chuckled and lightly punched Dad on the arm. "Let's just see if laggy is in the dictionary." She reached for the large hardcover dictionary at her elbow, but Dad's hand darted out and covered the book.

"Have I ever told you how beautiful your eyes are?" Dad asked. "Like two priceless emeralds." He batted his eyelashes and grinned.

Kelsey laughed. "You're full of it, mister," she said. She reached for the book again, but Dad lifted it overhead and out of her reach. I smiled at their playful antics.

I turned to survey the second table, which was home base for what appeared to be a cutthroat game of Monopoly. No surprise, Mom looked like she was winning, at least if you went by the piles of brightly colored bills arranged neatly in front of her. She also had a stack of property cards sitting next to her elbow. She appeared to be beating the pants off of Kathryn, Simon, and Aries.

A quick scan of the room and a headcount told me I was short one guest. Ned was probably holed up in his room drawing owls. I hoped the noise from the games didn't bother him.

Simon's eyes lit on the pitcher of tea. Leaving his spot at the table, he grabbed a glass from the tray, tossed in several lemon slices, and filled it to the brim with tea from the pitcher. As I watched in wonder, he gulped down the entire glass in about two seconds, then reached for the pitcher again and refilled the glass. He gulped the contents of the second glass, then set it back down on the tray and wiped his mouth with the back of his hand. "I was thirsty," he said sheepishly.

"This game stinks!" Aries shouted, throwing her last twenty dollars at Mom. She stood up, sending her folding chair toppling to the floor. "Capitalism is what's destroying our planet!"

Kathryn gazed at Aries with a bemused expression on her face. Mom raised her eyebrows. Deciding to play peacekeeper, I hustled over to Aries' side.

"Maybe you would rather play a card game?" I suggested. "We have plenty to choose from." Taking her gently by the elbow, I steered her over to the shelf overflowing with games.

Aries didn't fight me, but she retained her sulky expression. She ran a listless finger over a deck of cards. I held my breath, worried she might continue to pout. Suddenly her finger landed on an ancient deck of cards, the edges of the cards creased and tattered from decades of use. "Old Maid!" she shrieked. She did a happy little shimmy as she yanked the deck from the bottom of the pile. "I haven't played Old Maid since I was little. I used to always win at this game." With a squeal she turned to her brother. "Leo! Look, they have Old Maid. Do you want to play?" She scampered over to the couch and sat down.

"Sounds like fun," Leo said. He poured two glasses of tea and joined his sister on the couch.

Aries shuffled the cards and began dealing. With that crisis averted, I looked back and forth between the two board games. Did I want Mom to beat me at Monopoly or did I want to let Kelsey clean my clock at Scrabble? Before I could decide, I heard a shout and the sound of something clattering down the stairs. I raced from the room, Bree close behind.

Ned lay at the bottom of the stairs. A gash on his head oozed blood. He lay flat on his back on the floor, staring at the ceiling. I rushed to kneel at his side. "Ned?" I called softly. He continued staring at the ceiling, his blue eyes vacant. "Ned?"

"Wha – what happened?" he asked. He lifted a hand to touch his head. He glanced down at his blood-smeared fingertips and winced.

"You fell down the stairs," I said. I looked up at Bree. "Would you please get the first-aid kit?"

Bree nodded and loped out of the room. Within a minute she was back with the kit. She knelt on the other side of Ned. "Do you think you broke any bones, Mr. Blankenberger?" she asked, opening the kit and pulling out an alcohol pad. While Ned checked himself over for injuries, Bree dabbed the alcohol swab on the cut on his forehead.

"Ouch!" Ned shouted. "That stings!"

"I'm sorry," Bree said. She spoke soothingly to Ned as she dabbed gently at his head. She applied ointment with a cotton swab, then taped a piece of gauze over the wound.

I gazed up at the top of the stairs, wondering what had caused Ned's fall. The stairs were steep, but I had made sure to put down runners so no one would slip on the wooden treads. I didn't see anything on the stairs that Ned could have tripped over.

I turned back to Ned, who, with Bree's help, was sitting upright. "Ned, do you know why you fell down the stairs?"

Ned shook his head, then winced at the pain the movement caused. "Not really," he said. "I was standing at the top of the stairs when a bird flying past the window caught my attention. I must have been so intent on watching the bird that I lost my footing and fell."

Hmmm. I looked back up at the second-floor landing. I heard the toilet flush and a minute later Simon started down the stairs. He did a double take when he saw Ned sitting on the floor.

"What happened?" Simon asked. "Are you OK, man?" he asked Ned when he reached the bottom of the stairs.

"I'll be fine," Ned said. "I've got a pretty hard head."

Simon laughed and rejoined Mom and Kathryn at the game table. "Is this game over yet?" he asked, eyeing Mom's growing stack of Monopoly money. "I'm tired of losing."

Kathryn admitted defeat and Mom let out a cheer. "I win again!" she said.

I was still concerned about Ned. "Are you sure you didn't trip on something?" I asked. "Maybe your shoe was untied and you tripped on the laces." I looked down at Ned's bare feet. Nope.

"Now that you mention it," Ned said. "You might not want to use so much polish on the handrails."

I frowned. I hadn't used polish to clean the handrails, just a mix of vinegar and water.

"I could really smell the lemons," Ned said. He rubbed his fingers together. "Maybe the polish was so slick I lost my grip on the railing and that's why I fell."

I didn't want to argue with a guest. Instead, I merely nodded and said, "Thank you for that advice."

Bree continued to tend to Ned, helping him stand and guiding him to a comfy recliner in the living room. I resumed handing out glasses of tea and offering the bowl of sugar cubes and slices of lemon. But an uneasy feeling began to unfurl in my gut. First Ned's sketches and camera equipment had been damaged, and now he had taken a tumble down the stairs. What sinister forces were at work at the B&B?

****

That evening all of the guests gathered around the big dining table for dinner.

"So, how's the investigation going?" Dad asked. "Are the police any closer to finding out who killed Shay?"

I shook my head. "No. I called the Police Chief, Potts, and he said they don't have enough evidence to charge anyone yet.

They're still following leads, but it sounds like they're hitting dead ends."

Dad frowned and reached for his glass of iced tea. "That's disappointing. I figured by now they'd have something."

"They're waiting on some lab results, too," I added. "Potts said those could take a while." I stared down at the tabletop and fiddled with my fork. "I just wish this was all over with so life could get back to normal."

Ned looked up from his plate, a forkful of fresh roasted vegetables paused midair. "I was supposed to go to the police station this afternoon to talk to the police chief," he said. "But after taking a tumble down the stairs, I forgot. I called and they told me I could head over first thing tomorrow morning instead."

Across the table, Kathryn raised an arched brow. She carefully set down her water glass and turned to Ned. "Oh, really?" she said, casting a sidelong glance at Simon. "How interesting."

Ned put down his fork and scanned the table. "Anyone seen the hot sauce?"

"It's in the caddy," I said, nodding toward the collection of condiments in front of Simon.

Ned stretched to reach for it, but Simon beat him to it. "Let me handle that, my man."

He extended his arm to reach for the caddy, but his elbow bumped his water glass, making it wobble. The glass tipped on its side, splashing water across the table.

"Oops," Simon muttered.

I jumped up, grabbing a towel from the sideboard to soak up the spreading puddle. As I worked, Simon righted the glass and fished the bottle of hot sauce from the caddy.

"Here's your hot sauce," he said, passing it over to Ned.

"Thanks," Ned replied, taking the bottle. I finished drying Simon's chair and returned to my seat, just in time to see Ned give the bottle a few brisk shakes over his food, then frown.

"What's wrong?" I asked.

"There's barely any left," he said, holding up the bottle. As he tilted it, I saw a glint of purple and gold.

Before I could say anything, Simon reached across and snatched the bottle from Ned's hands. "I'm sure that'll be plenty," he said quickly, peering at Ned's plate. "You only need a little anyway. Eat up."

114

Ned didn't look convinced. "Maybe we have another bottle in the kitchen," I offered, starting to rise.

Ned held up a hand. "Don't bother. This is fine."

I sank back into my chair as he took a generous bite of his dinner.

"Not quite hot enough for me," Ned said, chewing thoughtfully. "But it's good."

Thankfully for the sake of everyone's digestion, conversation switched from the topic of a stalled murder investigation to talk of what it was like to go without cell phones.

"The past two days have been blissful for me," Aries said, finishing her last bite of fresh-baked bread and dabbing her lips with a napkin. She leaned back in her chair. "What about you, bro-bro? Isn't it great not being tied to your phone all the time?"

Leo stared down at his plate. "I guess," he said.

"What does everyone else think?" Aries asked, gazing around the table at her fellow guests, her brown eyes shining.

Dad finished his last bite of chicken and pushed his plate away. "It hasn't been quite as bad as I thought it would be," he said, draping his arm over the back of Kelsey's chair. "I went fishing in the pond this afternoon and didn't even think about my phone once."

Kelsey nodded. "It was nice and peaceful. But I will admit, I kept reaching into my pocket and felt panicked when my phone wasn't there."

A murmur of agreement arose around the table.

Mom filled her water glass from the pitcher next to her. "I, for one, will be happy to get my phone back. I didn't sign up for this cell-free adventure like the rest of you did."

A hush fell over the table. Mom's comments were like dumping ice water on everyone's good mood. I stood up from the table and grabbed my plate. "Who's ready for fresh strawberries and homemade pound cake for dessert?" I asked.

A cheer went up around the table. I gathered a handful of plates and piled silverware on top to take with me into the kitchen. I kept a bright smile on my face until I was safely out of the dining room. I stepped into the kitchen and dropped the pile of dirty dishes into the sink with a clatter. Luckily, nothing broke.

"Something wrong?" Bree asked. She was slicing strawberries, gathering the sweet red pieces and distributing them on plates next to wedges of golden pound cake.

I wanted to scream in frustration, but I stamped my foot instead. "Mom is complaining about not having her cell phone," I said. I grabbed the bowl of whipped cream from the refrigerator and pulled a spoon from the drawer. "Everyone else is enjoying themselves. Why can't she?" I began to drop dollops of whipped cream next to the pound cake on each dessert plate.

"Well, she didn't exactly sign up for going without her phone," Bree said.

"That's what Mom said." I placed several dessert plates on a tray. Bree grabbed a second tray and loaded it up with plates. Before we went into the dining room, I took a few deep breaths and plastered a smile on my face. I would deal with Mom later. As long as I kept my guests' spirits up, nothing else mattered.

Chapter 13

Yawning and stretching, I stepped into the kitchen early the next morning. The pink hint of sunrise was just starting to tickle the gray clouds gathered over the fields. I shivered and wrapped my arms around myself. Why was the kitchen so cold?

The red front door was open. *Did I forget to lock the door last night?* I wondered. I distinctly recalled shutting and locking the door promptly at ten o'clock. *Perhaps Ned went out last night to look for owls and forgot to shut and lock the door behind him.* I moved to close the door to block out the cool morning air, then glanced down at the lock. I pulled my hand back as if I had been burned. Deep gouges marred the metal around the lock.

Had a thief broken into the B&B? Had I been robbed? I retreated to the safety of the kitchen, then realized the thief could still be inside the house. I quietly pulled open a kitchen drawer and removed a heavy marble rolling pin. I lifted the rolling pin over my head, ready to strike should someone suddenly jump out at me. I walked slowly through the downstairs, peering behind chairs in the living room and under the big dining room table. I saw no one. I lowered the hand holding the rolling pin and massaged my shoulder. Brandishing a marble rolling pin was no easy task.

I paused to think. The farmhouse looked completely undisturbed. Nothing was out of place and it didn't look as if anything was missing, either. Who would break into a house and not take anything?

The safe. I rushed to the front entry and my heart plummeted to my feet. Not only did the safe show signs of being tampered with, the door swung wide open when I grasped the handle.

Oh, no. Terror seized me like the powerful jaws of a lion. What if something had happened to my guests' cell phones? Not only would I be financially on the hook to replace the stolen devices, but my guests would be inconvenienced and possibly in financial jeopardy. So many people had their credit cards and bank accounts on their phones. What if someone had drained a guest's bank account? Or, even worse, more than one guest's back account?

The B&B's reputation was at stake, too. If the guests' phones had been stolen, they would no doubt rush to social media the moment they got home to complain to the world about what had happened to them at the Yesteryear Bed and Breakfast. No one would want to stay here ever again if they thought there was a phone thief on the loose. The B&B would be out of business almost as soon as it had started.

I held my breath as I scanned the contents of the safe. All of the boxes holding guests' cell phones were where they should be. I reached into the safe and pulled out the box marked *Kent. Please, please let the phones be here,* I prayed silently. I let out my breath when I removed the top, pulled the soft cloths aside, and saw Dad's cell phone on top of Kelsey's. I went through the rest of the boxes: Simon, Sanchez, Blankenberger, Malton. All of the phones were unharmed and resting in their respective boxes.

Whew. I sagged against the check-in counter, weak with relief. Thank goodness. All of my guests would be leaving at the end of the week with their cell phones. I straightened up and frowned. If none of the guests' cell phones had been taken, then what had the thief been looking for in the safe? I peered into the back corner of the safe, where I kept a few of Grams' valuables: her plain gold wedding band, a lovely emerald brooch, and a pair of pearl earrings. They weren't the Crown Jewels, but altogether they had been appraised at several hundred dollars.

The boxes holding the jewelry were gone. Rage boiled in my veins. Some lowlife had stolen Grams' jewelry!

I wasn't concerned about the money. I would never have sold those pieces anyway. They had meant too much to Grams and, therefore, meant the world to me. Grams had continued to wear her wedding ring until the day she died, although Gramps had passed away decades before. I could recall her wearing the pearl brooch to church. She wore the emerald earrings with her favorite green dress when she went to a wedding. Those items were pieces of Grams' life, and someone had taken them.

I stewed for a while, thinking about what I would do to the creep when I caught him. Then sadness sat in. *If* I caught him. With a heavy heart, I realized I might never see Grams' jewelry again.

I slammed my hand against the side of the safe, causing the door to swing open. And that was when it hit me. What else wasn't there that should be? Shay's cell phone and the paper towels I had wrapped it in were missing. Although the safe wasn't large, I bent down to examine every shelf and peer into every corner. I ran my hands over the shelves, just to be sure. Nope. The phone was gone.

Confusion mixed with anger inside me. I could understand someone stealing jewelry. They wouldn't be millionaires after pawning Grams' ring, brooch, and earrings, but they would make a few bucks. But a cracked, dirty cell phone? Who would want that?

While I pondered those questions, I heard footsteps coming down the stairs. A stream of people entered the kitchen. The guests were calling out good morning to each other, but went silent when they saw me standing in front of the open safe. I knew I must look like the world had just come to an end.

"Rachel?" Dad stepped around the counter and put a hand on my shoulder. "Are you OK?"

Mom was right behind him. "Honey, did something happen? You are white as a sheet." She placed a hand on my forehead. "Are you sick?"

I shook my head. Dad stepped back and Mom slowly lowered her hand. I pointed at the front door. "Someone got into the farmhouse." I gestured at the open safe. "And they broke into the safe."

Pandemonium erupted in the front entry.

"Are our phones OK?" Leo asked. Lifting his hand to his mouth, he began to chew on his fingernails like a deranged beaver.

"Was anything taken?" Kelsey asked.

"Someone broke into the B&B?" Aries asked. She looked wildly around the front entry, as if perhaps the thief were still there, just waiting to ambush her.

"My phone!" Simon wailed. He stepped toward the safe, but Kathryn pulled him back.

"I will sue if anything has happened to my phone," Kathryn said, her voice calm and cold. "You, young lady, need to have better security than some cheap safe to protect your guests' valuables."

I hung my head in shame. Kathryn, although rude, was absolutely right. I vowed right then and there to replace the broken safe with the sturdiest safe money could buy.

"Please don't speak to my daughter that way," Mom said. I lifted my head and watched Mom address Kathryn. "It's not her fault someone broke into the house."

Kathryn lifted one perfectly plucked eyebrow at Mom, then turned to me. "Is my phone still there, or has some thief taken it?"

I nodded. "Yes," I said, my voice shaking. "Everyone's phone is exactly where it should be, unharmed and in one piece." I wasn't sure why, but I didn't say anything about Shay's phone being stolen. Everyone let out a sigh of relief.

"Is anything damaged or missing?" Dad asked.

I shook my head. "No. I went through the house myself and nothing is out of place." I felt tears pricking my eyelids. "But a few pieces of Grams' jewelry were in the safe, and now they're gone."

"Oh, dear." Mom rubbed my back and made sympathetic noises.

"Is that all?" Kathryn asked, waving her hand dismissively.

Before I could reply to Kathryn, a troubled look crossed Dad's face. "Wait a minute. You went through the house, alone, after you thought someone might be in here? Rache, what were you thinking? The robber could have still been in the house. What if he had tried to hurt you?"

"I know that wasn't the smartest thing to do," I admitted. I grabbed the marble rolling pin I had placed on the counter. "But I did have this for protection."

Dad raised his eyebrows. "A rolling pin? What were you going to do, bake him a pie if he threatened you?"

I rolled my eyes. "It's a marble rolling pin, Dad. I would have clobbered him with it."

Dad didn't look convinced. "I think it's time to call the police," he said, taking the rolling pin from my hand. "Don't you?"

I nodded and walked into the kitchen to pick up the phone. I was getting tired of calling the police. After I called the police, I wandered back into the mudroom where Dad was assessing the safe.

"Do you think it can be repaired?" I asked.

Dad shook his head. "I don't think so, Rache." He pushed the door of the safe shut, but the door sprang right back open. "I do think I could duct tape it closed. Then, when it's time to return the phones, you can just cut the tape off."

I sighed. It wasn't a perfect solution, but it would work. I pulled a roll of tape from a drawer and handed it to Dad, who set to work winding the tape around the safe. Before the next group of guests arrived, I would have to buy a newer, much sturdier, safe.

****

When Bree arrived for work, she raised her eyebrows at me when she saw Dad winding duct tape around and around the safe.

"We had a break in last night," I said, showing Bree the gouge marks on the door lock.

"Oh, no!" Bree gasped. She reached out a finger to touch the marks slashed into the metal. "Who would do such a thing?" Without waiting for me to answer, she looked wildly around her. "Did they take anything? Is anyone hurt?"

"The thief broke into the safe and took Grams' jewelry I kept in there," I said. Bree's eyes darkened and her hands clenched into fists at her sides. Although Bree hadn't known Grams, I had told her numerous stories about Grams and the wonderful memories we had made together at the farm. My kindhearted employee knew how much Grams' jewelry meant to me, and she was taking the theft personally.

"I don't think anyone was hurt," I said, surveying the guests gathered in the kitchen. I did a quick head count. "We're short one guest," I said. "I don't see N—"

An unearthly moan coming from upstairs interrupted me in midsentence. The hairs on the back of my neck stood straight up. I hurried up the stairs, followed closely by Bree and the rest of the guests. The guests gathered in a knot in front of Ned's closed bedroom door, murmuring anxiously and exchanging questioning glances. The horrible moans were coming from inside, along with an unpleasant retching sound from the bathroom.

Anxiety fluttered in my chest. Thoughts of food poisoning rushed into my head. Was Ned ill because of something he consumed last night at dinner? I put my hand on my stomach. I

121

had eaten the same thing as Ned, and I felt fine. I glanced at the guests clustered in the hallway. Although they looked sleepy, no one looked sick. My mind flashed back to Ned sprinkling the food on his plate with hot sauce and I winced. Ned had bragged that he had a gut of steel, but did he really?

Since I was the owner of the B&B and the one in charge, it was my duty to see if Ned was alright. I knocked lightly on the door and called his name. The only response was another ghastly moan. I opened the door a crack and poked my head inside. Ned was laid out on the bed, one arm clutching his stomach and the other dangling off the bed. He emitted another terrible moan as I stepped into the room.

"Ned," I called softly to the distraught guest on the bed. "Are you OK?"

A stupid question, I admit. Ned was not OK. His skin was deathly white and he had red rings around his eyes. His clothing was rumpled with wet blotches down the front. I didn't want to think about what had caused those.

"Oooohhhhhhhhh," Ned moaned in response.

"Would you like me to call a doctor for you?" I asked. The bruises from Ned's tumble down the stairs were blooming furious shades of purple, green, and yellow under the bandage taped to his head. At the rate this poor man was going, he would leave the B&B flat on his back on a stretcher. I shivered. *Or worse.*

Ned slowly shook his head. The motion must have been too much for him, because he let out another moan. Standing so close to him when he made that sound caused the little hairs on my arms to shoot straight up to the ceiling. "I'll be fine in a few hours." Ned whispered so softly that I had to strain to catch the words. "I just need to lay here for a while."

"No problem," I said, infusing my voice with a chipper tone. "Just let me know if you need anything."

I stepped out of Ned's room and closed the door behind me. Bree had joined the small knot of people clustered on the landing. Concern clouded her normally open expression.

"What is going on?" she asked.

"Ned isn't feeling well today," I said. I didn't want to alarm the other guests by providing a graphic description of how Ned looked like death warmed over. Instead, I clapped my hands and smiled at each guest in turn. "For everyone else, it's another great day at the farm!" I said. I hated myself for using forced cheer, but it seemed to do the trick. The guests all shuffled back to their rooms, leaving Bree and I alone on the landing. Once the last guest had disappeared behind a closed door, the fake smile fell from my face like a heavy weight.

"What's really wrong with him?" Bree asked, turning accusing eyes on me.

I held up my hands in front of my chest. Pitching my voice low so the guests wouldn't hear, I said, "Don't blame me. Ned is a little under the weather today. Maybe from all that hot sauce on his food last night at dinner. He probably just needs to let it work its way out of his system. I have to run over to Kurtis' Garage to get a new tire on my car before Shay's funeral today. Can you take care of Ned?"

Bree nodded, smiling. She would do a much better job of tending to Ned than I ever could. While I headed downstairs, Bree opened the linen closet in the hallway and removed several washcloths. "Do we have any ginger ale?" she asked, following me down the stairs. I directed her toward the pantry and she pulled the bottle of ginger ale from the shelf. After filling a tumbler with ice and pouring ginger ale into it, she balanced it on a tray along with a package of crackers. She nestled the washcloths under one arm and headed back up the stairs to nurse Ned, the sick bird nerd.

I made a pit stop at my bedroom. I undid my hair from its usual ponytail and let the brown locks spill down over my shoulders. I dabbed on a little lip gloss and a tiny bit of perfume behind my ears. I felt silly for primping, but at the same time I recalled how disheveled I must have looked when I met Kurtis for the first time. I wanted to look good for our second meeting.

About ten minutes later I pulled into the parking lot of Kurtis' Garage. A young woman with short blonde hair was working on a car up on a lift. When I approached the garage, Kurtis stepped out of the main office with a clipboard and a pen. He smiled when he saw me.

"Rachel!" he said. "So good to see you." He glanced over at my car. "Did you come to get that tire replaced?"

"Yes," I said. "Do you want me to make an appointment?"

"No way," Kurtis said, shoving the clipboard under his arm. "Give me your keys and I will take care of replacing the tire personally."

I handed Kurtis the keys and he ushered me into the main office and told me to take a seat. For the next twenty minutes I divided my attention between an informercial playing on the small TV bolted to the wall and a cooking magazine I found on the coffee table in the waiting room.

When Kurtis came back into the office, I met him at the front desk and pulled out my wallet. Kurtis said he didn't want to charge me, but I insisted on paying.

"Do you know if the hardware store in town carries door locks?" I asked. Kurtis looked at me quizzically and I explained how someone had gotten into the farmhouse and broken into the safe. I wanted to change the lock on the front door as quickly as possible.

"I think they do," Kurtis said, handing me my receipt. "Do you need any help installing the lock?"

I did, but I didn't want to tell Kurtis that. He had already done so much to help me, and I didn't want to take up any more of his time. Kurtis noticed my hesitation.

"How about I stop over at your place tomorrow afternoon?" he asked. "I usually leave here around three. Will that work?"

"You don't have to go to any trouble."

"It's no trouble," Kurtis said, handing me a copy of the receipt to sign. "One of the perks of being the owner." He pointed across the street at a tidy redbrick ranch. "I live just across the street, so I can change out of my work clothes and be at your place tomorrow about three thirty."

I protested, but he wiggled his clipboard back and forth, waving away my complaints.

"I won't take no for an answer," he said. "I insist."

I looked up into Kurtis' clear blue eyes. "Well, if you insist," I said. He handed me a copy of the credit card receipt and I stuffed it into my purse. Kurtis handed me my car keys and I stepped out of the office. With one final wave, I was back on the road.

As I drove back to the farmhouse, I thought about who might have broken into the safe. I thought about Dad asking me for special treatment by letting him look at his phone. I quickly dismissed that thought from my mind. Dad would never break into the safe. Simon had tried to bribe me the same night Dad had asked to look at his phone. I thought about Leo, and how sad he had looked when he told me how much he missed his phone. Simon and Leo both acted innocent, but were they?

Chapter 14

I stood in front of my closet, assessing the contents with a critical eye. What should I wear to the funeral of a woman I hadn't particularly cared for in life and whose body I had discovered under a rhubarb leaf in my garden? *Hmmm.* I opted for a simple black dress. In fact, it was the only little black dress in my closet, a holdover from my time in Chicago. Finn and I had dined out often, and Finn preferred fancy restaurants. The fancier the better. When I moved to Hillsville, I quickly realized I was much more comfortable in a pair of well-worn jeans and a T-shirt. I had kept one little black dress, though, for old times' sake, and now I was glad I had. I pulled the dress from the back of the closet and removed it from the plastic garment bag. I held the dress, hanger and all, in front of me and studied my reflection in the mirror. The dress had a modest neckline and short, lacy black sleeves. The hem fell well below the knee. Perfect for a funeral.

I took a quick shower, blow dried my hair, and applied makeup. Mom came into the bedroom just as I was zipping up the dress. "You look nice," she said.

"Thanks." I slipped my feet into a pair of low black heels.

Mom went over to the bed and frowned at the clothing in her open suitcase. She had not packed for an extended stay, and she certainly hadn't packed for a funeral. I watched as Mom sorted through the contents of her small suitcase. Once again, I wondered why on earth she had come to the B&B. Had she been planning on staying somewhere else instead? Why else would she have come prepared with a suitcase? But then, if she had been planning to stay somewhere else, why had she come to the B&B?

Mom glanced up and caught me staring at her. I quickly turned away and lifted a pair of pearl earrings from my jewelry box. I fastened one earring to my right earlobe and realized with a pang that the earrings had been a gift from Finn. I let out a deep sigh. I had been in Hillsville for months now. Would Finn and I ever be able to untangle the mess our relationship had become?

Mom closed her small suitcase with a loud bang and I jumped. "I have absolutely nothing to wear," Mom declared, sitting down on the end of the bed. "What am I going to do?"

I thought Mom was acting rather dramatic about the funeral of a woman she didn't even know. "Well," I said. "You didn't really know Shay, so I'm sure it would be OK if you missed the funeral."

Mom shot straight up off the bed, her face crimson. "I would not miss this funeral for anything," she said. Her body began to shake and her lower lip trembled.

I held up my hands. Mom looked like she was on her way to a major meltdown. I had no idea why, but I wanted to avert disaster. "I'm sorry," I said. "I didn't realize Shay's funeral was so important to you." I guided Mom over to my closet. "We're about the same size. How about you borrow something from me? I don't have any other black dresses, but I do have a dark gray dress, as well as some black slacks and a few dark blouses."

Mom quickly thumbed through the clothing in my closet. She selected a pair of black slacks and a slate-gray short-sleeved blouse. I bent to retrieve a pair of black flats from the closet floor that would pair well with the outfit. Mom accepted the shoes without a word and began getting dressed.

I drove Mom into town to the Hutchins Family Funeral Home. The parking lot was packed, but I managed to claim the last spot at the far corner of the lot. Before we reached the front door, a woman with a mass of white curls wearing a long navy dress approached us. She squinted through thick glasses and squealed. "Trishie Walters, is that you?" she asked.

I watched as Mom's face turned a flaming shade of scarlet. Then, in a meek voice, Mom said, "Hello, Miss Dobson."

Miss Dobson put a hand on Mom's shoulder and squeezed. "I remember when you were just learning your ABCs," she said. She turned to me. "Trishie was one of my first-grade students, you know. Cute as a bug, and such an independent little thing. She always had her own plans and never wanted to do what the other kids in class were doing."

I snickered. Mom shot a dirty look my way. I managed to cover the sound with a cough and smiled at Miss Dobson. "Sounds like some things never change," I said. Miss Dobson nodded and walked slowly up the steps of the funeral home. I followed her, but Mom pulled me back.

"That was so humiliating," she hissed in my ear. "I haven't been called Trishie in more than forty years."

"So what?" I said. "It's just a silly little nickname."

"What if everyone here remembers me as just little Trishie Walters?" Mom asked. She gazed at the funeral home, doubt clouding her features. "But how can I stay away?" she asked. For a moment I thought she was asking me, then I realized she was talking to herself. Apparently she received a satisfying internal answer, because she squared her shoulders and marched up the front steps. She pushed open the funeral home door and stepped inside. I followed behind.

A man in a dark suit smiled at us as we entered. "Welcome," he said in a quiet voice. He handed each of us a copy of the funeral program. "The Clarke funeral is being held here in Room A," he said, guiding us toward an open door. We thanked him and stepped inside.

I looked around the room in amazement while Mom signed our names in the register. It looked like everyone in the county had turned out for Shay's funeral. Dozens of flower arrangements were arranged around the room. The air was thick with the scent of the many blooms. A large posterboard covered with photos of Shay from her childhood to more recent shots was positioned near the casket. Mourners clustered in groups, whispering to each other.

I caught a glimpse of Miss Millie talking animatedly to a woman in a burgundy dress. I hardly recognized her without her postal service uniform. Today she wore a soft gray sweater and a matching skirt. A plain gold necklace and a pair of gold hoop earrings completed her outfit.

I caught sight of Carter amidst the crowd. At first, I didn't recognize him. His hair had been washed, combed, and cut. He wore a dark suit and was fidgeting with the collar of his white dress shirt. He appeared frozen, no doubt overwhelmed by everything going on around him. My maternal instincts kicked in. Carter was so young and had been through so much already. What he really needed, I realized with a pang, was a father. As I watched Carter shake hands with an older man dressed in dark jeans and a western shirt, the germ of an idea began to form in my mind. Maybe there was a way I could reunite Carter with the father he so desperately needed and Dwight with the son he so desperately wanted to see.

Someone bumped into me and I apologized. "Excuse me," I said. "I didn't mean to . . ."

The words died on my lips when I saw the woman standing next to me. She wore her brown hair in curls around her face. She wore a black dress with a short skirt and a plunging neckline. In her spiked black heels, she stood several inches taller than me.

"I'm Erica Lane," the woman said, extending her hand. I took her hand limply, stunned by her choice of funeral attire. Eventually her words penetrated my brain.

"Erica Lane." I said her name slowly. "You live in that log cabin on Hillsville Lake, right?"

Erica nodded. "That's me."

"Were you friends with Shay?" I asked.

"About as close as anyone could be to Shay." Erica craned her neck, peering over my shoulder at the casket. "I'm here because I wanted to see with my own eyes that Shay was really dead."

If Erica's revealing outfit had shocked me, it was nothing compared to how bowled over I was by what she had just said.

"Excuse me?"

Erica laughed loudly at my stunned expression. Several mourners turned to look disapprovingly at us. I felt my face flush, but Erica either didn't notice the dirty looks aimed our way, or chose to ignore them. She pulled me over to a few available chairs, and we sat down.

"I wouldn't put it past Shay to fake her own death," Erica said, crossing her legs and leaning back in her chair. "Shay would do anything for attention."

I finally found my voice. "That's insane," I whispered.

Erica shrugged. "That was Shay," she said. "She thrived on pushing people too far."

"You really think she would fake her own death?" I asked. "What did you think she would do, pop up out of the coffin halfway through the funeral service and shout 'Gotcha'?"

Erica tilted her head, seeming to seriously consider such an outlandish scenario. "Shay always said she wanted to go out with a bang," she said, shrugging again. She caught sight of someone over my shoulder and her eyes lit up. "Gotta run," she said. I turned in my chair and watched Erica sidle up to a man wearing a white dress shirt and a pair of black slacks.

With Erica gone, I couldn't put it off any longer. I steeled myself to approach the casket. The last time I had seen Shay she had been face down in my garden under a rhubarb leaf, great-grandma's gardening shears sticking out of her back. The thought made me want to turn and run, but I forced my feet forward. It was my obligation to pay my respects to the deceased.

I gazed down at Shay and a wave of relief washed over me. Shay lay on her back in the white satin-lined casket. Her blonde hair with the red tips was clean and framed her face. Her makeup was tasteful and she wore a simple white dress. She looked so lifelike that I expected her to sit up at any moment, just as I had said she might. Instead, she lay still, her hands wrapped around a spray of white carnations. She looked so peaceful and serene.

I admired the different flower arrangements positioned around the casket. Dwight's name was written on a colorful arrangement of gerbera daisies. I shuddered when I saw Erica's name on a bouquet of white lilies. How Erica could be so callous about her friend's death was beyond me. An arrangement of gorgeous red roses sat next to the lilies. The name Cody Lane was printed neatly on the little white card. *Cody must be Erica's brother*, I thought. Then my gaze landed on an enormous vase overflowing with roses, mums, carnations, and daisies, all white. The huge arrangement was accented with lush greenery. The large arrangement towered over all of the others. I peeked at the name on the card and sucked in my breath. The name *Trisha Malton* was written on the card in Mom's flowing script.

A feeling of shock rocked me all the way to my toes. Mom hadn't mentioned she was going to buy flowers for Shay, let alone such an opulent arrangement. Then I felt a flood of embarrassment. I had discovered Shay's body, but I hadn't even thought about buying flowers for her funeral. I chided myself for not being a very good neighbor. No matter how loathsome of a person Shay was, I still could have bought an arrangement to honor her at her funeral.

But why would Mom buy such a large, elaborate flower arrangement for Shay? As far as I knew, Mom only met Shay briefly at the B&B when Shay stopped in to taunt the guests with her cell phone and try to convince them to come stay at her campground. Why would Mom feel the need to go all out for a woman she saw for only a few minutes?

I looked around for Mom. I spied her standing in a corner, partially hidden by a large funeral wreath with the word "Mother" written on it. I discreetly waved Mom toward the casket, but she shook her head and didn't move.

The soft music playing in the background suddenly stopped. I threaded my way through the mourners, took Mom's arm, and guided her to two empty seats in the back row. Pastor Morris stepped to the front of the room. He wore a black suit with a white carnation in the breast pocket that matched the carnations in Shay's hands. He spent several moments looking down at Shay, then turned and faced the crowd jammed into the room. He cleared his throat, welcomed everyone, and began to talk about Shay's life.

As I listened to Pastor Morris' soothing voice, I felt my head grow heavy and my chin drooped toward my chest. The warm room and the smell of flowers were lulling me to sleep. I blinked rapidly in an effort to keep myself awake. *The stress of the grand opening of the B&B and running around town trying to figure out who killed Shay must be starting to catch up with me,* I thought. I felt my eyelids flutter again and decided to close my eyes, just for a second. Then, dimly, as if from a distance, I heard Pastor Morris ask if anyone would like to say a few words about Shay. Next to me I felt Mom stand up. She walked past me toward the front of the room. Suddenly I was wide awake. What on earth could Mom possibly have to say about Shay, a woman she barely knew?

Mom seemed confident as she approached the front of the room, but when she got to the casket, her body crumpled and she fell to her knees on the funeral home's plush carpet. I gasped and shot out of my seat. Pastor Morris helped Mom to her feet and she gripped his arm for support. Then Mom opened her mouth and spoke: "The young woman in this casket was my daughter."

It was as if a bomb had exploded in the room. People let out shrieks and gasps. Pastor Morris looked stunned. I stood rooted to the spot, unable to breathe. I felt shocked to my core. Was my mother losing her mind? I flashed back to Mom's bedraggled appearance when she suddenly showed up at the B&B. She had been acting secretive and so unlike her usual confident, put-together self. Then a terrible thought struck me. What if Mom really was losing her mind? What if she had Alzheimer's disease or dementia? Maybe she had no idea what she was saying.

"That's right," Mom said. She let go of Pastor Morris' arm and stepped toward the casket. She gazed down at Shay for several long moments. When she looked up, there were tears streaming down her cheeks. "I got pregnant in college and gave the baby up for adoption. Shay contacted me recently to tell me she was the baby I had given up. I came back to Hillsville to meet her and was so happy to reconnect with her." Mom let out a strangled moan. "And now I have lost her all over again!"

A large woman stood up from her seat in the front row. "Liar!" she shouted. The woman swayed up to the lectern and shook a finger in Mom's face, her black dress billowing around her. She wore several rings on each finger. "I gave birth to that girl," she said, swinging her right index finger in the direction of the casket. The five rings on her index finger sparkled in the sunlight beaming through the window. "I spent nineteen hours in labor with her and I remember every minute of it. I don't know who you are, lady, or what's wrong with you, but that is my daughter in that casket, not yours."

Everyone's gaze pivoted to Mom. Mom covered her face with both hands and began to sob. She dashed down the aisle and around the corner. I didn't hesitate for a second before running after her. Behind me, I heard the crowd erupt into loud chatter. I knew that Mom's outburst would be the juiciest bit of gossip to hit Hillsville in years.

After a brief search, I found Mom in the women's restroom. She had locked herself in the larger of the two stalls. A trail of toilet paper snaked along the floor under the stall door. When I entered the bathroom Mom let out a huge honking sound and the trail of toilet paper unrolled further from the spool.

"Mom?" I watched as under the stall door more toilet paper lurched across the floor. Mom loudly blew her nose and didn't reply.

"Mom, are you OK?"

Silence.

I didn't know what to expect. My mother was never at a loss for words. What could I say? As far as public embarrassments go, this went far beyond lipstick on her teeth or the back of her skirt tucked into her pantyhose. Finally, I decided to just blurt out my worst fear. "Mom, do you have Alzheimer's?" I squeezed my eyes shut, terrified yet anxious to hear the answer. Once the problem was spoken out loud, we would be able to deal with it and everything would be OK.

The stall door squeaked open. *"What?"*

I opened my eyes. Mom was virtually wrapped in toilet paper from head to toe. Tear-stained, crumpled tissue draped around her neck like a feather boa and fresh toilet paper swathed her waist, ready to be pressed into service at any moment.

"It's OK, Mom," I said, engulfing her in a hug, toilet paper and all. "You're not the first person to go through this. We'll find you the best doctors. I'll take care of you every step of the way."

Mom swiped a clean sheet of toilet paper across her face and stepped over to the sink. The toilet paper fluttered in her wake. She splashed water on her face, snatched a paper towel from the holder by the mirror, and dabbed it against the skin under her eyes. Turning to me, she said, "I don't have Alzheimer's disease, Rachel. Whatever gave you that idea?"

Once again, I recalled the disheveled state in which my mother had arrived at the B&B. I thought about how uncharacteristically quiet she had been during her stay. And I thought about the scene she had just caused next to the casket.

Mom seemed to be able to read my thoughts. "Every word of what I said was true," she said. Then she closed her eyes. "Or at least I thought it was all true." Mom took a deep, shuddery breath, as if she were marshalling every last bit of courage in her body. "I got pregnant in college and I gave the baby up for adoption." The words rushed out of Mom's mouth and she sagged against the sink, tears spilling from her eyes. "I have kept this secret for decades," she said. She pressed her fist against her mouth and let out another anguished sob. "And then I go and spill my guts to a room full of *strangers*."

I felt dizzy and collapsed onto a padded bench along the wall. I couldn't believe any of this was happening. This morning I had woken up in my bedroom at the B&B, completely sure of just about everything in my life. And I thought finding a dead body would be the biggest surprise of the week!

What Mom had said suddenly hit me. "I have a sister?" I whispered. A sibling was one of the things I had always wanted most in my life and never gotten. The idea that I had a half-sister and she had lived right next door to me and I didn't even know it was almost too much to bear. Shay and I never got along, but if I had known we were half-sisters maybe I could have tried harder. I *would* have tried harder. My one shot for a sibling, and now it was gone forever. Then I remembered the woman in the black dress berating Mom in front of Shay's casket. The two women couldn't both be Shay's mother. And what had Mom meant when she said she "thought it was all true"?

The restroom door opened and a woman stepped across the threshold. It was Grams's mail carrier, Holly Granger. I almost didn't recognize her. Usually, I saw her sitting in her beat-up car surrounded by baskets of mail, dressed in a baggy T-shirt with her hair in a ponytail. Today she wore a dark gray dress with matching high-heeled shoes. Her lustrous black hair hung loose around her face and she wore makeup that highlighted her green eyes. She pulled up short when she saw Mom and I.

"Oh!" she exclaimed, holding a hand to her chest. She kept her head down, staring at the floor and not making eye contact with either of us. Her face turned bright red. "I didn't realize anyone was in here," she said. She started to back up. "I'll come back when you're done."

"Holly, wait," I said. But Holly had already turned and fled down the hallway.

"She must think I'm insane." Mom moaned. "I can't believe I made such a huge scene in there. What must everyone think of me?" I thought about going after Holly, but then Mom let out a fresh sob. "I am going to be the laughingstock of Hillsville," Mom said. She was still wrapped in toilet paper like a mummy. My urge to laugh died away when I saw how small and vulnerable Mom looked. I hugged her again and she hugged me back. When we let go of each other, she stood up straight and ripped away the toilet paper she had swaddled herself in.

"Shay lied to me," Mom said. She stuffed the wadded-up toilet paper in the trash can. She retrieved her purse from the hook on the back of the stall door. She pulled a hairbrush from a zippered compartment in her purse and ran it through her hair. She plucked a compact from a small makeup bag and dabbed the powder on her cheeks and over her forehead.

Uh-oh. Mom was humiliated, but she was also angry. When Mom gets angry, she's sort of like the Incredible Hulk. But instead of getting all green and muscly, she stands up super straight and fixes her makeup. Once she's finished doing that, look out! She may not be as big as the Hulk, but she is certainly just as strong and twice as fierce.

"Let's go, Rachel," Mom commanded. She squared her shoulders, opened the door, and marched down the hallway. I followed in her wake, feeling like a submissive lady-in-waiting as Mom, the queen, resumed her royal duties. My mind churned with questions I wanted to ask Mom, but I realized now was not the time to ask them. However, when the two of us got back to the B&B, Mom would have *a lot* of explaining to do.

Mom held her head high as she passed the other mourners. Shay's mother stood in the receiving line, and before she could say a single word Mom squeezed her hand and said, "I'm so sorry for your loss." The depth of emotion in Mom's voice cut right through me. Mom may not have been Shay's mother, but she was a mother and she could sincerely share in the other woman's pain. Shay's mother nodded but didn't speak. She gave Mom a faint smile and held Mom's hand for several beats. No one said a word as the two women made a silent agreement. Mom let go of the other woman's hand, nodded to the others in the receiving line, and spun on her heel. It was time to go.

Chapter 15

Mom and I drove home from the funeral in silence. I dropped Mom off at the B&B, then decided I would take a trip to Skyler Industries. I wanted to give Mom time alone, and maybe I could talk to someone in human resources and finally find out why Bree had lost her job. I changed out of my black dress and into my regular clothes before heading out.

Skyler Industries was located on the other side of Hillsville in a small industrial park. I drove with the windows down, enjoying the warm breeze. The smells of spring drifted in through the open windows, the scent of flowers mingling with the sweet aroma of freshly turned earth from the area's acres of farmland. Birds swooped above the power lines, chattering to one another.

I passed the tiny town square that was half park, half monument to the town's most famous resident, Elias Whitmore, an inventor who had lived in the town back in the 1800s. His claim to fame was that he had invented a device that would allow farmers to shell corn more effectively. A bronze statue of Whitmore stood in the center of the square, surrounded by a ring of flowers in bloom. Whitmore carried an open book in one hand and an ear of corn in the other. Every summer the town held Whitmore Days, a festival to honor the area's esteemed farmer, scholar, and inventor.

I turned into the industrial park and wheeled into the factory's parking lot. The Skyler Industries building looked almost brand new. It was a long, L-shaped building painted gray. The grass was thick and green, trimmed carefully around the sidewalks leading to the front entrance. Shrubs blooming with pink blossoms had been planted on either side of the front door. The American flag flapped high atop a flagpole next to the building.

When I pushed through the front door into the lobby I was greeted by a woman with short brown hair. She wore a green blazer and matching skirt. She smiled at me when I entered. "Welcome to Skyler Industries," she said. "How can I help you?"

I approached the woman's desk. A metal plaque on the desk read *Anita*. I smiled at her. "Well, Anita, my name is Rachel Kent and I own the Yesteryear B&B."

Anita smiled blandly but didn't say anything.

"I just hired a terrific employee by the name of Bree Foster," I continued. "She used to work here and I wanted to get a little more information about her employment at the factory."

Anita's smile remained glued to her face. "Let me contact Human Resources," she said. She lifted the receiver of her desk phone, dialed a few digits, and waited. When someone answered on the other end, she turned and spoke into the receiver in a low voice. I couldn't make out what she was saying.

When the call was over, Anita hung up the phone and turned back to me. She still wore the same bland smile, but her eyes no longer exuded professional friendliness. "I'm afraid we don't share information about previous employees," she said.

"But, what about—?"

"Thank you for visiting Skyler Industries," Anita said. "I hope you have a wonderful day, ma'am." She turned to her computer and began typing.

Well, I knew when I was being dismissed. I didn't like it, but there was nothing I could do. I headed back to the car. Miss Millie had mentioned that Shay's boyfriend, Bobby, also worked at the factory. I scanned the parking lot, wondering what the chances were that Bobby would be at work today. My gaze landed on a dented blue Ford Ranger with several Campfire Junction bumper stickers plastered across the back window. Bingo.

I got back in my car and turned on the radio, preparing to wait as long as I had to for Bobby to emerge. But before I could even finish singing along under my breath to one song on the local country music station, the back door of the factory opened and a stream of employees gushed out. A few people stopped to chat with coworkers or to sit on the picnic tables near the exit, but most people looked like they couldn't get away from the factory fast enough.

A minute later a man with the mother of all mullets approached the Ford Ranger. He stuck his key into the door lock and twisted it. Wrenching open the door, he was about to hoist his heavy frame into the driver's seat when I lunged out of my car. I hadn't thought too far ahead about what possible reason I would have to talk to a complete stranger in a factory parking lot after work, and I wished I had dedicated a little more brainpower to the mission.

The casual approach seemed to be the best idea. "Bobby?" I said it like it was a question, hoping it would sound less awkward that way. Bobby had levered himself into the driver's seat by the time I arrived. He poked his head out of the open door and looked around. When he saw me, he leered. It wasn't a pretty picture as he was missing several teeth in important spots in his mouth. The teeth he did have were various shades of brown and yellow. I managed to keep the fake smile plastered on my face and I mentally patted myself on the back for not retching.

"Got a minute?"

"Sure do."

"I wanted to talk to you about Shay."

Bobby's easygoing demeanor immediately hardened. His expression didn't change, but his entire body went rigid. I watched his Adam's apple bob up and down. Squinting at me suspiciously, he pulled a round container of chewing tobacco from his back pocket. He unscrewed the lid and placed a generous wad between his gums and lower lip. That explained the brown and yellow teeth. "What did you say your name was again?"

I hadn't introduced myself on purpose. For one thing, I was sick and tired of hearing people say that I was a cell phone thief. For another, I didn't want Bobby making the connection between my B&B and Shay's death. I decided to go with little bits and pieces of the truth. "My name is Rachel." Totally true. "I knew Shay." Also true. "I wanted to tell you how sorry I was to hear about her passing." True.

That explanation seemed to satisfy Bobby. If he thought it odd that a complete stranger would track him down in the parking lot after work to offer condolences, he didn't let on. The suspicious look lifted from his eyes like morning fog vanishing in the sunlight. He went back to staring at my chest and grinning.

I wrapped both arms around my torso as if I were giving myself a great big bear hug. "Brr," I said, faking a shiver. "It's cold out here."

Bobby squinted up at the blue sky, where the afternoon sun blazed high overhead. The temperature well exceeded the average for the month of May in Michigan. I could feel beads of sweat popping out on my upper lip. Bobby stopped looking at the sky and instead shot me a quizzical look. Still keeping my arms clamped tightly across my chest, I shrugged. "I have a condition," I said.

Bobby stared at me like he thought I might have a mental condition, and at this point I was wondering about that myself. Doubt reared its ugly head, but I tamped it down. I reminded myself why I was in this situation: the farm. I had to find the killer who had viciously murdered someone in my backyard.

"Was that it?" Bobby had stopped smiling and now looked annoyed.

"Um. Well."

"Hey, Bobby." I turned my head at the sound of the voice. A woman with curly red hair and pale, freckled skin approached the truck. She shot me a dirty look before bouncing over to Bobby and beaming at him brightly. "Are you ready to go?"

"You bet, honey bunch." Bobby ogled me one more time, then started up the truck. Thick black smoke belched out of the tailpipe and I stepped back, coughing and waving a hand in front of my face to chase away the fumes. Bobby laughed and put the truck into gear, zooming out of the parking lot.

I watched the truck pull out in front of a car, which had to swerve to avoid ramming into Bobby's truck. The driver of the car laid on the horn and Bobby stuck his middle finger out the window. My arms dropped to my sides and my mouth gaped open. Bobby was already seeing another woman just days after his former girlfriend had been murdered?

Even though Bobby wasn't going to win any Boyfriend of the Year awards, I wasn't sure if such callous behavior was solid proof he was a murderer. Bobby seemed more like lazy mooch, not someone who would go to all the trouble of killing someone else. However, my talk with Bobby certainly hadn't removed him from my suspect list.

On the way back to my car I saw two men and a woman sitting at a picnic table, absorbed in their phones. All three wore light blue T-shirts with the name Skyler Industries on the left breast, jeans, and work boots. Bright orange earplugs dangled from plastic cords slung around their necks. The woman appeared to be in her mid-fifties, pudgy with a heavily lined face. She wore her curly salt-and-pepper hair cropped short.

As I passed the picnic table, my shoulders hunched in disappointment, the woman looked up from her phone. "Hey," she said. I stopped and looked behind me, thinking the woman must be calling to one of her coworkers, certainly not to me. When I didn't see anyone else around, I turned back to the woman, pointed at my chest, and raised my eyebrows. The woman nodded. "Yeah, you. Come here."

I walked over to the picnic table, simultaneously wondering what this woman could possibly want with me, as well as why I instantly felt compelled to do whatever she told me to.

"Have a seat," she said, waving a hand at the spot across the table from her. I sat down heavily next to one of the men. He briefly glanced up from his phone and nodded at me.

"My name is Rita," the woman said. She pointed at the man sitting next to her. "This is Rodney." Rodney was probably in his early twenties, with short blonde hair already thinning on top. He didn't even look up from his phone, just lifted a hand and waved in my direction. The woman pointed at the man sitting next to me. "That's LeWayne." LeWayne was a middle-aged African-American man. His goatee was flecked with gray and a paunch hung over his belt. He looked up from his phone and reached out to briefly shake my hand before returning to whatever he was absorbed in on the screen.

Rita assessed me with shrewd brown eyes. "Seen you talking to Bobby," she said.

I nodded.

"Thought I heard you mention that woman that got murdered, Shay." I nodded again. Rita shook her head, and I assumed she was about to lament Shay's passing. Instead, she lowered her voice and said, "I don't like to speak ill of the dead, but that girl had it coming. I seen Shay sometimes here at the factory when she visited Bobby, but I seen her up close and personal when me and my family went to Campfire Junction." Rita paused, and a dreamy

140

look came over her face. "I remember Campfire Junction back in the good-old days, back when Shay's parents were still in charge." She shook her head and sighed. "What a great, clean campground it was back then. Perfect for families. Shay ran the place into the ground and now it's a shadow of its former self.

"I don't believe for one single minute that Bree Foster murdered Shay," Rita continued. "There are plenty of people in this town that would have stood in line for a chance to kill that woman, but Bree wasn't one of them." I opened my eyes wide, surprised at the vehemence in Rita's voice. "It's shameful the way the head honchos at this factory treated Bree," she said.

I decided subtlety wasn't necessary with Rita, so I dove right in. "What exactly happened to get Bree fired?" I asked.

Rita's eyes widened. "Don't Bree work at your place now?" she asked. "Didn't she tell you what happened?"

I shook my head. "She told me she worked here and that she left after four months. She wouldn't give me any details." I gestured at the building next to us. "That's why I came here. I wanted to find out why Bree was fired, but no one would tell me why."

Rita clamped her lips shut and her expression turned stony. I felt my heart sink. All of a sudden this woman didn't want to talk?

"Please," I said. "What you tell me could help put a killer behind bars, and clear Bree's name."

LeWayne stood up suddenly. "Whatever you're going to say, I don't want to hear it," he said. "Ain't none of my business. The less I know about what other folks do, the happier I am."

Rodney also rose from his seat. He slipped his phone into his pocket. "I'm outta here, too," he said. "Gotta get the car home so my wife can drive it to work."

When we were alone, Rita stared at me across the picnic table, wringing her hands in her lap. She was waging a mental war about whether or not she could trust me. I smiled brightly, hoping that would help win her over. Her scowl deepened. Hmm, maybe my winning smile wasn't as winning as I had hoped. I stopped smiling and let Rita continue to assess me. Finally, she let out a huge sigh. The mental war was over, but I still wasn't quite sure which side had won out.

"Do you promise not to repeat a word of what I tell you to anyone?"

I resisted the impulse to pump my fist with victory. I kept my expression solemn. "Absolutely."

Rita stopped wringing her hands and placed them in front of her on the table. "I told Bree I would never breathe a word of this to anyone. We were friends and she trusted me." She pointed at the factory building. "You can't trust very many people in that snake's den."

Rita bent over the picnic table and pitched her voice so low I had to strain to hear her. "Bree knew one of her coworkers was being sexually harassed by her supervisor, but the coworker wouldn't stick up for herself," she said. "Then one day the supervisor saw the woman was in the breakroom by herself, so he went in and locked the door behind him. He thought he and the woman was alone, but Bree had gone to the bathroom. When Bree heard the woman arguing with the supervisor, she burst out of the bathroom and threatened to kill him if he ever laid another hand on her friend. She saved her friend but lost her job. That slimy supervisor went straight to HR and told them about Bree's threats, but didn't say what really led up to them. He made up some excuse about how Bree was angry about a poor employee evaluation she had received. Since Bree had gotten a bad eval just a week before, HR didn't even question him."

"Why didn't Bree's coworker come forward with the truth and defend Bree?" I asked. "Surely they would have believed her if she had told them what happened."

"That's the saddest part," Rita said. She glanced around to make sure we were still alone. Everyone from the previous shift had gone home, and everyone who had shown up for the current shift had already gone inside the building to begin work. "Bree's coworker is married to a jealous, abusive man. If he finds out another man so much as said hi to his wife, he takes his anger out on her."

My gut churned at the awful visual Rita's words created in my mind. The truth started to become clear. "Her husband would have blamed her if the story had gotten out that another man had harassed her?"

Rita nodded. "Sick, huh?"

I sat stock still, thinking about Bree's bravery. Not only had she stood up to a man in power who was harassing her coworker, she had also kept the secret so the other woman wouldn't suffer at the hands of her abusive husband.

Rita resumed wringing her hands on the picnic table. "Oh no, no," she said. "I did the wrong thing. I knew I shouldn't have told!"

I reached out and placed my hands over hers. Her fingers stopped twisting, but tears glittered in her eyes. "No, you did the right thing," I said. "I knew Bree wasn't capable of murder, and this is proof."

"Are you going to tell Bree I told you?"

I shook my head. "No, but I can't promise I won't have to tell the police."

Rita's lined face seemed to fold in on itself, creating even more lines and cracks. She sighed and nodded. "I understand," she said. "So long as it helps Bree, I understand."

Chapter 16

When I got back to the farmhouse, I went looking for Mom and found her in the barn with the cats. Mom sat on one of the straw bales, Biscuit sitting on her lap. I could hear his purr, loud as a lawnmower, when I entered the barn. I smiled as Mom ran her hand down the cat's back. Thick clumps of hair wafted off her hand when she reached the base of his spine and drifted lazily in the shafts of sunlight pouring through the dusty window.

I pulled down the soft long-sleeved flannel shirt I always wore to visit the cats from the nail I used as a makeshift hook. I slipped my arms into the shirt. There was a rip in one elbow and the flannel fabric was wearing thin in spots, but the shirt was comfy and kept the cat hair off my clothing. I buttoned the shirt as I walked.

"Mom?" I approached cautiously, as if I were afraid she would bolt like a skittish deer if she saw me coming. Mom looked up briefly, then returned her attention to stroking Biscuit. For a woman who had always seemed most at home in a power suit and heels, she looked remarkably happy to be sitting in a dusty barn covered in cat hair.

"Rachel, we need to talk." Mom kept her eyes trained on Biscuit.

"Yes, I think we do." I took a seat on the straw bale across from her. Cupcake and Muffin, eager for some kitty lovin', jumped up on the bale with me, one on either side like fuzzy bookends.

Mom took a deep breath, then let it out slowly. "First of all, I owe you an apology."

Thank goodness for the cat on either side of me. If they hadn't been sitting next to me, I might have fallen over and toppled onto the straw-strewn barn floor. Never, in all my life, had Mom ever apologized to me.

Mom apparently didn't need a reply, because she kept on talking. "You have been working so hard to start a new business and now you are involved in a murder investigation. And my secrets are only adding to your problems. You deserve to know the whole truth."

I leaned forward, eager to hear the complete story from my mother's youth. With my left hand stroking Cupcake's sleek fur and my right hand rubbing Muffin's fluffy head, I settled in.

"I was so excited to leave Hillsville and go to college in a big city." Mom's eyes took on a faraway look. She stopped petting Biscuit and he let out an indignant meow. Mom once again reached up to absently stroke his fur and he closed his eyes in kitty bliss. "I had never even been out of Hillsville before, other than a visit to the campus. I would lay awake in bed at night and imagine all the great things that were going to happen once I left small-town farm life. I would live in a dorm, eat in the cafeteria, meet wonderful, exciting new people."

I smiled. It seemed Mom had been focused on the social aspect of college, not the studying aspect.

Mom continued. "You don't know this, but before I was an international business major, I majored in paleontology."

For the second time in about five minutes, I almost toppled off the straw bale. At the rate I was going, I would have to look into installing seatbelts on these things. The last thing I needed was a head injury or a broken bone due to a fall.

"You wanted to study dinosaurs?" I asked, incredulous. I tried to imagine Mom digging in the dirt under an unrelenting sun, wearing khaki shorts and a matching bucket hat. Then I pictured her running from a T.Rex in some real-life version of *Jurassic Park*, but neither one fit my hard-charging, corporate-type mom.

Mom laughed. "Can you believe it? I thought it sounded glamorous to travel around the world to different sites. I dreamed of one day discovering a new species of dinosaur and having it named after me." She shook her head. "Luckily, I came to my senses and switched my major to international business, but that wasn't until my sophomore year. As a freshman I was about as green as I could be. Everything was new to me: the classes, the dorm, the boys." Her expression took on a misty sadness as she mentally wandered back to those years. "Within my first month on campus I met a paleontology grad student who taught one of my intro classes. His name was Guy Durand. He was so handsome. He had amazing green eyes and thick black hair. He also had a terrific sense of humor. I loved his laugh."

Mom stopped talking and wiped at the wetness gathering at the corners of her eyes with her fingertips. "He was several years older than me, but that just added to the allure. He asked me to meet him at the local coffee shop one Saturday morning, and then after that we were practically inseparable."

"All of that happened during your first month at school?" I was shocked. In my first month at college, I was still trying to remember which way to turn the key to unlock my dorm room and where the library was.

Mom nodded. "By the time I found out I was pregnant, Guy had taken off to Asia for a dig and I was trying to muddle through my classes the best I could." She took a deep, shuddery breath. "The baby was due in June, and I was terrified because I would have to go home to my parents' farm looking like a blimp. There was no way I was ever going to be able to hide my pregnancy at that point."

"So then what happened?" I imagined my mother as a young college student, pregnant and scared. My heart ached for that young woman.

"I had gone to the medical clinic on campus and they gave me the contact information for a local church that helped young women who were expecting. One of the volunteers there helped me when I needed it. Because I was technically an adult, they didn't have to tell my parents." She opened her eyes and looked straight at me. "Rachel, that was the hardest time in my life. I was young, alone, pregnant, and scared. When the baby came early, I was even more afraid."

Neither of us spoke for a minute. I busied myself scratching Cupcake and Muffin behind the ears while Mom took deep breaths.

"After the baby was born, I held her for a few minutes before they took her away. She was so small and wrinkly." Mom smiled at the memory. "I loved her so much my heart hurt, but I knew I wouldn't be a good mother for her. She needed adult parents with jobs, who had the maturity and the ability to care for her and give her what she needed. The church group had arranged for a married couple to adopt her right away, and I signed the papers. I never knew what the couple named her, where they lived, or even what their names were. I thought it would be better that way."

"Did you go back home that summer?" I asked.

Mom nodded. "Yes. In a selfish way, I was glad the baby had come early. I did call the church group and asked if the baby was doing OK. I worried about her being born premature. The woman I spoke with said the baby had only spent a few days in the hospital and that the adoption had gone smoothly. She told me the parents were overjoyed because they had been trying for many years to have a baby and couldn't. She also said the baby was healthy and happy. That was all I needed to hear."

I let all this sink in. My mom had been a teenage mother and I had had no idea. Then it hit me: If Shay had lied and she wasn't the baby my mother had given up for adoption decades ago, then I still had an older half-sister out there in the world somewhere. I couldn't even begin to grapple with that idea right now, so I changed the subject.

"Does Dad know about this?"

Mom shifted on the straw bale. "No. I never told him. He has no idea. In fact, I lied and told him I had never been with another man before him."

Yikes. This conversation had taken a sharp turn and was entering some dicey territory. As much as I loved both of my parents, there were some details I just didn't need to know. Time for another question.

"Did Grams and Gramps ever find out?"

Mom tilted her head to one side, thinking. "I think Mother suspected something was wrong, but I certainly never told her what happened. Whenever she asked me about school that summer, I would answer as vaguely as I could. So, no, I don't think they knew."

"No one ever knew about the baby but you?"

"Well, the doctors and nurses at the hospital knew, but they didn't know anything about me. To them I was just another patient. The people in the church group knew my name, but they kept all of my information confidential. I requested that the adopting couple not know anything about me, either."

I thought of Miss Millie, standing on a milk crate and peering intently at me over the counter. Miss Millie knew everyone's secrets. Did she also know Mom's? "Did you go to the post office that summer?" I asked.

Mom looked confused for a second, then she snorted, a sound I had never heard her make before. Staying at the farm was really helping her overcome her prim and proper ways. "Absolutely not. I stayed as far away from Miss Millie and her X-ray eyes as I could. I just knew that one look at me and she would see all of my secrets glowing like neon lights in Las Vegas. Whenever Mother asked me to go to the post office to buy stamps or to pick up a package, I told her I had a stomachache." Mom rested her hand on her abdomen, as if the very memory gave her cramps. "And usually I wasn't lying."

Wow. Mom had carried this secret around for more than thirty years, never telling another soul. All of this new information was interesting, as well as overwhelming, and I had a lot to think about. But right now, I needed to get to the most pressing matter: Shay's murder.

"If you never told anyone you had a baby you gave up for adoption, then how did Shay track you down?"

Mom sighed and shrugged. "I have no idea. One day several months ago my assistant answered a call from a woman named Shay Clarke who said she wanted to speak with me about an urgent matter. I didn't recognize the name and I was busy with a massive project that was overdue and over budget, so I didn't have time to get back to her. She called again a few months ago and since I finally had some breathing room at work, I called her back. She told me she was my long-lost daughter and that she lived in Hillsville, of all places."

"Did you ask her to prove who she was?"

Mom shook her head. "Not at first. When I first talked to her, I was so shocked that I dropped my cell phone and it shattered. I had to call Shay back on my desk phone. I was terrified and excited at the same time. On the one hand, I lived in fear that the secret I had been hiding for decades would come out and people would find out the truth. On the other hand, I was over the moon thinking about how wonderful it would be to see my child again."

148

I nodded. It would indeed be a tremendous shock to have someone call up out of the blue and announce she was the child you had given up so many years before. "Did you talk to her again?"

"I did, several times. After our first phone call I lived my life in a daze for about a week. When we spoke again, I had gathered my wits a little bit and realized this could very well be a scam. I asked her questions about when she was adopted and through which organization, and she knew all the answers. She knew when the baby had been born and at which hospital. That was enough to convince me."

I thought about Mom's disheveled appearance when she had shown up at the farm. The mother-daughter reunion must not have gone well. "Why didn't you stay with Shay?" I asked. "Why did you come to the farm instead?"

Mom sighed loudly. "Shay demanded money almost within minutes of us meeting," she said. "I had imagined a tearful reunion, the two of us embracing and smiling with joy at being reunited." Mom clenched her fists in her lap. "Getting hit up for money was a slap in the face. I told Shay I would have to think about it, and then she made a comment about how maybe I wouldn't be able to see my grandchild if she didn't get the money."

I gasped. What a disgusting, horrible thing for Shay to say. Seems like she had a knack for knowing just what to say to make people angry at her.

"It was the last thing Shay said to me as I was on my way out the door," Mom continued. "I heard those cruel words echoing in my head while I wept and drove around the countryside." Mom spread her hands wide. "Then I showed up here at the B&B."

I didn't know what to say. I remained silent and continued to stroke Cupcake and Muffin.

Mom squeezed her hands into fists in her lap. "I was so stupid. I should have asked for more proof. I'm such a fool."

"Don't say that," I said. "You were taken by surprise, and then she was able to answer all of your questions. If you never told anyone, how could she have had all that information?"

Mom sighed and tipped her head back, staring up at the dusty rafters. "If I knew that, Rachel, I think we would have our murderer."

A shudder rippled down my spine. Never in my wildest dreams did I ever think I would be having a conversation with my mother about murderers. I wanted to get this ordeal over with so I could return to cooking, gardening, and looking after guests. Tracking down murderers was not what I had signed up for when I opened the B&B.

I walked slowly back to the house from the barn. I had always believed myself to be my mother's first – and only – child. While I had always yearned for a sibling, how would it feel to suddenly have an older half-sister? It would definitely change the family dynamic. I felt a pang of fear mixed with jealousy. Would Mom get so excited about finding her first child that it would change her feelings for me? I chastised myself for even thinking such a silly thought. I was an adult and needed to take a more proactive role in my relationship with my mother. Even though Mom and I were both busy, I vowed to make time to call her more often. Maybe I could even take some time off around Christmas and make a trip to Grand Rapids to stay with her for the holidays. While I was there the two of us could look into genealogy sites online and search for the adopted child together. Why not?

Of course, Mom's firstborn wasn't a child anymore. I quickly calculated my half-sister would be about thirty-five years old now. I remembered all the daydreams I had had as a child about what it would be like to have a sibling, especially a sister. The two of us would share a room and we would stay up late, talking. We would share our deepest secrets and talk about boys. I laughed out loud. That scenario wouldn't fit my current lifestyle, that was for sure. Even though I had plenty of boy problems to share with a dozen sisters, I didn't have the time to stay up late when I had to wake up early to make breakfast for a houseful of guests.

Maybe I could modify my childhood daydreams to fit with my current adult circumstances. Perhaps my half-sister, if she was ever located, could stay at the B&B. I wondered if my sister looked at all like me. Would she like the same things I did? A terrible thought entered my mind. What if I finally got my wish of having a sister and the two of us had absolutely nothing in common?

I shook my head to clear my thoughts. Too many what ifs. I opened the front door of the farmhouse and stepped inside. *One step at a time,* I thought. *I need to find my sister first, then worry about whether or not we will get along.*

Chapter 17

That night after dinner I decided to pay a visit to Erica Lane. She and Shay had definitely had a twisted relationship, but could Erica hold a clue about who might have wanted Shay dead? There was only one way to find out.

I guided the car up the curving driveway and parked in front of the immense log cabin-style house overlooking Hillsville Lake. I opened the car door and the moment my feet hit the ground two large German Shepherds came racing around the side of the house. I clutched the strap of my purse and almost jumped onto the car roof.

"Diesel! Heidi! Down!"

Immediately the dogs plopped onto their behinds, tongues lolling out of their open mouths. I breathed a sigh of relief and released the death grip on my purse strap. Erica appeared from behind the house. She wore a purple tank top and black shorts. The dog wearing a spiked black collar, presumably Diesel, let out a little whimper of joy when he saw Erica. She placed a hand on the dog's head and I swore he smiled. I thought about revising my opinion of Erica. Could she be all bad if dogs liked her?

"What do you want?" Erica asked. In a fit of mental whiplash, I once again changed my opinion of Erica. Her dogs might like her, but so far, she didn't appear to have very good people skills.

"I –"

"Wait a minute." Erica's hand slid from the dog's head. Her nails were long and painted a deep shade of red. She pointed her index finger at me. "I met you at Shay's funeral. You were with that crazy lady who thought she was Shay's mother."

I bristled at Erica calling my mother crazy. Mom had genuinely believed Shay was the child she had given up for adoption. Shay was the dirty rotten liar.

"That 'crazy lady' is my mother," I said icily, quickly making the decision to forego diplomacy. Erica Lane did not seem like a woman who appreciated pleasantries or tact. "Shay lied to my mother and told her she was my mother's long-lost child."

Erica returned to petting Diesel, who looked like he was in doggie heaven. The other dog, Heidi, wore a neon pink collar. Heidi nudged Erica's other hand and she absentmindedly began stroking the dog's ear. "Is that what she did?"

Erica's reaction was what I would expect if I had told her I had stopped by to borrow a cup of sugar or to comment on the weather.

"You don't sound all that shocked," I said.

"I'm not." Erica turned and motioned me toward the house. "Let's go inside. It's time for me to feed the dogs."

The dogs followed behind Erica single file and I fell in line, bringing up the rear. Erica pulled open the front door and I followed the dogs into the house. The dogs' toenails clicked against the wood floors in the spacious entryway. Erica led the way through the open interior of the house to the kitchen, where she bent down to open a cupboard. She reached into a metal container, loaded up a metal scoop with dog food, and deposited a healthy portion into each of the two bowls next to the counter island.

While Erica filled bowls with dog chow I gazed around me. Erica's house was a showpiece. The kitchen was outfitted with new appliances, each one fingerprint free and sparkling. The kitchen flowed seamlessly into a large living room, which was dominated by a massive stone fireplace. Leather and wood chairs were grouped around the fireplace. The entire interior of the home was pine, like living inside of a tree.

Erica, finished with her task, came to stand next to me. I could hear the dogs crunching their kibble, the sound echoing through the large, open house.

I opened my mouth to explain why I was there, but Erica beat me to it. "I know why you're here," she said. I closed my mouth. Was Erica going to make this easy on me and just confess to killing Shay? I leaned forward in my chair.

"You're here because you heard Shay was having an affair with my husband."

My mouth dropped open again. Not what I had been expecting. Erica noticed my shocked expression. "You mean you didn't know?"

"Uh, no. How long had this been going on?"

Diesel finished his meal and sauntered into the living room. Erica sat in one of the upholstered chairs and Diesel plopped down next to her. She reached down to stroke his back. "About a year."

Erica's husband had been having an affair with Shay for an entire year? I sat down slowly on the leather couch across from Erica. Heidi wandered in from the kitchen and lounged on the floor on the other side of Erica's chair. Erica had both arms down at her sides, petting the dogs. She didn't look like a woman who was filled with rage over the antics of her cheating husband. But then again, if she had killed Shay, what did she have to worry about?

"Does your husband know that you know about the affair?"

"Of course. He's the one who told me."

OK, now I was confused. Erica did not seem like the kind of woman who would tolerate her husband having a mistress on the side. She seemed more like the kind who would demand every second of her husband's attention.

I searched my mind for a follow-up question, something tactful. My search came up empty, though. I felt foolish sitting there with Erica staring at me. I jumped when the back door slammed open and a man carrying a knife dripping with blood entered the house.

"Don't come in here!" Erica shouted, leaping up from her chair.

I shrank back into the couch, wondering if one of the dogs would go after the man. The dogs stood up and wandered over to the man, sniffing his mud-covered boots.

"Take that nasty knife outside," Erica told the man. "You're dripping blood and fish guts all over my clean floors." She let out a huffy sigh. "And how many times have I told you not to wear your muddy boots in the house?"

"Oops." The man backed out of the door, the dogs following him. Erica went into the kitchen, opened a closet door, and pulled out a mop and a bucket.

"That man never listens to a word I say," she said to me as she passed by. She quickly cleaned up the mess on the pine floors.

A few minutes later the man returned without the knife and barefoot. He was tall, over six feet. He wore a pair of shorts and a tight black T-shirt. His biceps, covered in tattoos, bulged as he pushed the back door shut.

"This is my husband, Cody," Erica said, gesturing at the man with the mop. She went back into the kitchen to put away the mop and the bucket. "This is Rachel Kent," she said, closing the closet door and pointing at me. "She's here to talk to about Shay."

Cody's face turned white, but Erica didn't notice. She had her back to her husband, washing her hands at the sink. By the time she turned around, Cody's color had returned.

"I meant what I said when I told you Shay was having an affair with my husband," Erica said, pointing at Cody. "She *thought* she was having an affair with him, but it was purely one-sided and all in her mind. Shay absolutely threw herself at Cody, but he didn't want anything to do with her." She smirked. "Isn't that right, hon?"

Cody ran his hand through his rumpled hair and laughed. "I wasn't interested in the least."

"Cody told me how pathetic Shay was about her seduction attempts, too," Erica continued. "She would wear the skimpiest skirt and a flimsy top that was nothing more than a bra when she visited him at work. She had no reason to be at his shop, but that didn't stop her from coming up with some crazy excuse."

"Wow," I said. "That's bold."

Erica nodded and sat back down. Cody joined me on the other side of the couch. "Yep. It was even more embarrassing that she had apparently forgotten to put on panties before she stopped in to 'visit' my husband."

My eyes went wide. Cody and Erica both laughed. "Cody told me about it as soon as Shay walked out the door. He called and told me how pathetic Shay was in her attempts to seduce him."

Cody leaned back on the couch. "I run an outdoor supply store downtown," he said. "Lane Sports. Ever been there?"

I shook my head. "I'm not into hunting or fishing, and I don't really have time for either. I run the Yesteryear B&B and some of my future guests might be interested, though."

"Send them my way," Cody said. He heaved himself up from the couch, walked into the kitchen, and cracked open the refrigerator. "You want anything to drink?" he asked. I shook my head, but Erica asked for a beer. Cody pulled two beers out of the refrigerator, popped the tops off both, and handed one to his wife. Erica smiled up at him.

I wanted to get my conversation with Erica back on track. "So, were you and Shay best friends?" I asked.

"Shay wasn't capable of having a best friend," Erica said. "She was only out for herself. Everyone thinks we were besties, but that wasn't true. I figured out pretty quick that Shay only thought about herself and her needs.

"Shay and I grew up together," Erica continued. "We both thrived on competition – sports, drama club, beauty pageants. You name it, we both fought like hell to win. We even went head-to-head in a watermelon seed spitting contest once at summer camp." Erica grinned wickedly. "I won."

I thought about my friends growing up. My family had moved several times because of my parents' jobs, but over the years I still managed to make a few close friends. We used to braid each other's hair and exchange friendship bracelets. That seemed pretty tame compared to the brutal frenemy relationship Erica was describing.

"Then why were you friends with her at all?" I asked.

Erica shrugged. "I enjoy the challenge of constant competition. I was with her all the time, but I wouldn't have trusted Shay for a second. I also wouldn't be stupid enough to tell Shay anything, because she would find a way to use it to her advantage."

Cody took a huge gulp of beer and started choking. Erica leapt up to thump him on the back, but he waved her away. He continued to cough, his chest heaving and tears streaming down his face. Finally, his breathing returned to normal and he sagged against the back of the couch. "Went down the wrong pipe," he said, his voice strained.

All three of us sat in awkward silence for several moments. I wanted to ask Erica more questions about Shay, but the convivial mood had been shattered by Cody's choking fit. I stood up and hoisted my purse strap over my shoulder. "Thanks for taking the time to talk to me," I said. I glanced over at Cody. "Nice to meet you." Cody nodded and lifted his beer bottle toward me.

Erica followed me to the door. Diesel walked at her side, while Heidi remained at her master's feet. "Don't worry about Cody," Erica whispered to me as she opened the front door. "Even though he thought of Shay as a major pest, her murder has really thrown him for a loop."

I glanced over Erica's shoulder at Cody. He took another swig of beer and reached down to scratch Heidi's ears. "Murder does that to people," I said. I walked out the door and over to my car. Erica shut the huge wooden door and I navigated the car down the steeply sloping driveway.

On the short drive home, I replayed my conversation with Erica and Cody. What woman would let her supposed best friend flirt shamelessly with her husband? Was Erica telling the truth when she said she thought it was funny, or was she really enraged and willing to kill?

By the time I pulled into the driveway at the B&B I had many questions, but few answers.

Chapter 18

On Wednesday morning Mom, Bree, and I worked together in the kitchen to clean up after breakfast. Our discussion turned to all of the bad luck that had befallen Ned—his camera and sketchbooks damaged, his tumble down the stairs, and getting sick after eating hot sauce on his dinner.

"You know something," I said. "I made scrambled eggs for Ned Sunday morning and he dumped a ton of hot sauce on them." I recalled Ned pouring on the hot sauce like ketchup and shuddered. "He ate the whole plate of eggs and sauce and didn't even break a sweat."

I plucked the hot sauce bottle from the caddy on the kitchen table. The red and yellow bottled sported a small cartoon chile pepper wearing a sombrero.

Bree glanced at the bottle I held, her brow furrowed. "Are you sure that hot sauce didn't bother him?" she asked. "I mean, that stuff is so hot it could set your mouth on fire."

I shook my head. "No, he ate it like it was nothing. I thought it was strange at the time, but he didn't seem bothered at all. In fact, he said his nickname in grad school had been 'Iron-gut Blankenberger.'"

Mom stared at me. "That's quite the nickname," she said.

"Yeah, it doesn't really roll off the tongue, does it? But it sure seemed accurate at the time."

"How could Ned eat all that hot sauce on his eggs with no problem and then get so sick with just a little bit of hot sauce on his dinner?" Bree asked.

I studied the bottle I held in my hand, noting the size and color. My mind flashed back to dinner on Monday night. Something lingered in the far corner of my mind, but I just couldn't reach it. I felt like I was reaching blindly toward the back of a shelf in a high cupboard. I knew the memory was there, I just couldn't get to it. "There was something that seemed different about that bottle of hot sauce at dinner the other night, but I just can't think of what it was." I replaced the bottle in the caddy on the kitchen table and groaned in frustration.

Bree exchanged a look with Mom. "Do you think it could have something to do with his fall?" she asked, her voice tinged with unease. "It's weird that he said he smelled some fruity furniture polish when we don't even have a bottle of that stuff here."

I shrugged, still lost in thought. "Maybe, but Ned said the fall was an accident."

Mom laid a reassuring hand on my shoulder. "If it's important, it will come to you," she said.

I nodded. Mom was right. If there was a memory that needed to resurface, it would emerge in time. "Well, I think we can all agree that something suspicious is going on with Ned," I said. "But what could it be?"

"Could Ned be connected to Shay's murder?" Bree asked, her hazel eyes wide.

I paused to consider Bree's suggestion. Could Ned somehow be connected to Shay's murder? He was outside the night she was killed, but other than that there was no evidence pointing to him as the killer. Could he be hiding something? Maybe he was covering up for someone else?

"I guess anything is possible, but how could he be connected?" I asked. "Ned said he had never even been to Michigan before, let alone Hillsville. If he is a stranger here, how could he have connections with anyone in town?"

"Ned could be lying," Mom pointed out.

"True," I murmured.

"A person doesn't have to go to a certain place to know someone there," Bree said. Mom and I swung our heads to look at her. "Duh. The internet? Ned could have met Shay online."

I recalled Ned's ancient flip phone. Ned could have texted Shay, I supposed, but that didn't feel right. The image of Ned sitting in front of a computer writing messages to Shay clicked into my brain, and that seemed even more bizarre. So far as I knew, the overzealous ornithologist and the conniving campground owner had absolutely nothing in common. But, then again, the anonymity of the internet could have given Ned the confidence to shed his nerdy image and engage in some salacious conversation online with a woman he didn't know.

"Maybe he's hiding something," Bree said, her voice thoughtful.

I swallowed hard, the words sinking in. It was possible. Ned *could* be hiding something. But what? I didn't want to believe he had any connection to Shay's murder, but all of the bad luck he had been having at the B&B, and now the nagging feeling gnawing at my gut made me wonder if I was missing something.

"If he was connected to Shay," I said slowly, trying to fit the pieces together, "then why now? Why here at the B&B, of all places?"

Mom shook her head. "I agree, it just doesn't make sense. But we can't ignore the fact that he was outside the night of the murder. That's suspicious, at the very least."

I nodded, but something still seemed off. I could feel it, like a puzzle with missing pieces, the whole picture just out of focus. Even though Ned might not be an obvious suspect, that didn't mean he wasn't involved in some way.

And that memory, the one I couldn't quite reach . . . it would surface eventually. I was sure of it. I just hoped it wasn't too late when it did.

****

True to his word, Kurtis arrived at the B&B that afternoon around three-thirty. He jumped out of the van, pulled a box of tools from the back, and jogged up the steps. I met him on the front porch.

"Where are the boys?" I asked.

Kurtis placed the toolbox next to the front door. "At a neighbor's house. I thought they might get in the way over here."

I felt a little twinge of disappointment that Jason and Mason hadn't come to the farm with their dad. I enjoyed the two little boys' energy and enthusiasm.

"Is this the door lock that needs to be changed?" Kurtis asked, gliding his index finger over the gashes scratched into the metal.

I nodded and handed Kurtis the new door hardware I had bought in town. Kurtis took the package I handed him. He quickly got to work on removing the old knob and lock.

160

I watched him work, his calloused hands expertly going through the motions. His hands gracefully moved from one task to the next. It was like watching a ballet. Kurtis glanced up, caught me watching him, and his face flushed deep red. He returned his gaze to the front door.

I couldn't help but find Kurtis endearing and caring. This was the second time in just a few days that he had so humbly come to my aid. *Could he possibly ever be interested me?* I wondered. I pushed that thought out of my mind. I couldn't be interested in another man when I still had no idea where Finn and I stood with our relationship.

Kurtis' voice interrupted my musings. "Rachel, I realize we haven't known each other long, but would you—"

At that moment a sleek, shiny BMW pulled into the driveway, but I couldn't see the driver through the dark tinted windows. When the driver's side door opened and Finnegan Peale, my ex-fiancé, stepped out, my knees felt weak. I reached out a hand to steady myself against the porch railing.

Finn was immaculately dressed in a white Gucci polo shirt and a pair of designer khaki shorts. His bare ankles stuck out of a pair of crocodile loafers. Finn lifted a pair of "if you have to ask you can't afford it" sunglasses off the bridge of his nose and slipped them into a monogrammed case. Although Finn looked like he always did, something about him was different. Standing in the B&B driveway, with the big red barn rising behind him, somehow Finn looked like a completely different person.

I wasn't sure how to greet Finn, especially with Kurtis standing next to me trying not to be obvious about staring at the two of us. I could tell Finn expected to be greeted as if he were still the man I loved, but the tension hanging between us was awkward. I made my way down the steps and hugged him like I had a million times before, but it felt unnatural and uncomfortable. I broke away from him with a nervous laugh.

"Finn, what are you doing here?" I realized right away that didn't sound welcoming and rushed to change my tone. "It's so great to see you! What do you think of the B&B?" I opened my arms wide, encompassing the farmhouse, the barn, and the sprawling but tidy garden.

As Finn spun in a circle, his lips pursed, the grin on my face began to fade. By the time he had shaded his eyes to grimace up at the painted Star of Hope barn quilt hanging on the red barn, the smile had slipped completely from my lips. "It's nice," he said.

Nice? I had poured my entire heart and soul into refurbishing Grams' farmhouse, not to mention every last dime in my bank account, and Finn thought it was *nice*?

"Ahem." Kurtis cleared his throat and I jumped. I had been so focused on Finn that I had completely forgotten about Kurtis. Kurtis walked down the porch steps to join Finn and me.

Finn stopped scrutinizing the farmhouse and turned his critical gaze upon Kurtis. His upper lip curled back. "This is Kurtis Tellke," I said quickly, before Finn could open his mouth to speak. "He was kind enough to volunteer his time to change the lock on the front door."

Kurtis extended a hand in greeting. "Nice to meet you."

Finn ignored Kurtis' outstretched hand and Kurtis pulled it back as if he had been burned. Finn inclined his head in Kurtis' direction, sunlight glinting off his thickly gelled hair.

"Well, looks like my work here is done," Kurtis said. Keeping his head down and avoiding my eyes, he hurried back onto the porch and stuffed his tools back into his toolbox.

"Kurtis, at least let me pay you for your time," I said. Kurtis' face flamed red again and he shook his head. Had I embarrassed him by offering to pay him?

"I'm just happy I could help," Kurtis said, quickly loading his toolbox into the van and jumping behind the wheel. He backed the van out of the driveway and onto the road.

I watched Kurtis go. I was pretty sure he had been on the verge of asking me out when Finn arrived, and I was surprised by how disappointed I was that he hadn't been able to finish asking me. Even though he had plenty of other competing demands in his life, Kurtis had still made it a priority to help me out. I was not happy with how Finn had treated Kurtis. I turned to Finn to tell him just that, but forgot everything when he flashed his killer smile at me. The same smile that always charmed me after every fight and made me forget why we had even argued in the first place.

"Would you like to come in?" I asked. Maybe Finn would be more impressed with the B&B once he was inside the house. No one could resist the farmhouse's welcoming embrace, after all. As Finn walked through the red front door, I wondered what he was doing in Hillsville. Was he going to tell me he missed me? Maybe he had changed his mind about the B&B and was going to offer his unconditional support for both me and my new venture.

Although selling Origins had been tough, losing Finn had been tougher. Every task I had had to do in order to cancel our wedding plans had taken another little bite out of my soul: Stopping the order for my wedding dress, telling the caterer and the florist the ceremony had been called off, returning the huge diamond engagement ring Finn had slipped on my finger the night he proposed.

When Finn had started to call me again at the farmhouse, I had been hopeful that he wanted to revive our relationship. However, we hadn't had a lot of time to talk because I had been so busy with the renovations to turn the farmhouse into a B&B, and entertaining guests meant my time was stretched even thinner. But now that Finn was here in front of me, perhaps we could sit down and talk—really talk—and figure out a way to make things work. I was deep in thought about ways Finn and I could make a long-distance romance work when something Finn said caught my attention.

"Wait a minute," I said. "Could you repeat that?"

"I said the Nibble Network has given you the greenlight for your very own cooking show," Finn said.

I frowned. "What's the Nibble Network?"

"It's this great new food-themed network that is getting its start in Chicago," Finn said enthusiastically. "The network is looking for fresh new talent and they can't wait to work with you. Filming for *In the Kitchen with Rachel Kent* starts next week." Finn bounced on the balls of his feet and grinned.

I was too shocked to respond. When did Finn plan all of this? Why didn't he talk to me about it? Finn rattled on, oblivious to my shock. "One of my clients knows someone who was able to connect me with an executive at the Nibble Network," he said. "After a lot of back and forth I was finally able to connect with this guy. We have been working on getting this project off the ground for the last six weeks."

Something clicked in my head and I counted back mentally. Finn's phone calls to the farmhouse had started just about six weeks ago. Anger bubbled in my stomach and I felt sick. Had Finn been sweet talking me into coming back to Chicago just so he could get me to take part in a new cooking show? Finn rambled happily on, talking about production schedules, scripts, and wardrobe choices.

"When were you going to tell me about this show you were putting together behind my back?" I asked, interrupting Finn in the middle of his description of what the set for the show would look like.

"I was saving it as a surprise for you, Rachel," Finn said. He wrapped an arm around my shoulders and pulled me close.

"Finn, I have a new business and a new life in Hillsville. How am I supposed to juggle a new cooking show as well? And in Chicago, no less. I can't be in two places at once."

Finn nodded. "I've got it all figured out. You can come back to Chicago and shoot the show for a few days during the week, then return . . . here . . . for the weekend." Finn gazed around the kitchen, wrinkling his nose as if he smelled a foul odor. "Think of the exposure this show will offer us," he said, focusing his attention back on me. "Think of the future endorsements and new product lines. Think of all the money we could make from this."

Exposure for *us*? All the money *we* could make? Suddenly, it all became clear. "Is that what all this is about? Money?" I shoved Finn away. His thick cologne was making my head ache.

"Rachel," Finn said. "You know how much I love you. This show would give us a chance to spend more time together, to get our relationship back on track. Maybe we could even set a new wedding date."

As I gazed at Finn it was as if he had been wearing a mask that was dropping away right before my eyes, exposing his true personality. Finn went behind my back to make plans for me to star in a new cooking show without asking me first. Then all he could talk about was the money *he* would get from that show. And now he was trying to convince me that he had done it as a surprise for me because he still loved me and wanted to get back together? How could I have been so blind?

"Get out, Finn," I whispered, rage causing my voice to tremble.

Finn looked stunned. "Rachel, you can't mean that." He reached out his arms toward me.

"I said GET OUT!" I screamed. I yanked open the front door of the farmhouse. "Get out of this house and get out of my life. I never want to see you again."

Finn's insincere smile melted from his face, replaced by an arrogant sneer. "Fine," he said. He gestured around the farmhouse's kitchen. "But you'll come back to me on your hands and knees, begging for another chance, when this dump goes under." His loafers clattered across the front porch and down the stairs. He slammed the door of his car and peeled out of the driveway, spewing gravel as he went.

I stood in the kitchen, Finn's hideous parting words echoing in my head.

****

I had to get away. I got into my car and drove. As I steered the car down the empty country roads, I felt the pain in my chest begin to ease. Watching the rolling green fields through the windshield was therapeutic. I felt my heartrate slow down to normal. I stopped crying. I took the back way home to the farmhouse. On the way, I passed Campfire Junction. I put the car in reverse and drove into the campground.

The sites closest to the road were basic, no-frills camping sites. Each had space for a large tent or a couple of small tents, as well as a firepit edged with bricks and a charcoal grill for cooking. I drove slowly down the dirt roads crisscrossing the campground. As I got farther into the campground the camping sites gave way to small log cabins. Each cabin had a wooden porch on the front and lacy white curtains at the windows. Cars were parked at a few of the cabins, and I saw a lone truck at one of the rustic camping sites, but overall, the place was empty and desolate. No wonder Shay had come over to the B&B to try to poach my guests.

I shook my head. That was ridiculous. Shay had said Campfire Junction was hopping. Perhaps everyone had checked out and a new batch of campers was heading this way right now to check in. I chalked up my negative feelings about the campground to Shay's recent death affecting my frame of mind. Discovering a corpse lurking under a rhubarb leaf in my garden was a sure way to sour my outlook on the world.

Touring the camping sites and cabins took only a few minutes, and soon I was in front of Shay's trailer. Across from the trailer was the main office. Next to the office was a small playground. A little boy chased a little girl around the jungle gym while their mother sat on a bench nearby, head bent over her cell phone. A young woman with straight brown hair hanging down to her waist

165

sat behind a counter where guests could rent sports equipment and buy ice cream.

I pulled into the small parking lot next to the main office. Maybe I could talk to a few employees and find out if they had noticed anything different about Shay in the days leading up to her death. Before I could approach the young woman at the counter, the two small children suddenly let out shrieks. "Ice cream! We want ice cream!" They ran toward the counter and jumped up and down. Their mother, engrossed in her cell phone, looked up briefly when she heard their shouts. With a deep sigh she stood up, rooted around in her large tote bag, and pulled out her wallet.

While the woman headed over to the ice-cream counter, I peered through the clear glass of the office's front door. A middle-aged man sat in a chair in front of a computer, scrolling through his Facebook feed. No one else was in the office. I pushed open the front door, setting off the bells overhead. The man looked up quickly, blocking the computer screen with his upper body. When he saw me, he relaxed and turned back to the screen.

"Can I help you?"

I leaned against the counter that separated us. "I've never been here before and wanted to check the place out," I said.

"OK." The man didn't even blink as he continued to scroll through photos and his friends' status updates. I could have screamed that I had explosives strapped to my chest and I was going to blow myself up and take him with me and I think I would have gotten the same bland response.

It was obvious this guy wasn't interested in working too hard since his boss had expired in my garden and was no longer in any position to give him a poor performance review. Since he didn't seem to care one way or the other, I decided to be a bit bolder in my quest for information. "I wanted to stop by and offer my condolences about Shay's passing," I said. I pulled a pen from the cup on the counter and twiddled it between my fingers.

The man finally turned to face me. He wore a lopsided, scratched nametag that read *Keith*. He looked to be in his late 30s. Male pattern baldness had already obliterated the hair on the top of his head and was quickly staking its claim on the remaining follicles. He wore a pair of bent wire glasses low on his nose, along with a T-shirt with a large campfire emblazoned on the front. Underneath were the words *Campfire Junction* in white block print. A pair of wrinkled black shorts and a beat-up pair of sandals finished off his look. Gnarly toes with large, thick nails poked out of the sandals. I quickly pulled my gaze back up to his face.

"I said, is that all?"

I must have been so focused on my assessment of Keith that I hadn't heard him address me.

"Look, lady, I'm almost forty years old and I'm stuck spending my summers at a stupid family campground. Either you need something or you don't."

The girl with the long brown hair entered the office through the back door. Out the window I watched the mother and the two children heading away from the playground. The little boy leaned over and took a big bite out of the ice cream cone the little girl held in her hand. She let out an ear-piercing howl and ran toward her mother. The little boy laughed and polished off the rest of his popsicle in one bite. The girl, whose nametag read *Samantha*, cast a dark glare at Keith.

"This campground is a joke," Keith said. "Shay made a lot of promises on the website and in the brochures that she couldn't keep. People came here expecting a huge virtual-reality game room and top-of-the-line jumbo TVs." Keith snorted. "What they got was some old video games, a broken flat screen TV, and a vending machine that ate all their money."

"It's not that bad," Samantha said, trying to do some damage control. She gestured at the pool, the clear blue water rippling in the light breeze. "The pool is nice."

Keith snorted again but didn't bother to respond.

I thought about what Keith had said. When Shay had showed up at the B&B, she had bragged about all of the amazing amenities guests could enjoy at the campground. Apparently, Shay had done more than stretch the truth; she had created a full-blown fantasy, painting a picture of a high-tech paradise that didn't even exist, let alone live up to the hype.

Keith continued with his bitter tirade. "Shay spent all her time talking up the amenities, then when the guests showed up and were disappointed and angry, who do you think had to deal with them?" Keith jabbed a finger at his chest. "Me, that's who. And when I told Shay about all the complaints, she just laughed and pointed to the fine print on the website that said 'No refunds.' As long as she had their money, Shay didn't give a hoot about the guests or their complaints. She left all the dirty work to her employees."

Yikes. Keith looked angry enough for three people. Could he have been angry enough to kill Shay?

As if reading my mind, Keith said, "I didn't kill her, but I won't lie and say I wasn't tempted to on more than one occasion." He logged out of Facebook and spun his chair around to face Samantha and I standing on the other side of the counter. "As soon as I get my last paycheck, I'm outta here. I got a new job offer and I start tomorrow." He looked around the office, his gaze flickering over the cracked countertops and the worn carpet. "I can't get away from this dump fast enough." Keith stood up from his chair, yanked open the office door, then slammed it behind him. He disappeared down the dark hallway.

"Well, I guess that's my cue to get going," I said to Samantha. "It was really nice to meet you." I opened the office door and walked toward the parking lot.

"Keith didn't mean what he said," Samantha said, her words coming out in a quick stream as she followed me. "Shay was working on getting all of those great things for the campground. She just needed more time."

I stopped and looked at Samantha. She was young, probably no more than seventeen or eighteen years old. This was most likely her first job and she wanted to remain loyal to her employer, especially since that employer had just been brutally murdered. Unlike Keith, most people weren't in a hurry to speak ill of the dead.

Samantha took my silence for doubt and rushed to reassure me. "It's true," she said. "Shay told me she was having money problems. She said her main source of funding had dried up and that she was trying to get the money from somewhere else." Tears pooled in Samantha's brown eyes. "She said she just needed a few more days and then she would have all the money she needed."

Ah, to be so young and so trusting. "What are you going to do for a job now?" I asked.

Samantha's shoulders sagged and she hung her head. "I'm going to spend the summer working at my dad's insurance agency," she said. She pushed a pebble around with the toe of her sneaker. "I really wanted to work here by the pool all summer, but

168

it looks like I'm going to be stuck in an office filing paperwork and answering the phone before I start college in the fall."

I patted Samantha on the shoulder. "It'll all work out," I said. "You'll see."

"Yeah, I guess." Loud shrieks and whoops filled the air. Samantha and I both turned toward the pool. Three young men ran toward the pool, leaped into the air, and jumped into the cool blue water. A few seconds later all three bobbed to the surface, pushing their wet hair out of their eyes. One young man splashed his friend, and soon all three were engaged in an all-out water war.

"I have to get back to work," Samantha said. "Thanks for stopping by."

I opened my car door and slid behind the wheel, deep in thought. Shay had flat-out lied about all of the amenities she offered at her campground. If she had lied about that, what else had she lied about? What had Shay meant when she told Samantha her "main source of funding had dried up"?

I glanced at the trailer across from the main office. Maybe Carter could provide some answers. I got out of the car and walked toward the trailer. I crossed my fingers, hoping Bobby wasn't there. I remembered the casserole I had dropped off for Carter the last time and felt bad that I didn't have anything with me today. However, retrieving the casserole dish made a handy excuse for this impromptu visit to Carter.

I knocked on the front door of the trailer, but there was no answer. I knocked on the door again, but after another minute or two there was still no reply. I was about to head back to my car when I decided to see if the door was unlocked. I looked across the way at the main office, but didn't see Keith or Samantha. The boys were taking turns dunking each other's heads in the water and weren't paying any attention to me. The knob turned easily in my hand. I looked up, but didn't see any cameras on the trailer. In one quick move I was inside.

The trailer wasn't any cleaner than the last time I had seen it. There were still stacks of paper plates and empty TV dinner trays on the floor, along with mounds of clothing and other odds and ends.

"Carter?" I called. "Are you here?"

Silence. I felt guilty for being in someone else's home without permission, but I also realized this was a golden opportunity to do some snooping to learn more about Shay and who might have wanted her dead. I quickly checked out the kitchen, living room, and small bathroom. I peeked into Carter's room, but didn't feel like picking through a teenaged boy's possessions.

On the opposite side of the trailer from Carter's bedroom was Shay's bedroom. I poked my head into the room, feeling goosebumps rise on my arms. I was sneaking into a dead woman's bedroom. I shook off the heebie-jeebies and gazed around the room.

Shay's bed was neatly made. I pulled open drawers in the bureau and nightstand, but only saw what I expected to see: clothing, a phone charger, and some loose change. I pushed open the closet door. The closet was stuffed with clothing hanging on the rack and shoes lined up on the floor. In the very back of Shay's closet were several shoeboxes. I lifted the lid on one of the boxes. It was filled with letters. I glanced at one of the letters and saw it was from Dwight. It was addressed to Shay at a Denver address. The postmark on the envelope was from five or six years ago.

The letters were all neatly filed according to date. I skipped ahead several years to read some of the most recent letters, which were sent just a few weeks before Shay's murder. In those notes, Dwight talked in glowing terms about how much he wanted to see his son again and activities the two could do together once he got out of prison. Dwight talked about taking Carter fishing. He asked if Carter was shaving yet. Said his biggest regret about going to prison was that it took him away from his son. Said he had changed and that he wanted to make things right with Carter.

I felt tears form in my eyes. It was obvious Dwight loved his son and being unable to see Carter or hear news about him was tearing him apart. Although I felt guilty for reading someone else's personal letters, I couldn't stop. I continued reading and found multiple notes Dwight wrote begging Shay to let his son visit him. Or, if he couldn't see him, to at least get a letter from him or even a letter from Shay telling him how his son was doing. One letter pleaded for even just a school photo. While I could understand how Shay could hate her husband for what he had done, keeping a father from even the tiniest detail about his son's life was just wrong.

After reading the letters, I was completely convinced that Dwight had nothing to do with Shay's murder. He was intent on getting his life back on track. He wanted to be with his son. He would not have jeopardized all of that by murdering Shay.

I was so engrossed in the letters that I didn't realize an hour had slipped by. I had to get out of the trailer before Carter returned home. I deliberated about what to do with the letters, but the sound of the trailer's front door opening made the decision for me. I heard someone rattling around in the kitchen, then Carter appeared in the bedroom doorway. "What are you doing here?" he demanded.

I felt foolish crouching on the bedroom floor, so I quickly stood up. I wanted to tell Carter about the letters I had just discovered, but I wasn't quite sure how to bring up the topic of his father. I pointed to the stack of shoeboxes on the floor. Carter looked at it dubiously. I opened the lid on the top box and handed it to him.

"What is this?" Carter asked, wrinkling up his nose.

"These are letters," I said. Carter looked at me and frowned. "They are what people used to send before there were texts and social media."

Carter rolled his eyes. "I know what a letter is. I'm not stupid." He didn't make a move to accept the box. "Why do I care about some smelly old letters?"

"I found them in your mom's closet. They're addressed to you."

This caught Carter's attention. He plucked one of the letters from the shoebox and read the name on the return address. "This is from my dad!" he shouted. He yanked the shoebox out of my hands so fast several of the letters spilled onto the floor. He bent and gathered them up, then flopped onto the bed, hugging the box to his chest. I tiptoed out of the trailer, leaving Carter to read the letters from his dad in private.

Chapter 19

My nerves were still jangled after my fight with Finn, but I felt a little better after reading Dwight's letters and giving them to his son. I glanced at the clock on the car radio. I had enough time to visit Kurtis and apologize for Finn's poor behavior before attending midweek services at the church.

Kurtis had mentioned he lived across the street from his business, so I pointed the car toward Kurtis' Garage. I parked the car in the driveway and surveyed the modest red-brick ranch house. A tire swing hung from a large maple tree in the front yard. Two bikes were propped against the closed garage doors, helmets and kneepads dangling from the handlebars. Jason and Mason didn't seem like they had the ability to stay still long enough to put on their clothes, let alone protective gear.

The curtains in the front window moved as if blown about by a mighty wind. Every few seconds I saw a little boy's head bob past the window – red for Jason and light brown for Mason. I heard muted shrieks of glee as I stepped out of the car and headed up the walkway.

I pressed my finger against the doorbell and heard chimes echo throughout the house. Almost immediately cries of "Doorbell! Doorbell! Someone's here!" took the place of the chiming bell. The front door swung open. Kurtis stood in the small front entry. Jason, a handheld video game in one hand, grinned up at me from under Kurtis' right arm. Mason was draped over Kurtis's back, his arms clasped around his dad's neck. I smiled at all three.

"Rachel, hi." Kurtis unhooked Mason's arms from around his neck and lowered the little boy to the floor. "What brings you to our neck of the woods?"

"Did you bring us presents?" Mason asked. When he smiled, I could see the tooth fairy had recently paid a visit to the Tellke home.

"Mason!" Kurtis sounded embarrassed, and I rushed to tell him it was OK, but he waved off my words. "Just because a pretty lady shows up at the house doesn't mean she brought you a present." He winked at me and I felt heat creeping across my cheeks. He pulled Jason to him with his right arm and Mason toward him with his left. He tickled each boy under the chin, eliciting more shrieks and peals of laughter. "How about you boys go play in your room until dinnertime?"

"Aww, Dad!" Jason protested. "Do we gotta? We're hungry now! We haven't had our afternoon snacks yet."

Kurtis made an exaggerated thinking expression, pursing his lips and narrowing his eyes while he stroked his chin with one hand. "How about this? You can each have *one* chocolate chip cookie that you can eat in your room."

The boys hollered and high-fived as they headed for the kitchen. I heard the sound of a lid being lifted from the cookie jar. Jason and Mason, armed with their loot, streaked past us down a short hallway to the other end of the house. I couldn't be sure, but I thought maybe the little boys weren't too good at arithmetic.

"I think your two little fiends took a couple extra treats," I said, laughing.

"Doesn't surprise me," Kurtis said. "They are opportunists to the core, my boys. I almost never let them eat in their rooms." He gestured at a coatrack next to the couch and I hung my purse on it. "So, what does bring you here, Rachel?" Kurtis looked puzzled. "Is there a problem with the new door lock?"

I shook my head. "No. I'm here for another reason. I want to talk to you about what happened when Finn showed up at the farmhouse."

Kurtis's gaze drifted to a spot on the wall just over my right shoulder. "You don't owe me any explanation, Rachel. He's your boyfriend. I respect that."

"He is my fiancé."

173

Kurtis's shoulders slumped and his gaze remained fixed on the wall.

I mentally kicked myself. Why had I just said that? "He *was* my fiancé," I amended. "We were supposed to get married, but then Grams died and I inherited the farm and decided to turn it into a B&B. Finn wasn't too happy when I left Chicago."

Kurtis shifted his gaze to meet mine. His light-blue eyes were crystal clear. "Would you like to have a seat? I have a feeling we should be having this discussion sitting down."

I nodded and took a seat on the soft gray sofa.

"Can I get you something to drink?" Kurtis asked. "We have soda and bottled water and lots of juice boxes. Or I can make coffee."

The offer of a juice box made me laugh, but Kurtis looked confused. I guess he hadn't meant that as a joke. "Just a bottle of water would be great," I said.

Kurtis turned toward the kitchen. "The boys might have left a cookie or two if you would like one. I made them myself."

"You made chocolate chip cookies?" I asked. "From scratch?" I winced at the note of surprise in my voice. Kurtis was a grown man, capable of baking cookies. I was just so used to being with Finn, a man who didn't even know how to turn on the oven, let alone whip up cookie batter.

Kurtis didn't sound offended when he replied. "Yep. I didn't even use that log of premade cookie dough they sell at the grocery store, either." He returned with the chocolate chip cookies. He handed me a napkin with two cookies on it, along with a bottle of water dripping condensation. A drop of water fell onto the knee of my jeans, creating a dark blue spot. "Shoot, sorry. Let me take care of that." He took the water bottle from my hand, lifted the hem of his T-shirt, and wiped the moisture off the bottle before opening it and handing it back to me. "Would you like a glass?"

I shook my head. "This is fine." I took a bite of cookie, stalling for time. Suddenly I had no idea what to tell the man sitting next to me on the couch. My history with Finn was so convoluted and confusing, I had no idea where to begin.

"Do you mind if I turn on some music?" Kurtis asked, shooting up from the couch like a wild jack-in-the-box. He was obviously uncomfortable, too. He opened a glass-fronted cabinet and started fiddling with an impressive stereo system. "Billy Joel is my favorite," he said, twirling a knob and pushing a few buttons. "Is that OK with you?"

"Billy Joel is perfect," I said, searching for a place to set the water bottle. There were no coasters on the coffee table in front of the couch, but there was a car magazine with numerous water rings on it. I assumed that was what passed for a coaster in a house with three males living in it. I put the water bottle down on the magazine as Billy Joel began to sing about his uptown girl.

Kurtis rejoined me on the couch. "So, what did you want to talk about?" He avoided looking directly at me. Instead, he picked up the cookie he had placed on the arm of the couch and stared down at it in his hand.

I didn't respond right away. I listened to the sounds of Jason and Mason playing in their room. Based on the snippets of their conversation I could hear, it sounded like they were inventing rules for a baseball-football hybrid that also involved some aspects of magic and wizardry.

So many thoughts flew through my mind as I searched for what to tell Kurtis. He undoubtedly thought Finn and I were a happy couple and he was an unwanted third party. Nothing could have been further from the truth. Finn had proved what a selfish, condescending jerk he was when he showed up at the B&B and scolded me like a naughty child, demanding I return to Chicago with him as if I were his property. But Kurtis didn't know any of that. Rather than get into the details, I decided to be direct.

"Finn and I broke up," I said. Kurtis' shoulders relaxed and he slowly turned his face to meet my gaze. "We were talking about getting back together, but that was before I found out what a controlling, manipulative jerk he is." I took a deep breath. I hadn't planned on telling Kurtis the truly horrible parts, but I felt so comfortable sitting next to him that they just slipped out. "He didn't want me to come back to Chicago with him because he loved me. He wanted me to come back because of the money he could have made with a new cooking show he was pitching behind my back, as well as future endorsements and product lines." I felt tears stinging my eyelids, but I promised myself I wouldn't cry over Finn, that louse. "Turns out he only ever saw me as a walking dollar sign."

I grabbed the bottle of water off the coffee table and took a huge gulp, trying to distract myself from the emotions that threatened to overwhelm me. A new song drifted out of the speakers, and this time Billy Joel was singing his ode to Allentown. I twisted the cap back on the empty bottle and replaced it on the table.

"Oh, Rachel," Kurtis said. The tenderness in his voice almost undid me. When he placed a hand over mine a wave of warmth rushed through my whole body. "I'm sorry."

I drew in a ragged breath. "Yeah, me too." I cast around for something else to say. I had just spilled my guts to this poor innocent guy. He must think I was a complete basket case. There he was, enjoying a relaxing afternoon with his kids, and I had barged in as if I were a neurotic guest on a TV talk show, ready to tell my secrets to the world. I jumped to my feet, but Kurtis, whose hand had never strayed from mine, gently pulled me back onto the sofa.

"It's OK," he said. "We've all been through bad breakups."

I leaned back against the couch. "I just wanted you to know the truth. Finn treated you so badly and I was so ashamed."

"You have nothing to be ashamed about," Kurtis said. "You aren't responsible for Finn's behavior."

I nodded. "I know that. Still, you had been so sweet and helpful and there he was treating you like an anonymous hired hand. It made me sick to think I had ever loved him, let alone wanted to spend the rest of my life with a man like that."

"My ex-wife was like that," Kurtis said, leaning back on the sofa and finishing off his cookie. "Her real name is Victoriana, but behind her back I always called her Queen Victoria. Thought the world and everyone else in it existed purely to serve her."

"The boys told me you were a widower." Kurtis stared at me, his brows turned down in a frown. I wanted to sink into the sofa cushions and disappear. "It's none of my business, really," I said. I stood up again, but Kurtis laid a hand on my elbow and gently pulled me back down.

"My wife and I divorced about a year ago," he said.

"Then why do the boys think you're a widower?" I asked.

Kurtis shook his head, then his expression cleared. His cheeks tinged pink as he explained. "The wife of one our elderly neighbors passed away recently and the boys heard someone refer to him as a widower. They wanted to know what the word meant. I didn't have the heart to tell the boys the man's wife had died, so

I told them being a widower meant that the man wasn't married anymore." Kurtis shook his head. "I had no idea the boys would take that to mean that any man no longer married was a widower, let alone use that word to describe me."

Before I could respond, Jason and Mason burst into the room, spinning in circles. Shrieking and giggling, they fell onto the living room carpet.

"Looks like it's time to get these two their dinner," Kurtis said, glancing at the time on his cell phone. He picked Jason up with his right arm and Mason with his left and dangled them upside down in the air. Both boys howled with laughter. Kurtis looked over at me. "Would you like to join us for dinner, Rachel?"

I shook my head. "No, thanks. I want to attend midweek services." Kurtis opened the front door and I smiled up at him. "Thank you."

Kurtis dipped his chin toward me. "Anytime."

I walked down the concrete steps and Kurtis shut the front door behind me. "Boys!" I heard him shout. "Let's make dinner!"

Getting into my car, I could still feel the touch of Kurtis' warm hand on mine.

****

I had just enough time to go back to the farmhouse to change my clothes before heading to the church for midweek services. I changed into a long flower-patterned skirt, a white blouse, and a pair of comfy flats. To finish, I twisted my hair up into a loose bun. The small church, while cozy and quaint, did not have air conditioning. Keeping my hair off my neck would help to cool me down. Otherwise, I would end up sweating bullets during Pastor Morris's sermon, which wasn't a good look.

The small white church was surrounded by towering maple trees, their branches heavy with thick leaves. I parked along the street and strolled toward the open front doors. Pastor Morris stood on the top step to welcome guests. He shook my hand and smiled. Piano music swirled through the front doors and surrounded us like a musical cloak.

"Rachel, it's wonderful to see you," he said. "How are things at the B&B?"

The smile on my face faltered, and though I silently commanded it to stay in place, it didn't listen. Pastor Morris noticed my change of expression and his eyes suddenly widened.

He winced. "I am so sorry. I forgot you were the one who found Shay." He patted my hand. "She's with the Lord now, Rachel."

I nodded and entered the church. I had no idea where Shay was at this moment, but I knew that I was on the hook to track down her killer. The thought cast a gray cloud over my mood, so I decided to tuck it away in another part of my brain. I enjoyed attending services in the same church Grams had taken me to when I was young. I had fond memories of attending Sunday school in the basement with the other children, watching puppet shows and playing with felt cutouts of Bible characters. Thoughts of those innocent times chased away the murderous shadows as I settled in to enjoy the service.

Suddenly a hush fell over the church. The women stopped chatting with each other and the men trailed off in the middle of their stories. Even the small children sitting with their parents and grandparents noticed the change in the air and went silent, no longer jumping up and down and chattering at each other. I swiveled in my seat and saw Dwight standing in the doorway. His huge frame dwarfed Pastor Morris, who had noticed his entire congregation staring at him. He had been shaking Dwight's hand. He slowly released his grip from Dwight's and gazed at his congregation, perplexed by their silence. I realized Pastor Morris must not be aware that Shay's ex-husband had just recently gotten out of prison and a potential pick for the title of her murderer.

Dwight fidgeted under everyone's accusing stares. He wore what looked like a brand-new blue plaid button-down shirt, straight out of the package and still with the sharp creases showing how the shirt had been folded. He also wore a pair of stiff-looking khaki pants. On his feet were the same heavy, worn work boots he had been wearing when we met. Apparently, his post-prison budget hadn't stretched far enough for the purchase of new footwear.

Pastor Morris strode up the aisle toward the pulpit, the confused look still on his face. He smiled and nodded to everyone as he passed. Dwight shuffled to a spot in the very back pew near the door. My guess was that he wanted a clear shot if the normally placid congregation turned into a bloodthirsty mob and he suddenly had to bolt.

I glanced around at my fellow parishioners. Many of the women were clutching their purses as if they worried Dwight might run up to them at any moment to snatch their worldly goods right from their hands. I noticed several men clenching their fists, their jaws tight as if ready to fight should Dwight come any closer. It was obvious no one trusted Dwight any farther than they could throw him, and since Dwight was a mighty big man, that wasn't very far at all. Most seemed to carry a spark of fear in their eyes.

To his credit, Dwight seemed to be taking the scorn in stride, but it was obviously not fun nor easy for him. He scrunched down as far as he could in the back pew, where he sat all alone. It must have taken a great deal of time and effort for him to work up the courage to even come to the church, let alone step foot inside. After talking with Dwight, I knew what a struggle it had been for him since being released from prison. Although I could understand why people might be afraid, I didn't agree with the way he was being treated. I myself had made the assumption that he was a hardened criminal based on his appearance and his record, and I wasn't proud of that. I had also seen the kind of person Dwight was now and I firmly believed he should be welcomed to the church like anyone else, not treated as if he were a homicidal maniac wielding a bloody chainsaw.

At a glance from Pastor Morris, the pianist stopped staring at Dwight and turned to her keyboard. Everyone pulled hymnals from their spots on the backs of pews and turned to the page for the first hymn. As the strains of the music started and voices began to swell, filling the church, I made a decision. Clutching a hymnal in one hand, I slipped my purse over my shoulder and made my way out of the pew. People sitting in my pew had to turn their legs sideways or stand up to let me through. As I passed, I heard several whispered comments, including, "I wouldn't if I were you" and "It's your funeral."

I ignored them, walked down the aisle, and made my way to where Dwight sat. He looked up at me and I could see in his eyes that he was struggling mightily to contain his emotions. His expression was a mix of anger and hurt, and I thought anger might be winning.

"Do you mind if I sit with you?" I asked, raising my voice loud enough to be heard over the singing. Dwight nodded. Cracking open the hymnal, I found the correct page and pointed at the spot in the song. Normally I disliked singing in public, but I decided I would make my voice heard in more ways than one today. Dwight seemed to have no problem singing in front of strangers. He opened his mouth and unleashed the most pleasant baritone I had ever heard. I swung my head in his direction, but he didn't notice my shocked expression. He faced forward, singing for all he was worth.

Chapter 20

After breakfast the next morning, Leo and Aries took off on a long bike ride down the two-lane country roads. Dad and Kelsey went for a walk in the woods. Kathryn and Simon stayed in their room. Ned was still sleeping after another long night communing with owls.

"Do you want me to pull weeds in the garden?" Bree asked.

"That would be great," I replied. I pulled a cookbook from the shelf. "I have a lot of baking ahead of me today."

Before getting started on a fresh batch of bread, I peeked my head into the living room. Mom sat on the couch, one of Grams' old photo albums open on her lap. Mom smiled as she flipped through the album.

With all my heart I hoped that Mom's opinion toward the farm was softening, now that she no longer carried the burden of the secret she had kept for decades. I didn't want to intrude on Mom's reminiscences, so I headed back to the kitchen.

Someone knocked on the door and I opened it. Carter stood on the front porch, his bike propped up at the bottom of the stairs. He wore a striped polo shirt and a pair of slightly wrinkled khakis, along with a pair of new sneakers.

"Hey, Carter," I said. "What's up?"

"I was wondering if you could give me a ride to the Corner Basket," Carter said. He looked up at me, squinting in the morning sunlight. "I want to fill out a job application. It's too far for me to ride on my bike."

I looked back over my shoulder at the cookbook spread out on the counter and hesitated. I had a lot of baking that needed to get done.

Carter noticed my hesitation. "You don't have to do it," he said, stomping down the porch steps and grabbing his bike. His voice quivered when he spoke.

"Carter, wait," I said. Carter stopped, his back to me. He was so young and had already been through so much. I couldn't disappoint him. "I'll take you over there. Just let me grab my things."

I gathered my purse and car keys. I ran over to the garden to explain to Bree what was happening and to ask her to take over baking duties. I hadn't worked with her on baking yet, but she thought she could handle it.

Carter and I got into my car. Immediately he whipped out his cell phone and started scrolling through his social media. At a stop sign, I glanced over at Carter's phone.

"Are those photos of you and your mom?" I asked.

Carter nodded. "Yeah, back when we lived in Colorado," he said. He flicked through the photos on the phone screen. In the photos Carter appeared to be about eight years old. I did some quick math and figured the photos were taken about five or six years ago. Shay appeared more carefree in the photos. She had an arm around Carter's shoulders. Next to her stood an attractive young man with blonde hair and green eyes. He looked familiar, but I couldn't place where I might know him from. I had been to Colorado a few times. Once on a skiing trip with Finn and another time for a conference for restauranteurs. I had met lots of people in Colorado, but I didn't have any close friends there. I chalked it up to having encountered so many people in the restaurant business. After a while I was bound to see people who looked familiar, even if I had never met them before.

We arrived at The Corner Basket and I parked in the lot. Before I could even unhook my seatbelt Carter shot out of the car and was halfway to the store. Either the kid was part bunny or he really wanted to get away from me. I lifted my arm and subtly sniffed. I was wearing deodorant, so I didn't smell. Then I realized Carter was a teenaged boy. On the teenage list of horrors, being thrown into an erupting volcano was preferable to being seen in a car with an "old" lady. I hurried out of the car, grabbing my purse from the backseat. I broke into a sprint and managed to catch up with Carter just as he was stepping through the automatic doors.

"You're quick, I'll give you that," I said, panting slightly. Carter just shrugged. "We need to go over to the customer service desk to get you an application," I said, pointing the way.

Carter rolled his eyes. "I *know* that." He sauntered toward the man standing behind the customer service desk as if he had all the time in the world. Now it was my turn to roll my eyes. He had no problem dashing away from me in the parking lot, but in front of other people he wanted to come off as Mr. Cool.

Carter politely asked for an application and I silently cheered. Shay had no doubt had many faults, but she had taught her son how to behave properly in public. Carter took the application, said thank you, and grabbed a pen from a cup on the counter.

At that moment Dwight strode toward us. He grinned when he saw me. I put a finger to my lips and pointed at Carter. Dwight looked at Carter, then back at me. I nodded and Dwight swung his head back around to stare at his son. He clutched his apron with both hands and looked ready to bolt to the back of the store. I loudly cleared my throat and Dwight looked back at me. I made a shooing motion toward Carter with my hands. Carter was engrossed in filling out the form, so he hadn't yet noticed Dwight.

Dwight placed his hands behind his back and whistled tunelessly as he slowly inched toward the customer service desk. I wasn't quite sure what Dwight was trying to do. He acted like he wanted to sneak up on Carter and catch him unawares so he could toss him into a cage like a feral cat.

Carter was partway through filling out the job application when Dwight reached his side. I quickly moved toward the two, eager to make an introduction.

Dwight bounced in place, his grin nearly splitting his whiskered face in two. Before I could even open my mouth, Dwight blurted out the truth. "Hi, Carter," he said. "I'm Dwight, your dad."

Carter was much shorter than his father. He lifted his gaze and looked up, up, up, at Dwight. He stared, disbelief written all over his face. "Prove it," he said.

Dwight was more than happy to oblige his son. Straightening his spine and clasping his hands in front of him as if he were about to recite a poem in front of an audience, Dwight said, "Your middle name is Eugene and your birthday is June eleventh."

Dwight unclasped his hands, opening his arms wide so his son could come rushing into his waiting embrace.

Carter's skeptical expression didn't change. He remained rooted to his spot in front of the customer service counter, the pen still gripped between his fingers. "Anyone could find basic information like that online," Carter scoffed. He glanced down at the partially completed application, where he had filled in his middle name and his date of birth. "You must have read it on my application," he said, anger creeping into his voice. "You're going to have to do better than that."

Dwight let his arms fall back at his sides and he thought for a moment. Then he broke into a huge smile. "You have a big, round birthmark on the right side of your fanny!" Dwight looked pleased with himself for remembering this tidbit. "I saw it when I was changing your diaper when you were a baby."

My eyebrows shot all the way up to my hairline. For a moment I feared they might shoot clear off my forehead and land in someone's shopping cart. My first thought was that I couldn't believe Dwight would ever use the word "fanny," but there it was. My second thought was about how Carter would react. I whipped my head to the left to watch his reaction. I crossed my fingers, hoping he wouldn't get too upset.

Carter's face flamed crimson. He looked around at all the people watching him. The two nearest cashiers had stopped ringing up groceries. One cashier, a middle-aged woman, was as still as a statue, a package of cream cheese dangling from her fingers over the scanner. No one said anything until a young man bagging groceries, who appeared to be about the same age as Carter, snickered and said, "Dude, you've got a big birthmark on your itty-witty fanny?"

Carter glared at Dwight. "I don't know who you are," he shouted, "but stay away from me, you freak!"

Dwight was crestfallen. Although he was a big guy, after Carter yelled at him and ran out of the grocery store, he seemed to deflate about three sizes. I put my hand on his arm, but he shrugged it off. I could tell he was doing everything he could to keep his temper from taking over.

"I'm sorry," I said. "I was only trying to help."

Dwight's glare made me take a step back. "Do me a favor," he said through gritted teeth. "Don't ever help me again."

He turned and disappeared through the swinging doors behind the customer service counter and disappeared into the back of the store, the doors flapping in his wake.

I turned around to find everyone still staring at me. "Show's over, folks," I said.

I hustled back to the car and found Carter slouched in the front seat, playing a game on his phone. I slid behind the wheel and turned the key in the ignition. Neither of us spoke all the way back to the farmhouse. Mentally I kicked myself for botching the reunion attempt between Dwight and Carter. Before the car came to a complete stop, Carter threw open the door and leapt out. He got on his bike and pedaled furiously away.

"What was that all about?" Bree asked. She stood on the front porch, leaning against the railing.

I looked up at Bree and gasped. Her hair was white. She looked like she had aged several decades since I left. "What happened to your hair?" I asked.

Bree lifted a hand to touch her hair, then pulled it away. Flour coated her fingertips. "I guess I got a little flour in my hair while I was baking," she said ruefully.

I trotted up the steps and walked through the red front door. Flour covered every flat surface of the kitchen. A blackened lump in a baking pan sat on the counter. Smoke hung in the air. I turned back to Bree, speechless.

"Things got a little out of hand," Bree said, wringing her hands in front of her. "I'm sorry."

I poked at the charred lump with one finger. "Is this all the baking you did?" I asked.

"Yes."

One look at Bree's distraught face made me swallow any comments I might have wanted to make. "Do we have any more flour?" I asked, looking at the empty container on the counter. Bree shook her head.

I picked up my car keys and purse. "I'll go back to the store to get more," I said. "Can you clean up in here while I'm gone?"

"Yes." Bree's voice was small and sad.

I put an arm around her shoulders and squeezed. "Accidents happen," I said. "Don't worry about it."

****

I made the trip back to the Corner Basket and grabbed several bags of flour. I passed the meat counter, but didn't see Dwight. Thank goodness. On the way home I passed Erica's house. Her two German Shepherds were in the road. I slowed down and stopped. I didn't want the dogs to get hurt.

I rolled down the car window and called to the dogs. They whined and turned in circles. *This is definitely strange,* I thought. *What should I do?* I looked up at the large log cabin home. I didn't see Erica or Cody. I looked back at the dogs. They were clearly agitated and I couldn't leave them in the road.

I decided to take a chance and stepped out of the car. The dogs immediately ran toward the car and I quickly shut the door again. Diesel sniffed the closed door and let out a pitiful howl. The hair on my arms stood straight up. Something was wrong, very wrong. I pulled into the winding driveway and the dogs followed.

I stepped out of the car and walked to the front door, the dogs at my heels. I rang the doorbell, but no one answered. I pounded on the wooden door a few times with my fists, but still no response. I peered into the window next to the front door, cupping my hands around my face to block out extra light. The interior of the house looked undisturbed. A loaf of bread sat out on the kitchen counter next to a container of mustard and a package of deli ham. An open laptop sat on the coffee table in the living room. A glass of wine on the end table next to a comfy recliner completed the cozy domestic scene.

It didn't take Sherlock Holmes to figure out what Erica had been up to. She had been in the process of making a sandwich, sipping wine, and working on her laptop when she had been interrupted. But interrupted by whom? And where was Erica now? Had something happened to her husband and she rushed out of the house to help him? Surely Erica wouldn't have dashed away and left her dogs alone outside to fend for themselves. A sense of unease slithered through my gut. None of this looked right.

"Erica!" I shouted, pounding on the door. I grabbed the doorknob and twisted, but the door was locked.

The dogs whined and spun in circles next to me. Their odd behavior was unnerving. Diesel took off back around the side of the house, then stopped to stare at me. He gave me such a plaintive look that I finally realized he wanted me to follow him. I felt like I was in an old *Lassie* rerun, but I followed the dog anyway. Heidi raced past me to join Diesel, and the two dogs stood together at the edge of the tall bluff overlooking the lake.

At first, I didn't see anything out of the ordinary. Looking around, I saw what I expected to see: rocks, a dirt patch worn in the grass, some sticks, and a chewed-up yellow tennis ball. I looked back at the dogs. "What do you want?" I asked. Diesel cocked his head at me. Heidi let out a howl that turned my blood to ice in my veins. "Do you want to play fetch?" I asked, looking down at the ratty tennis ball. I didn't really want to pick it up with my bare hands, but at this point I would do anything to distract the dogs and make Heidi stop howling. Maybe I could throw the ball just once. If I threw it really far, I could sprint back to the car before the dogs could return.

I bent over to pick up the tennis ball. It had been at least a decade since I had played softball, but I had been a pretty good pitcher on my high school team. My spirits started to perk up a bit as I gripped the ball in my hand. Maybe a little fetch would be fun. I lifted my arm to toss the ball, and when I did, I caught sight of something bright pink fluttering at the bottom of the bluff. I turned and stared down at the water lapping the shore. A bundle of pink fabric was lodged among the rocks. I looked closer and my breath stuck in my throat. It wasn't a bundle of rocks – it was a body.

Without thinking, I slipped and slid down the steep incline, the dogs hot on my heels. I scratched my arm on a protruding branch on the way down, but ignored the sting and the rising red scrape on my skin. I made my way over to the pink bundle and sucked in a breath. It was Erica. She wore a ruffly pink sleeveless top and a pair of black shorts. Her feet were bare. She was lying on her side, one arm bent under her at an unnatural angle. Her brown hair swirled in the water. There was a deep gash on her forehead. Dried blood streaked down her face and had pooled in the sand and on the rocks. I felt nausea rising in my throat but tamped it down. I had to do something to help her.

"Erica?" My voice came out in a whispered croak. I cleared my throat and tried again, louder this time. "Erica? Can you hear me?" Erica didn't reply. I crouched next to her, lake water lapping over my sandals. I shivered as the cold water closed over my toes. I gently touched Erica's arm. Her skin felt cool and clammy. I felt for a pulse on her wrist, but didn't feel anything. Taking a deep breath, I placed two fingers on Erica's neck. Still no pulse.

I stood up and backed away. Not another dead body!

Diesel and Heidi stood next to Erica's body, whining softly. Diesel nuzzled his head under my right hand, while Heidi licked my left hand. I put a hand on each dog's head. "It's going to be OK, guys," I said, doing my best to comfort them, although I didn't believe a word of it. Their mistress lay dead at my feet, after all. I continued to stroke the dogs' heads, looking all around me. Numerous houses surrounded the lake. Surely someone must have seen something. I had to call the police.

I looked back up at the steep incline. It had been a lot easier to come down than it would be to climb back up. I spied a small dirt path to the left and followed it, coming out on the road. I realized the post office was only a few minutes away. I could go there and have Miss Millie call the police. Once I had that idea in my mind, I felt a jolt of relief. Miss Millie, with her no-nonsense attitude, would know what to do. She would help me. With that thought firmly in mind, I jumped into action, lurching into the road. The sound of screeching brakes made me take a step back. A horn blasted in my ear.

"Watch where you're going!" yelled a man in a rusted red truck. He shook his fist at me as he accelerated in a cloud of dark exhaust fumes. My heart beat wildly in my chest. I had come within seconds of being roadkill. I placed a hand over my heart and took several deep breaths. When my heartbeat had slowed down to normal, I looked both ways before crossing the street and walking to the post office.

The police arrived within minutes after Miss Millie dialed 911. An officer asked me to come to the police department to answer some questions. He gave me a ride over to Erica's house so I could retrieve my car. I kept my head down, doing my best to avoid all of the emergency vehicles clogging Erica's driveway.

I answered all of the officer's questions to the best of my ability. After I had been asked all of the questions half a dozen different ways, I was finally free to go. All I wanted was to get back to the farmhouse and work away my tension with a lump of soft, fragrant dough.

I was shocked to see Dwight being led down the hallway by a police officer. His hands and legs were bound. His long hair was matted and his clothes were streaked with dirt.

"What is going on?" I asked.

Dwight didn't respond.

"Why have you arrested Dwight?" I asked, turning to the officer at his side.

"We found him at Hillsville Lake, not far from where the body was found."

My jaw dropped open. The police couldn't possibly think Dwight had killed Erica.

"Can I talk to him?" I asked, gesturing at Dwight. He stood next to the officer, his head bowed, staring at the ugly industrial carpeting.

"I'm afraid not, ma'am," the officer said.

I had reached my limit. Tears began to flow down my cheeks. I dashed down the hallway and burst through the front door onto the sidewalk. I wiped at my eyes with the palms of my hands. I couldn't believe I had cried in front of the cop and Dwight.

I walked down the street to where I had parked my car. Along the way I passed Cody's store, Lane Sports. The inside of the store was dark, and the closed sign hung on the window. I stopped when I thought I saw someone moving inside the store. Was Cody in there? If he was, I could offer him my condolences.

I stood on tiptoe in front of the large front window and cupped my hands around my eyes so I could see inside the store. At first I didn't see anyone, and I thought maybe my eyes had been playing tricks on me. Then I saw Cody emerge from the back of the store. I raised a hand to knock on the glass. Cody looked up, startled, as he walked toward me.

Cody opened the front door and stuck his head outside. "We're closed," he said. His eyes were red rimmed and his brown hair was rumpled. He stared at me for a moment, then finally recognized me. "Hey. Rachel, right?"

I nodded.

"It's great to see you again, but the store is closed," Cody said. "There's been an . . . accident." His voice broke on the last word. I gulped, the vision of Erica's dead body floating into my mind.

"I know," I said. "I'm the one who found Erica's body."

Without a word, Cody stepped back and opened the door all the way and motioned me inside the store.

"I'm so sorry about Erica," I said, looking up into Cody's green eyes. He was a big guy, easily six-three or six-four.

"Thanks," Cody said. "I wish I could have been there. If I had been there, I could have saved her." He grabbed his head and ran his fingers through his hair, causing it to stand straight up. "God, Shay, why?"

Shay?

"Don't you mean Erica?" I asked.

Cody lowered his hands and stared at me. "What?"

"You said Shay, but your wife's name was Erica." My voice slowed as realization dawned. I recalled the flower arrangement bearing Cody's name at Shay's funeral. No man would buy a flower arrangement for his wife's best friend's funeral when his wife would do it for him. Cody went out of his way to buy Shay flowers. Why? Because he was her lover? Because he felt guilty for killing her? I thought back to my discussion with Erica and Cody at their house. Erica had explained all the ways Shay had tried to seduce Cody. But what if Cody had welcomed those advances, instead of rejecting them?

At Shay's funeral Erica had talked about how she believed Shay would have had no problem with faking her own death to get attention. A woman who would be willing to fake her own death would have been completely capable of seducing her best friend's husband. Stealing him away from Erica and forcing a divorce would be an even bigger accomplishment, at least it would be from Shay's demented viewpoint.

The thought hit me like a dropped plate shattering when it hit the floor—sharp, messy, impossible to ignore. "You were having an affair with Shay and lying about it to Erica," I whispered.

Cody looked stunned for about two seconds, then laughed. "You can't be serious," he said with an uneasy laugh. He walked around the counter to stand behind the register. I stood across from him, the glass counter packed with colorful fishing lures between us.

"Shay was getting tired of being the other woman," I said, jabbing my finger against the counter for emphasis. "She and Erica were major frenemies, always trying to one-up the other. The two thrived on the competition and there were no rules. The ultimate one-up would be to steal Erica's husband away from her. Shay wanted you to divorce Erica and marry her, but you didn't want to lose out in the divorce. You knew how vicious Erica was and that she would do everything in her power to ruin your life if she found out you were having an affair with her best friend."

"I just lost my wife," Cody said. "I don't have time to listen to crazy nonsense." He turned his back on me and fiddled with a fishing rod on the counter. My blood boiled at his rebuff, but I had obviously hit a raw nerve and I wasn't about to back off.

"Erica wouldn't just ruin you financially, either. She was too vengeful for that." I was talking to Cody's broad back, but I didn't care. By the tense set of his shoulders, I could tell he was listening to every word I said. "If you divorced her, she was going to trash your reputation and your business. You couldn't bear the thought of losing your business and having your dirty deeds become public knowledge, so you killed Erica and tossed her body off the bluff."

"This is ridiculous," Cody roared, turning and glaring down at me. The thick, ropy muscles in his neck strained against his skin, his gleaming white teeth bared in a snarl. I felt like cowering in a corner, but I stood my ground, glaring back at him and hoping he wouldn't see my knees knocking together in fear.

"You want the truth?" Cody growled. He clenched his right hand into a fist and I closed my eyes, preparing myself for the blow. Instead, he punched his fist into a nearby display of hiking boots, the boots bouncing out of the boxes and scattering across the floor. "Yes, I was screwing Shay. Does that make you happy?"

I opened my eyes and looked at Cody. "If you were having an affair with Shay, then why did you tell Erica about it, even as a joke?"

Cody stared at the boots and boxes scattered on the floor, then bent over and began to pick them up. "I told myself that I was telling Erica the truth—Shay did all those things I told Erica about." Cody began to restack the boxes. "What I didn't tell her was what me and Shay did after she did those things. I made Shay out to be desperate and pathetic, and in a way, I really thought she was." Cody replaced the last box on top of the stack and sighed. "I'm not proud of that, but I liked the way I felt when I was with Shay, like I was the one in command, with all the power."

I could see Cody's side of things. Erica wasn't exactly a doting wife. However, that was no excuse. "If you had problems in your relationship, you needed to address them," I said.

Cody looked down at me. "Are you married?" he demanded.

"Well, no," I admitted. I thought of my relationship with Finn and how I couldn't even officially break up with him, even after moving to another state and starting a new business. Although I had not started seeing another man and certainly hadn't murdered anyone – let alone two people – I could understand where Cody was coming from. It was tough to be honest with those closest to you. There were so many emotions and doubts and fears involved. It was easy for me to say what he should have done because I didn't have an emotional stake in the outcome.

Cody nodded. "Then you have no idea what you're talking about. Run on back to your little farm and go back to stealing cell phones, OK?"

I bristled. The cell phone thief line was really getting old. "Relationships aren't easy," I said. "But no matter what, murder still isn't the answer."

Cody scrubbed his hand over his face and ran his fingers through his hair. "That's just it. I didn't kill Shay or Erica." He dropped his hands to his sides and shook his head. "Lord knows I *felt* like killing both of them at one time or another because they drove me crazy, but I would never actually do it."

The bells over the front door jingled and an older man entered the store. Cody had not locked the door behind me. The man looked at Cody and I, his bushy gray eyebrows raised. I backed away and managed a strangled laugh, as if Cody had just said something funny.

"What a great story!" I said in a voice that was too high and too insincere, but I didn't care. I waved at the man and backed away from Cody. "See you later." I called out, pushing open the door and dashing down the sidewalk toward my car.

I gasped for breath, winded after the emotional confrontation with Cody. I wrenched open my car door and fell into the driver's seat. I sat draped against the steering wheel, panting, for several minutes. When I finally caught my breath, I twisted the key in the ignition and pulled out of the parking space, heading for home.

During the drive to the farm my mind was crowded with thoughts of Cody. He had absolutely everything to lose if he and Erica got a divorce—his business, his reputation, the respect of family and friends. No doubt Erica would have waged a bitter fight over every scrap of their shared assets. Fighting with Erica would have taken its toll on him mentally, physically, and emotionally. The same went for Shay. If he hadn't divorced Erica to marry her, she would have exposed their affair and his life would have been ruined. By killing both women he would have been free of their demands and able to play the role of grieving young widower.

Chapter 21

By the time I arrived back at the farmhouse, it felt like a million years had passed since I had left on my simple errand of buying flour at the grocery store. I rushed up the porch steps and into the kitchen. The counters, cabinets, and floor had all been cleaned. Not a trace of flour remained. The kitchen window was open, releasing the last wisps of smoke from the burned bread. But Bree wasn't in the kitchen.

"Hello?" I called. No answer. I spied a note scrawled on the pad on the wall by the phone.

Rache,

When you didn't show up, we decided to go into town to eat at a restaurant. We are going to raise a toast to six whole days without cell phones!

Love,

Dad

P.S. Since you weren't back in time to make dinner, Bree took off early.

I leaned against the wall and felt like crying. I was angry at myself for letting my guests down. I was upset that Dwight was in jail. I was pretty sure Cody had killed Erica and perhaps Shay. My head felt like it was stuffed full of wet cotton.

I needed to calm my nerves and sort out my thoughts. I went out to the barn to pet the cats and think about what I should do next. The dose of kitty therapy helped. Biscuit had been particularly friendly, and the oversized flannel shirt I wore for my visits to the cats was covered with cat hair. When I emerged from the big red barn, I was surprised to Kathryn and Simon walking down the steps. I wondered why they hadn't joined everyone else for the celebratory dinner in town.

Simon was loaded down with luggage, while Kathryn only carried her purse. Simon's old duffel bag was slung around his neck, the zipper gaping open. I rushed forward to help Simon with the luggage, forgetting about my cat fur-covered flannel. Simon raised his head, caught a glimpse of me running toward him, and let out a screech.

"Keep away from me!" he shouted, jerking to the side. As he did so, the duffel bag tipped and its contents came spilling out. A pair of boxer briefs, a tube of toothpaste, and a lone athletic sock tumbled onto the driveway. I looked away to avoid embarrassing Simon, but something green and sparkly caught my eye. I stared at the ground, where Grams' emerald brooch lay in the gravel.

No one said a word. The only sounds were the breeze whispering around the farmhouse and the sound of birds twittering in the trees. I lifted my gaze to Simon's face. "You broke into the safe and stole Grams' jewelry?" I stared at him, puzzled, then I felt something click in my brain. "You stole Shay's cell phone, too, didn't you?"

Instead of replying, Simon dropped the luggage on the ground. Kathryn let out a shout, but he ignored her. He reached behind his back and whipped a gun from the waistband of his jeans. Instinctively I raised my hands and glanced questioningly at Kathryn.

"What's going on?" I asked. My head spun, terror gnawing at my gut. "Kathryn, what—"

Before I could finish my sentence, Simon noticed the white door to the cellar at the side of the house. "We can kill her and stuff her body down there," he said, keeping the gun trained on me while he tugged at the door. The door hadn't been opened in years, and no doubt the hinges were rusted shut. I squeezed my eyes closed, praying Simon wouldn't be able to open the cellar door.

With one final yank, the cellar door flopped open. Simon grasped my arm, and I screamed when his fingers twisted my skin. "Shut up," Simon said, forcing me into the cellar and down the first step. All of the memories from the time I was trapped in the cellar while playing hide-and-go-seek with Amy Custer years ago were resurfacing, threatening to engulf me. I tried to fight it, but I could feel the panic winning. An image of my lifeless body tumbling down the cellar steps filled my mind. Then I had an idea.

Even though every muscle in my body was tensed up, I did my best to go limp in Simon's arms. For a moment I worried my actions would send both of us pitching down the cellar stairs, but Simon managed to right himself just in time. He tightened his grip, wrapping his arms around me to keep my lifeless body from slithering to the ground. He cursed me, but I did my best not to react. I could feel Simon's arm muscles straining to keep me upright. He stepped back out of the cellar, and that was when I wrapped my arms around his face, rubbing the cat hair-covered sleeves against his nose, eyes, and mouth.

My plan worked. Simon quickly let go of me and bent over, coughing and sneezing, tears streaming from his eyes and snot running from his nose. In between gasps he cursed me and the barn cats. The gun dangled at his side. Kathryn let out a huffy sigh, as if Simon were a misbehaving child, and snatched the gun from his hand. "You have been useless this entire trip," she spat out. "You aren't worth the money I'm paying you if I still have to do all the work myself."

What was Kathryn talking about? Then my whirling mind finally processed what she had said. "You killed Shay?"

Kathryn smirked. "Wow, Sherlock, it's about time you figured that out. You have been running all over town trying to find a killer when the killer was sleeping in the room above you the whole time."

I shuddered at the thought that Shay's murderer had been under my roof for an entire week. I took a close look at Kathryn. She was still impeccably dressed and composed, but something was different. The change wasn't in her wardrobe or her hairstyle. Her expression was different, and so was the way she held herself. She radiated a terrifying, demented energy that twisted her features into a grotesque mask. I trembled. Kathryn noticed and laughed.

My mind flashed to all of the bad luck Ned had been having at the B&B: his sketchbooks and camera being vandalized, the tumble he took down the stairs, the hot sauce making him sick. I gasped and stared at Kathryn. "You did all of those bad things to Ned?" I asked in a whisper.

"We thought he saw us the night we killed Shay," Kathryn said. "We heard him call out 'I see you!'"

196

A memory of Ned saying "I see you" flashed into my mind. When did I hear him say that? I struggled to recall what he had been talking about. Then, suddenly, I remembered. Ned had said he had been talking to an owl. I couldn't help myself – I laughed. All of the fear and terror I had been experiencing bubbled out of me in the form of laughter.

Kathryn scowled. "What's so funny?" she demanded.

"He w-was t-talking to an ow-owl," I said, panting.

"Whatever," Kathryn scoffed. "I'm not surprised. That bird dork can't see anything that doesn't have a beak and feathers." She snorted. "What a loser."

My laughter died in my throat, replaced with anger. "Ned is a bird *nerd*," I said. "And he may be a little spacey, but at least he isn't a cold-blooded murderer." Oops. I slapped a hand over my mouth. Not a good idea to antagonize a crazed woman holding a gun. Kathryn pointed the gun at me and sneered once more at Simon writhing on the ground. No one had rushed to Simon's aid and he was gasping for breath.

"Shouldn't we help him?" I asked. Even though Simon had just pointed a gun at me and tried to kill me, it still seemed inhumane to let him suffer. I knew some people could have severe allergic reactions. Was it possible Simon could even die?

Kathryn did not share my sympathy for Simon. She kept her gaze – and the gun – trained on me as she spoke. "That screw-up survived an allergic reaction a few days ago. He'll be fine."

I recalled standing in the bathroom of Kathryn and Simon's room at the B&B. All of those tissues. The box of Benadryl. Simon had been exposed to the barn cats. But how? Why would he go into the barn when he knew the cats would be there? A picture was starting to become clear in my mind. I looked up at Kathryn, who was wearing a smile the devil would envy.

"Why did you kill Shay?" I asked. "How did you even know who she was? You live in Colorado . . ." My voice trailed off and I recalled the letters Dwight had written to Shay. Shay's address had been in Colorado.

"Shay was a nanny for my two youngest children," Kathryn said. "It only took about five seconds for my oldest son, Teddy, to become infatuated with her. She had him wrapped around her little finger, always getting him to do things for her. Then, one night, they came home late from a party. Shay had been drinking, but she refused to give anyone else the keys. She ran into another car head-on and killed the driver of the other car. But before the police could arrive, she had talked Teddy into getting into the driver's seat." Kathryn closed her eyes, then took a deep breath. "Teddy had been drinking that night, too, and he was over the legal limit. It looked like a pretty open-and-shut case, and the police didn't ask too many questions."

"But why didn't Teddy just tell the police what had happened?" I asked. "Surely someone saw Shay driving away from the party and could back him up."

Kathryn shook her head. "I tried to tell my son that Shay was a conniving, self-centered monster, but he wouldn't listen. It was like she had him under a spell. I confronted Shay before the trial and told her I could prove my son's innocence. Shay said that maybe I could, but I wasn't going to do that. When I asked her why, she pulled out her phone and showed me photos she had of me in a . . . compromising position with a man who wasn't my husband."

I sucked in a breath. "You were having an affair?"

Kathryn nodded. "Yes. And I knew Shay meant it when she said she would show the photos to my husband and that I had to pay to keep her quiet."

An image of Shay at the B&B filled my mind. I strained to recall what she had said. Something about having her entire future in her phone. Had she meant the blackmail money she was getting from Kathryn because of the risqué photos stashed on her phone?

"If my husband ever found out about the affair, he would divorce me immediately," Kathryn said, interrupting my thoughts. "I couldn't let that happen." Her hand tightened around the gun. "I grew up dirt-poor and I remember how horrible that was," she said. "If my husband divorced me, I would only have my family to turn to, and I wasn't going back to that life." A tear streaked down her cheek. "I had to sit by and watch my son be convicted of a murder he didn't commit and be thrown in prison. Meanwhile, Shay was demanding money to keep quiet about the photos, and her demands kept increasing. I could no longer afford to pay her." She spread her hands, the gun glinting in the waning rays of the evening sun. "Don't you see? I had to kill her."

Kathryn stared at me beseechingly, trying to play the part of a grieving mother getting revenge for a horrible wrong committed against her son. But behind her pleading words I saw her true motive—greed. Kathryn stood by while her son was convicted of a crime he didn't commit just so her infidelity wouldn't be exposed and she wouldn't lose her cushy lifestyle. And Kathryn had the nerve to accuse Shay of being a conniving, self-centered monster.

"Why did you kill Shay here at the farm?" I asked.

"I told Shay I wanted to meet her in person to pay her, but what I really wanted to do was have Simon get rid of her," Kathryn said, her right index finger hovering over the trigger. "We were supposed to meet Shay out by the pond. But it started to storm. Mr. Tough Guy over there was freaked out by the thunder and lightning, and we all ran into the barn to take cover." She glared at Simon, who had flopped onto his back on the ground and was staring at the sky overhead, wheezing. "Meanwhile, he forgot all about the cats." She laughed as she recalled the scene. "Those cats mobbed him like he was covered in tuna fish." Her laughter stopped and her gaze grew hard. "He was just like he is now, on the ground and absolutely useless. Shay realized something was up and took off. I chased her, and on the way out the door I grabbed those antique gardening shears hanging on the wall. Shay was nowhere near as fit as I am," she said proudly, flexing the biceps of the arm not holding the gun. "She had gotten a big head start on me, and I still caught up to her within seconds. And, well, you saw what happened after that."

Kathryn had chased Shay down and stabbed her right through the back with great-grandma's antique gardening shears. A tremor raced up my back and my knees felt wobbly. If she was willing to do that, she would have no problem shooting me with the gun.

Kathryn glared at me. "Shay thought she could blackmail me for eternity, but she was wrong." She lifted the gun, pointing the barrel straight at my chest.

Suddenly I heard the sound of a lawnmower approaching. Kathryn was focused on me and didn't seem to hear. With a sinking heart I realized it was time for Ernie to mow the lawn. I was terrified that Kathryn would turn and shoot Ernie. I did my best not to let my expression betray Ernie's arrival. I couldn't afford to let my expression give anything away.

"Missus!" Ernie shouted.

Well, so much for not giving Ernie away.

The sound of the lawnmower grew louder as Ernie approached. He was driving his ancient lawnmower much faster than his usual sedate speed. The lawnmower kicked up dust and gravel behind him as he barreled down the road. Kathryn turned to face Ernie, the gun aimed right at him. But Ernie didn't slow down. He kept the lawnmower heading straight at Kathryn. She threw up her arms and dove to the side, the gun flying through the air. The gun landed on the grass several feet away and I breathed a sigh of relief. Not only did Kathryn not get a chance to shoot Ernie, Ernie also didn't run over the gun with the lawnmower. I wasn't sure what happened when a riding lawnmower passed over a handgun, and I didn't want to find out.

Kathryn landed on the grass with her leg tucked under her at a sickening angle and I heard the crack of the bone. Kathryn let out an inhuman howl and clutched her shin. "My leg!" she shrieked. "You broke my leg!"

Ernie brought his lawnmower to a stop. He leaned to the right and fished a flashy new cell phone out of his dusty pants pocket. He poked at the screen. When the dispatcher answered, Ernie calmly said, "Mister, I just hit a woman with my lawnmower."

Chapter 22

All of the guests gathered in the dining room for their final breakfast together on Friday morning. Bree and I joined them. Over vegetable and cheese frittata and fresh fruit, we all discussed what had happened the day before with Kathryn and Simon.

"So the two of them were only pretending to be married?" Dad asked, spearing a strawberry with his fork.

"Yes," I replied. "When the officer put handcuffs on Simon, he immediately turned on Kathryn and spilled the beans. Simon had been in the same prison as Kathryn's son and offered his services when he overheard Kathryn and her son discussing their plans to kill Shay during visiting hours. Simon was about to get out of prison and was looking for a way to make a quick buck." I shook my head. "Apparently he didn't get the memo that killing someone could land him right back in prison."

I thought back to the attack of hiccups Kathryn had during the hike in the woods. Simon had been stunned, as if he had never seen it before. If the two had been married for twenty-five years, as they had claimed, he would have been well aware of Kathryn's intense bouts of hiccups. I also remembered tripping over the pile of blankets and pillow on the floor of their room. Since they were not husband and wife, Kathryn had taken the bed and made Simon sleep on the floor.

"Did Kathryn and Simon also kill Erica?" Kelsey asked, taking a drink of orange juice.

I nodded. "Yes. The police were able to figure that out, too, with a little bit of help from Carter. Shay couldn't keep her mouth shut about her blackmail scheme and blabbed to Erica about how much money she was getting out of Kathryn, but she wouldn't tell Erica why. Erica wanted a piece of the action, so one day while Shay was taking a shower and Erica was over for a visit Carter saw her get into Shay's phone. He asked what she was doing, and she said her phone had died and she just needed to look at something online. Well, she found the texts back and forth with

Kathryn. She also found the photos and sent them to her phone, along with Kathryn's contact info. Before Erica could start sending Kathryn messages threatening to tell her secret, she saw Kathryn at the B&B and recognized her. Then she decided to do her blackmailing in person. Kathryn couldn't afford one blackmailer, let alone two, so she had to kill Erica, as well."

"Did the police find Erica's phone?" Bree asked, helping herself to more frittata.

"They found it in Hillsville Lake," I said. "Kathryn thought that if she threw a cell phone in the water that anything on it wouldn't be recoverable." I took a bite of fluffy frittata and chewed. Once I swallowed, I said, "She was wrong. The police were able to recover everything from both Shay's and Erica's phones."

Talk thankfully turned from the topic of murder to chatter about all of the activities everyone had taken part in while at the B&B. Everyone was brimming with pride over having gone a whole week without their cell phones or other devices. I wondered what would happen when all of the guests had their phones back in their hands.

After breakfast everyone stood in front of the safe in the mudroom. Mom stood next to me. I bumped her with my elbow as I cut through the layers of tape keeping the safe closed. I apologized and Mom nodded, but she didn't take a step back. *Can she really be this anxious to get her cell phone back?* I wondered, hacking away at the last of the tape. I bumped Mom with my elbow again and let out a frustrated sigh, but Mom didn't seem to notice.

The safe door swung open and I thought for sure Mom would lunge forward and trample me in an effort to get to her phone, but she didn't even look at the contents of the safe. Instead she stared at me, a tremulous smile on her lips. I pulled the box with Mom's cell phone in it from the safe and extended it toward her. She took the box, placed it on the counter, and wrapped her arms around me. Surprised, I rocked back on my heels, almost losing my balance.

"Oh, Rachel," Mom said. "I can't believe I almost lost you!" Tears glistened in her eyes. She hugged me tightly.

I hugged Mom back. "It's OK, Mom," I said. "I'm here and I'm safe. We can put all of this behind us now."

Mom let go of me and nodded, swiping at her eyes. "I want things to be better between us, Rachel."

"It will be better, Mom. It will." I felt tears forming in my eyes, but I didn't want to cry in front of my guests. Everyone was watching us with rapt attention.

I grinned at the assembled group. "My life's a real soap opera, isn't it?" I joked. Everyone laughed. I quickly pulled the box holding Dad's and Kelsey's phones from the safe. Dad picked up his phone and pushed the power button, then frowned. "Rats. It's dead."

Kelsey smiled at him. "What did you expect, honey? It hasn't been charged in a week." Kelsey turned on her phone. "Somehow I have two percent power," she said. "That won't last long, though." She slipped the phone into the back pocket of her jeans.

"I'm going to go get my charger," Dad said, hustling out of the room and up the stairs.

Next to receive his phone was Ned. With his gaze riveted on the hummingbirds hovering around the feeder, he took his flip phone and slid it into a pocket in his cargo shorts.

The next box had Kathryn's and Simon's names on it. A violent shudder passed through me at the mere sight of the name *Dillon* scrawled in black marker. Kathryn had been in too much pain to think about asking for her cell phone back when she had been loaded into the back of the ambulance. Once Simon's allergic reaction had subsided, he had been helped into the back of a police car. I had received a phone call from the police department saying both of them had eventually asked for their cell phones when the excitement died down. An officer was supposed to come to the farmhouse sometime today to pick up the phones.

The last box taken out of the safe contained the cell phones of Aries and Leo. Aries took her phone back and slipped it straight into her purse. She didn't even bother to check if the phone needed to be charged or if she had any messages.

Aries let out a contented sigh. "I *loved* being without my phone," she said. "This has confirmed my plans to pursue a low-tech future." She spread her arms wide. "I have also loved being at the B&B and seeing what it's like to live in a rural area. I can't *wait* to go back to California and start packing." Aries looked expectantly at her brother.

Leo reached for his phone, his hand trembling when he wrapped it around the cell phone. "I really enjoyed spending time at the B&B, too," he said. "I'm so glad I gave myself the opportunity to be without my phone." Aries grinned and nodded. Leo gulped and I watched his Adam's apple bob up and down in his throat.

"Aren't you excited, too, Leo?" Aries lifted her head and beamed at her brother. "All of our dreams are finally going to become reality!"

Leo shuffled his feet, his gaze darting around the room. The pained look on his face told me he would rather be thrown to a pack of ravenous wolves than tell his sister the truth. I gave him an encouraging smile.

Leo gulped. I worried he might chicken out. I closed my eyes and silently cheered him on. "I'm not going to move away from California, Aries," he said in a quiet voice.

Aries didn't look angry; she looked confused. "What about all of our plans?"

"You can still move wherever you want," Leo said. "But I want to go back to Los Angeles and work with Mom and Dad in the family business." Leo patted the front pocket of his shorts, where he had stashed his cell phone. "And I want to stay connected."

"But we're twins," Aries protested. "We have always done everything together. How can I live without my best friend?"

Leo clasped Aries' hand. "I will still be your twin and your best friend," he said, "we just won't be pursuing the same goals in the same way." He tightened his grip on his sister's hand and she squeezed back. "I have felt this way for a while now, and I finally feel strong enough to tell you. This is the right decision for me, sis."

"I understand," she said. "I'm not happy, but I understand." She smiled at Leo. "You can still come visit me at my new farm."

"And if you ever crave a taste of city life, you can always come back and visit me and the rest of the family." Leo grinned at his sister and she laughed.

"You bet I will," Aries said.

"This is a very special place you have here, Rache," Dad said after several beats of silence. "But don't you work too hard now." Dad winked at me and I rolled my eyes. Dad was one to talk about working too hard. No doubt he would jump back into his crazy work schedule as soon as he got off the plane in Seattle. Dad and Kelsey were leaving today, but they planned on returning to Hillsville in the fall for another visit. Dad had joked that they would stay in a hotel so he could watch cable news 24/7.

Mom stood quietly, listening to everyone around her talk. I studied Mom and the expression on her face. She had been through a lot. She thought she had reunited with the daughter she gave up for adoption, learned she had been lied to and manipulated by a world-class con artist, and humiliated herself at a funeral. It was a lot to process. When there was a lull in the conversation, I said, "How are you doing, Mom?"

Mom leaned her head against the door jamb and sighed. "I'm glad you're alright and that Shay's and Erica's killers are behind bars, but I wish things could have gone differently."

I nodded. Even though the identity of Mom's firstborn still remained a mystery, I was glad to finally put talk of murder behind me. I was looking forward to a busy summer season. The B&B was booked solid through Labor Day. Right now, though, I wanted to cherish the remaining moments with my family. I was proud that the Yesteryear B&B was so popular and I was happy I could offer people a brief respite from their phones and modern technology.

I watched Leo and Aries talk quietly, their heads together. For some people, like Aries, ditching a cell phone was a joy. For other people, like Leo, going without a cell phone was torture. Many other people, though, fell somewhere in between. They may not want to forsake their phones forever, but a little break felt good.

An hour later everyone was packed and on their way back home. I hugged Dad and Kelsey goodbye. Mom wrapped her arms around me and we both promised to call each other more often. I shook hands with Ned and waved goodbye to Leo and Aries.

After everyone had left, I sat on the porch and reflected on the Yesteryear B&B's grand opening. While a murder investigation certainly hadn't been part of the plan, the guests had still managed to enjoy themselves and take a break from their phones.

I could hear Bree through the screen door, singing as she washed the breakfast dishes. We had a full day of cleaning and prepping ahead of us so we could welcome a new batch of guests tomorrow, but I wanted to steal a few extra minutes for myself. I gazed around the farm, admiring the big red barn and the barn quilt gleaming in the morning sun. I was filled with a mixture of contentment and excitement, eager to welcome more guests to experience the happiness the farm offered its visitors. Best of all, I could feel Grams' presence all around me. I opened the red front door and walked into the farmhouse. It was good to be home.

Epilogue

The end-of-summer bonfire was in full swing. The round brick firepit had been heaped with wood and kindling. Flames twisted in orange spirals toward the star-speckled night sky. Bags of marshmallows, stacks of chocolate bars, and boxes of graham crackers were spread out over the picnic table, ready for everyone's favorite treat – s'mores. Two large coolers, one on either side of the picnic table, held cans of soda and bottles of water nestled in ice.

A variety of lawn chairs were arranged around the circle and were quickly filling up with all of the important people in my life. Dad and Kelsey sat on a lawn chair built for two. Kelsey was smiling and whispering in Dad's ear. Even though their honeymoon had ended several months ago, it was obvious they were still newlyweds. They had flown in from Seattle for a quick weekend visit. This time around, they were staying at a hotel in a nearby town. Dad said he had appreciated unplugging while they were here last time, but this time he wanted to binge watch all the cable news he could.

Mom sat by herself in a chair directly across the bonfire from Dad and Kelsey. She seemed to be lost in her own world, but every so often she would look up at the sky and smile. She was also staying at a nearby hotel, although not the same one as Dad and Kelsey. When she arrived, she had confided to me that she and Howard, her fifth husband, were separated and that the divorce would be final sometime around Christmas. She also said she would be taking a break from marriage for a while. Knowing both of my wedding-loving parents as well as I did, I decided to reserve judgment on that statement. Mom was a grown-up and could be trusted to make her own decisions.

The sound of a car door slamming in the driveway caught my attention. I heard two male voices and shortly I made out the burly figure of Dwight and the shorter, scrawny form of Carter next to him. Between them they carried the biggest cooler I had ever seen. Dwight nodded at me and hoisted the cooler onto one of the picnic table benches. "We brought dinner," he said proudly, gesturing at Carter. "Sandwiches, coleslaw, and potato salad for everyone."

"You didn't have to do that," I said, lifting the lid off the cooler. Inside were stacks of individually wrapped sandwiches and tubs of salads. "This is too much."

Dwight waved away my objections and slung an arm around Carter's thin shoulders. Carter hesitated for a moment, then wrapped an arm around his dad's waist. His arm only made it halfway around Dwight's massive middle, but that didn't matter. Dwight's smile lit up the night and flared even brighter than the bonfire.

"I can never repay you for what you did for me, Rachel," Dwight said. He squeezed Carter's shoulders then released his son so he could start unpacking the food. "You believed in me and gave me a second chance while everyone else in town was ready to throw me back in prison for murder." He stopped unpacking the food for a minute and gazed over at Carter, who was busy unwrapping a package of paper plates at the other end of the picnic table. "Plus, you reunited me with my son. I will always be grateful to you for that."

I felt tears pricking my eyelids. Instead of responding, I caught Dwight's gaze and held it for several beats. I think my eyes said everything Dwight needed to hear.

The red front door of the farmhouse opened and Bree bounced down the steps. She had been a tremendous help to me over the summer, and I couldn't run the B&B without her. She greeted Dwight and Carter and helped them spread the food out on the picnic table.

While everyone dug into the food, I sat down in my lawn chair and gazed up at the clear night sky. One of my favorite parts of living at the farm was being able to see so many stars. The twinkling lights scattered across the velvety blackness soothed away the stress of the day. I felt at peace knowing that Simon and

Kathryn were behind bars for killing Shay. Kathryn had been like a snake coiled in the grass, hiding and waiting to strike.

Without my noticing it, Mom had dragged her chair over next to mine with one hand. In her other hand she carried a plate overflowing with food. When she saw my eyes widen, she laughed. "I thought you might like something to eat, so I brought two of everything."

I smiled. "Thanks. I am kind of hungry."

Mom sat down and pulled a second plate out from under her heaping plate. She produced two forks from the pocket of her shorts. She placed a ham sandwich on my plate, along with a large helping of potato salad and a small pile of coleslaw. I wrinkled my nose. Mom knew I hated coleslaw.

As if reading my mind, Mom said, "The coleslaw is Dwight's special recipe. Try it; you might like it."

I dipped a spoon into the coleslaw and lifted it to my lips. I had never cared for the tangy taste of coleslaw, so I was pleasantly surprised when I tasted Dwight's special recipe. "This is really good," I said, settling into my seat to enjoy my meal.

When I was about halfway through eating my sandwich, Dad stood up and tapped his plastic fork against his can of soda. The sharp *tink, tink* sound made everyone lift their heads in Dad's direction. He was beaming from ear to ear. I felt a split second of panic. Oh no. Was Dad going to launch into his stand-up comedy routine?

But humor wasn't on Dad's mind. He extended a hand to Kelsey and she rose from her chair to stand next to him. "We have an announcement to make," he said. "We have decided to leave Seattle and move to Hillsville!"

Cheers and clapping broke out. I handed my plate to Mom and jumped up to hug first Dad, then Kelsey. "That's incredible news!" I said. "It will be so great to have you nearby. But what about your job?"

Dad waved his red plastic cup in a dismissive gesture. "Being with Kelsey has made me realize how much of my life was devoted to work. We have more than enough money, so I'm going to take an early retirement." He put his other arm around my shoulders. "And we both agreed we couldn't think of a better place to be than here in Hillsville, near my beautiful daughter."

For the second time that evening I felt tears threatening to flow. I reached out to hug Kelsey and noticed she, too, was grinning from ear to ear. Was she that excited to leave Seattle?

Kelsey cleared her throat. "I have an announcement to make, too," she said. She squeezed Dad's hand. "I'm pregnant!"

I let out a squeal of joy. Dad, a shocked expression on his face, dropped his red plastic cup, the contents of which flooded over his shoes. He didn't seem to notice. "Really, Kels?" he asked. When Kelsey nodded, he let out a whoop of joy, picked her up in his arms, and swung her around in a circle.

While Dwight slapped Dad on the back and Bree jumped up and down in delight next to Kelsey, I tried to process the thought that, at the tender age of thirty-one, I would finally get the sibling I had always wanted. I couldn't wait.

Then I caught sight of Mom. She had stood up and was coming over to congratulate Dad and Kelsey. She looked genuinely happy for both of them, but in her eyes, I could see she was thinking of the daughter she had given up all those years ago. Mom was still no closer to finding out the identity of her first child. We had talked about it several times over the phone after that fateful week at the B&B, so I knew she had come to terms with the fact that she would most likely never get closure, but that didn't mean she liked it.

The sound of another vehicle pulling into the driveway surprised me. Everyone who had been invited to the bonfire had already arrived. Perhaps it was just someone using the driveway to turn around? No, the car had parked. The driveway was dark so I had to wait until the visitor entered the light cast by the bonfire. When I did, I smiled and waved. "Holly," I said. "What are you doing here? Did you forget to deliver an important piece of junk mail?"

Holly smiled at my joke, but she looked nervous. She clutched a tissue paper-wrapped bundle in one hand and her purse in the other. "Am I imposing?"

"Not at all. Please join us. We have more than enough food to go around." I steered Holly toward the cooler full of food, but she shook her head. She also declined the offer of a soda.

"I just wanted to stop by for a few minutes," Holly said. She locked eyes with Mom and everyone fell silent. "I wanted to talk to Trisha."

Without taking her eyes off Mom, Holly unwrapped the parcel she carried. Taking a deep breath, she lifted a baby-sized gold bracelet from the box. The small heart-shaped charm dangling from the chain caught and reflected the light from the bonfire.

Mom walked slowly toward Holly, her gaze riveted on the baby bracelet. "Is that what I think it is?"

"It is." Holly's entire body trembled and I worried she would dash off into the woods like a frightened deer. She extended the bracelet for Mom's inspection, but Mom didn't care about the jewelry. She opened her arms and engulfed Holly in a hug.

I decided that the next time I hosted a bonfire, I was going to bring a truckload of tissues. This time I didn't even try to stop the tears. Carter, as a teenaged boy, was doing his best to look unaffected, but Dwight didn't seem to care. He pulled a napkin from the stack on the table and let out a big honk. The sound seemed to break the spell, and Mom and Holly broke apart, laughing and wiping away tears. Mom guided Holly to a lawn chair, then sat in the chair next to her. Mom didn't look like she was even capable of speech, so I asked the question on everyone's lips.

"Is it true? Were you the baby Mom gave up for adoption?"

Holly nodded. "It's true. I am."

I frowned. "But how did Shay know all of that information about your birth?"

Holly sighed. "I made the mistake of believing Shay was my friend and confiding in her." She looked toward the direction of Campfire Junction, a sad expression on her face. "I told her I had found my birth mother and that I was too nervous to call her myself. When Shay volunteered to make the call for me, I was relieved. I gave Shay all the information I had, in case she needed to answer questions. I never imagined she would claim she was the adopted child."

I recalled my conversation with Erica. She had told me Shay was incapable of being friends with anyone, and she had been right. It turned my stomach to think that Shay had tricked Holly into giving her personal information that she had then used for a blackmail scheme.

"But why didn't you say anything when Shay was murdered?" I blurted out the question and instantly covered my mouth after the words had escaped. "I'm sorry, Holly."

"No, it's OK." Holly looked at me fondly. "You're my half-sister. You deserve to know."

I smiled back. In the space of a few minutes, I had gone from being an only child to being a middle child. I now had an older half-sister in my life and a younger half-sibling on the way. Never in my wildest dreams could I have imagined any of this.

"I was too scared," Holly answered simply. "I was too scared to call my birth mother, and I was too scared and embarrassed to tell anyone after Shay was killed. I had confided in Shay and she had broken that trust in a terrible way. I wanted to just forget about everything and go back to the way things had been." She twisted her hands in her lap. "It took all the courage I had to come here tonight. I lost track of the number of times I got in the car, drove a few miles, then turned the car around and went back home." Everyone laughed. She turned her attention back to Mom. "But I decided I couldn't live with myself if I didn't get everything out in the open. I heard about the bonfire tonight and knew Trisha would be here, so I came to tell her who I was in person."

Dad recovered first. Still flush from the announcement of his big move and Kelsey's pregnancy, he lifted his refilled red plastic cup into the air. "To family!" he shouted.

"To family!"

Everyone went back to congratulating Dad and Kelsey, and Holly joined them. I pulled my chair closer to Mom's. "Are you OK?" I asked.

Mom smiled at me and reached out to clasp my hands. "Absolutely," she said. "I have two beautiful daughters. The divorce will be tough, but it's not like I'm not used to it." We both laughed. Her hands holding mine tightened. "I'll have plenty of time to think about my life now that I have sold my business."

My jaw dropped. Not just one, but both of my workaholic parents had decided to leave their careers.

"Are you going back to school to finish that paleontology degree?" I joked.

Mom shook her head. "No. I have absolutely no idea what I'm going to do. I sold the firm for a tidy profit, so I don't have to worry about money, but for the first time in my adult life I have no master plan and no idea what I will do next."

I let that statement soak in before I asked my next question. "How do you feel?"

"Free," Mom replied. "For the first time in a long time, I feel free."

THE END

Rhubarb Cake

Ingredients:
For cake:
1 ½ cup white sugar
½ cup vegetable oil
1 egg, beaten
2 cups all-purpose flour
1 teaspoon baking soda
½ teaspoon salt
1 teaspoon vanilla extract
1 cup buttermilk
1 cup of finely chopped fresh or frozen rhubarb (if using frozen rhubarb, thaw first)
For topping:
¼ cup sugar
½ tsp. cinnamon
Directions:
Preheat oven to 350 degrees F.

For the cake: In a medium bowl, with an electric mixer on medium speed, beat sugar, vegetable oil, egg and vanilla until combined and the mixture is creamy, about one minute.

In a large bowl, whisk together flour, baking soda, and salt. Add the sugar mixture to the flour mixture alternately with the buttermilk, starting and ending with the buttermilk.

Pour the batter into a greased 9x13 inch baking pan.

For the topping, mix ¼ cup sugar with ½ teaspoon of cinnamon. Sprinkle the cinnamon-sugar mixture evenly over the cake batter, making sure to sprinkle the mixture into the corners.

Bake for 30 minutes, or until a toothpick inserted in the center of the cake comes out clean. Serve warm. Add whipped cream if desired.

Acknowledgements

First, a big welcome to all of my new readers! I hope you have fallen in love with Rachel, Bree, and the whole gang at the Yesteryear B&B. Thank you so much for taking this journey with me. Please stay tuned for another cell phone-free adventure in the next book in this series, *Beets and Betrayal*.

Thank you to my first readers, Jeff Biggs, Janet Biggs, and Becky Biggs.

I thank Mariah Sinclair for the amazing cover design.

Infinite thanks to my husband, James, who makes it all possible.

Please consider leaving a review on Amazon when you are done reading. Every review is deeply appreciated and will help me continue my author journey. Thank you!

About the Author

Jamie McAllister writes cozy mysteries from her home in Southwest Michigan, where the weather—and the suspects—change often. When she's not plotting fictional crimes, Jamie can be found crocheting, sewing, or serenading her husband (and the cat) with her accordion.

Manufactured by Amazon.ca
Acheson, AB

30286259R00120